THE
CLEANSKIN

LAURA BLOOM

THE CLEANSKIN

the
author
people

First published in 2016 by The Author People
PO Box 159, St Ives, NSW, 2075 Australia
Copyright © Laura Bloom 2016

National Library of Australia Cataloguing-in-Publication entry

Author:	Bloom, Laura
Title:	The Cleanskin
ISBN:	978-1-925399-14-1 (paperback)
ISBN:	978-1-925399-15-8 (ebook)
Subject:	Australian Fiction
	Thriller
	The Troubles
	IRA
	Irish Australian
	Sectarian violence
	Espionage
Design:	Alissa Dinallo
Cover Photo:	Photo by Douglas Frost

Printed by Lightning Source

For my grandparents Mary Gallagher, Anders Bastian,
Nancy Macdonald and Alton Budd

AUTHOR'S NOTE

I would like to acknowledge the Arakwal people of the Bundjalung Nation who are the traditional custodians of the land around Mullumbimby, where much of this story takes place.

Unless the past is resolved, it will always be there and it will always damage what we do.

- Hugh Orde, Former Chief Constable of Police, Northern Ireland

The complete plan for any operation might well be known to very few people indeed, perhaps not until just before an attack begins, or perhaps never.

- Stella Rimington, Former Director-General of MI5
Open Secret, p.xiii, Arrow Books

PART ONE

CHAPTER ONE

2009

Forty-two hours after he got out of bed in London, Aidan was finished with flying. He limped out of the airport and found the motorbike he'd chosen online. It was a Ducati, a good one, and he lashed his bag onto the back with the elastic they'd given him at the car hire desk. He gazed at the map for a moment and then tucked it into his bag. South, they'd said. He should find his way out of the car park and turn right. After that, he was on his own.

The highway he turned onto was a scrappy affair. Broken-down holiday houses and brick blocks of flats lined one side of the road. He'd seen from the map that the Pacific Ocean lay metres away on the other side. The highway ran through dense woods and then emerged into a great plain. This must be the caldera, thought Aidan, the crater of a volcano that had erupted twenty three million years ago, splattering ash and lava and creating an area of extraordinary fertility – and extraordinary spiritual power, according to the local Aboriginals. He'd read about it on the plane.

The spiky cane fields gave way to rolling hills. He turned onto a side road and everything was a hypnotic, psychedelic green. A lushly wooded escarpment rose straight up from the flood plain. It could be the dawn of time if it weren't for the old wooden houses sitting in the cane fields, the car sales yard next to the disused railway track and cows grazing in the paddocks lining the road. He slowed as he came into town. The road became the main street and finally he was pulling up in front of the post office. They'd know what he was looking for, surely. And they did. It didn't take much before someone was leading him back out to the road and pointing out the direction he should go.

It was that easy. And that was a surprise. He'd followed a lead, something someone had said once to Liam, and it proved to be accurate. People, weirdly, were always trying to curry favour. Even from Australia, a world away, they somehow imagined that they might be useful to The Cause. That they might have an impact, however small. Like bit-players in a movie, Aidan imagined, taking their jobs more seriously than any of the actors in major roles. If only they knew how his brother talked about them. Despising them more, for some reason, than the ordinary man in the street.

'Who was it?' Aidan had asked, on his last visit to Liam in prison.

'Some guy.'

Liam's faulty memory, or selective divulging of information – you never could tell with him – was making all of this vague when Aidan needed it to be definite. He would be travelling to the other side of the world to look for her, after all.

'Someone she knew at school? Or went to church with? Some dude she was friendly with at youth group?' Aidan prompted him.

'This guy, he saw her up north near Byron Bay.'

Liam smiled. 'Dolphins,' he said, and Aidan couldn't help himself. He smiled too. Even in this serious place, Liam doing one of his impressions was irresistible.

'I see drumming.' Liam's hands slapped the table in front of him and he looked up, beyond Aidan, his face assuming a far-seeing gaze. 'Open-air markets full of unwashed people, and fire-twirling, no doubt.'

When they lived in Australia as teenagers they'd never been north of Sydney, but they'd heard enough to get the lowdown on Byron Bay. It was California thirty years ago – it didn't matter which year, just think of California thirty years before that and there you had it – with space. It was Glastonbury, with better food. Portland, with cheaper prices. It was any alternative place with fewer people and better weather.

'I can't imagine her living near Byron Bay,' said Aidan, doubtful. She definitely was not the type.

Liam shrugged. 'That's what I heard.'

'She could have moved.'

'Nah. Owns a business, they said. A family. The whole bit.'

So this was specific, thought Aidan. How typical of Liam, acting as if it was all a rumour when he probably had a photo. He probably had some kind of illegal web-streaming spying equipment set up and trained on her. When

Liam wasn't in prison he always had the latest phone, the latest computer. Click on Google Person and you'd see her on the toilet right now.

When Aidan arrived home that night he clicked on Google Earth. The town was called Mullumbimby. The map twirled and zoomed, giving him a slight feeling of seasickness and a very real sense of power. This must be how the CIA bosses felt back when this technology was exclusively theirs, coming round to show them a Contra strike on the Sandinistas, thought Aidan, or the Taliban – funded by them at that time, of course – on the Russians. Closer. It wanted an address. He opened a new window and typed Mullumbimby into the business directory. He just wanted to get a look at the place. A fuzzy picture came clear. Jesus Christ, you wouldn't want to be having it off with the woman next door at the wrong moment, or indulging in a naked slash in the garden. There it was. A low wooden fence, a grassy verge, a looming lowering sky. Trees and more trees. So much green. He zoomed along the street. Tennis courts and big gardens. More trees. Purple blooms. The verge of the road melding into grassy dirt.

And it turned out she was right where Liam's informer had said she'd be, working in her cafe, and looking just the same. You'd think she might have cut her hair, or dyed it or something – that thick black mane cut in a square fringe across her forehead was a dead giveaway, unless he had it all wrong and she wasn't hiding. Mullumbimby wasn't that far from Sydney, or London, for that matter – his own presence proving the point in question. She wasn't much aged, either – that skin. But without that bloom she'd had, that dusky rose-tinted blush. She looked washed-out, actually, underneath her olive skin. Not unattractive, if dark-featured, depressed-looking secretive women were your thing.

The evening of his arrival he'd followed her home right to her driveway, although she made an interesting detour to the pub – that wasn't her husband she was sharing a bottle of wine with, surely? He'd gone out there again this morning and Megan had almost bumped into him, reversing her car down her driveway at an unwise speed. He hadn't expected her to turn around so fast. Hadn't expected her to get such a good look at him – with his helmet off no less – so soon. She didn't recognise him, though, he could tell. It didn't surprise him. He'd been just a boy when they'd last met.

She was solemn and shy, not saying much, twenty years ago when Dom first brought her home. For months their mother, Nuala, had been begging for an introduction.

'She's not my girlfriend,' Dom would heatedly reply, whenever the topic came up.

'Of course not,' Aidan and Nuala would agree, straight faced. Dom was too good to have a girlfriend. Too pure. Dom had dedicated his life to God.

'My "calling" is not what you think. It's not what you're trying to make it out to be.'

What they were trying to make it out to be was a life of such saintly sacrifice and suffering that he would have to give it up and go back to university full-time to continue his economics degree. That's what Nuala wanted, and Aidan at that time was too young to disagree.

'It's exciting, Mum,' Dom told her. 'It's like being in a rock band. Or becoming an artist. I feel, every moment, like I'm doing the thing that I'm most meant to do.'

'Lucky you,' she sighed.

Nuala worked for a government department in town. She told Aidan it was even less exciting than it sounded.

'I feel like I'm improvising but at the same time I'm following directions.'

They had been sitting around the kitchen table, remembered Aidan. Their kitchen in Balmain had exposed brick walls from the seventies and organically-shaped wooden bench tops. When they moved into the house, Nuala said she should go out and buy a set of earthenware crockery for them to eat from, to match the decor. She was joking, of course. She'd brought their Wedgwood china out to Australia with them from Belfast, all twelve settings of it, finger bowls included. It comforted Aidan that in the new world their lives had been plunged into at least their dinnerware remained the same.

'I feel like I'll do whatever God wants me to do.'

Nuala sat back in her chair, still wearing her suit but with slippers on instead of her high-heeled shoes. Back in Ireland she'd worked from home, sharing an office with their father. She'd worn caftans and long, flowing velvet scarves, big fake flowers pinned about her person and clanking costume jewelry. When they moved out to Australia, though, all of that disappeared, and dull blue suits and silver stud earrings took their place. Aidan mourned the loss of his free-flowing mother as much as his dead father some days.

'But darling,' she said. 'How can you tell what God wants you to do?'

'I can't always. And you never know for sure. But it's listening. It's about listening.'

Aidan was young enough to be new to stuff like this, old enough to be interested. They'd never gone in much for religion back home.

'I'm listening every day. Whatever comes to me to do on this day I will do.'

'Whatever?' Nuala smiled, but she looked sad, thought Aidan.

'Whatever,' said Dom firmly. 'Don't worry, Mum. I think I'm meant to be helping young kids who come from difficult backgrounds. It's nothing radical.'

She smiled again and Aidan knew she was relieved.

But she was really relieved – really, really relieved – when they found hard evidence that Dom had a girlfriend. The thing that gave it away was the love bites on his neck. Liam, on one of his fleeting visits from London, spotted them immediately.

'Check it out!' he drawled.

Dom frowned, pulling up his collar and pretending he didn't know what Liam was talking about, but they were all watching out after that. He came home later all the time. Mass finished at eleven on Sundays, and he wouldn't get home until three – Nuala's sit-down roast lunches notwithstanding. He got home late from the church youth group he led, too, and would be on the phone, whispering and mumbling in his room until all hours. But still he wouldn't tell them anything, and he wouldn't bring her home.

This went on for months – Liam had gone back to London and Aidan had almost started to believe that there was no one special – until finally, one day, Dom phoned, the minute Mass finished, it must have been, and asked Nuala to set another place at the table.

'Oh, but she looks Irish!' Nuala's face cleared as the girl walked up the path.

She wasn't beautiful, thought Aidan, a runty fourteen-year-old at that time, all spots and unwanted sprouting hair. He felt disappointed in Dom. She wasn't even pretty. The girls he decreed to be good-looking at that age were blonde, with open faces and big breasts. Aidan had a poster of Farrah Fawcett on his bedroom wall, balancing on a skateboard, as if to say that apart from her goddess body and mane of long blonde hair she would have everything in common with a teenage boy. This girl was broad-shouldered and as tall as Dom, sturdy and athletic looking.

'That's because she *is* Irish,' said Dom proudly, catching the girl's hand and swinging it.

'Actually it was my grandparents who were from Ireland.' Her accent was clear and polished. 'I'm Australian.'

'Well, and it's a pleasure to meet you, my dear, such a pleasure!' said Nuala, sweeping her up into a hug.

Aidan didn't think Megan was the huggy sort, but she put her arms around his mother and seemed to be doing a fair job of squeezing her back when Aidan noticed Dom watching her. He had never seen Dom look at anyone like that before, and suddenly he felt like just a child.

—————

CHAPTER TWO

Matt was worrying about the local bat population. It had swelled recently, and been displaced, so now they were forced to spend their days in a straggling stand of trees next to the main road heading out of town.

'If they can't rest properly they'll get stressed,' he was saying, as he poured muesli into three bowls at the kitchen table. 'When they're stressed they spread disease.'

'The council's hiring a specialist to look into moving them somewhere safer,' said Halley, as she warmed a pot of milk at the stove. She'd overheard someone talking about it at the cafe, and listened carefully so she could tell Matt. 'For fifty thousand dollars, they're going to be okay.'

If it wasn't bats, it would be the threat of flooding or feral animals or the receding coastline on his mind, thought Halley, and she used to get as worked up about these issues as he did. It seemed to Halley now, though, that you could argue all you wanted, but the planet was well past saving, and the only person you should ever count on was yourself. The only responsibility that mattered was actual. Her husband. Her son. Her cafe. Her water-logged snake-infested piece of land. Of course you didn't want to sound heartless or cruel, but wasn't life sometimes that way? And weren't you better off making your accommodations with it and proceeding from there?

'Greek islands,' said Matt, as she handed him his coffee. He caught her hand and held it, startling her with his touch.

'Next year, you and me for a romantic holiday.'

Romantic? thought Halley, staring at their hands.

Last night she'd pressed her body all along the length of his. 'Look how well we fit together,' she'd whispered. He'd pressed himself back into her for a moment, sharing his warmth, and she'd begun slowly moving her hand up his thigh. 'Hang on,' he'd said, sitting up so abruptly he'd knocked her hand away, and turning on his bedside light. She'd held herself still, waiting for him while he'd fumbled with the alarm on his phone, but when he lay back down he'd kissed her lightly on the mouth and rolled away from her, taking more than his fair share of the doona.

'Why not?' Matt ran his fingers over hers, staring up at her.

'What about Benny?' she floundered, vulnerable from the sudden sense memory.

'He can stay with Cal.'

'Cal's only sixteen,' she said, pulling her hand away and turning back to the counter.

'I was thinking of Cal's parents as much as Cal. But he'll be seventeen in a year's time, anyway. Or maybe Cal could come and stay here.' Matt with his special brand of inexorable logic was oblivious to her panic. 'Could be just the thing for them. Make them take more responsibility.'

'They'd eat nothing but junk. He'd wear the same clothes to school every day,' Halley improvised.

'I'll stay here alone, I don't mind,' Benny piped up from where he was lying on the couch at the other end of the kitchen.

'You'll stay here with me.'

From the unnatural sudden silence, she realised that she'd spoken more harshly than she'd intended.

It happened again when they were eating breakfast. Benny was arguing the case for foster parents when Halley said, 'They should just put the babies up for adoption and be done with it.'

Benny flinched. Matt frowned at her.

'I don't mean to be mean,' said Halley, floundering again. 'But babies ... babies don't get a second chance. They either make it, being loved and helped and encouraged, or they don't.'

'Did you love and encourage me?'

'Benny! Of course I did. How can you ask me that?' What was happening between them? Halley wondered. He wouldn't let her go near his room when he wasn't there, he wouldn't let her do his laundry, and for the last few months he'd even refused pocket money, telling her with pride that he earned all he needed working at Sug's restaurant.

'I just think there's a crucial time in a baby's life,' Halley battled on. 'When you have a baby one day, you'll see. And you either give that baby what it needs or you don't, and it doesn't get a second chance.'

'What about the mother's life, though? Or the father's?' said Benny. 'Shouldn't they get a second chance?'

'Of course they should. Everyone deserves a second chance, but life doesn't always work that way.'

'What a hardarse,' Matt muttered.

And then she saw it. A conspiratorial look between the two of them. A quick glance. Raised eyebrows and a smile. For all her sins, she at least had somehow managed to bring together a father and a son who loved each other. She bent over her muesli, blinking rapidly, pretending not to have seen.

'Why won't you talk about travelling with me?' said Matt as he climbed into the car and tightened his seatbelt.

They were running late. People would be pouring in for breakfast soon, and she started reversing the car down the drive before she'd closed her door. She placed her left hand on Matt's headrest to steady herself as she steered with the right hand, craning her neck to check on the road before swinging the car around. A man was standing on the opposite verge. She slammed her foot on the brake so hard her handbag fell off her lap, wallet, lipstick and change cascading onto the floor of the car.

She ducked her head to check out the stranger in the rearview mirror. He was a biker by the look of him, dressed in a leather jacket, his light red hair standing up in tufts around his head like a baby chick's, his helmet cradled in his arms as he turned to look at her. She used to fancy bikers, remembered Halley, impatient already at the time he was going to waste. Used to imagine they were free-spirited or some such rubbish. He probably needed help with his bike, she decided. People drove down here, lured by the beauty of the narrowing valley. Their house was near the end of it, where the road began climbing steeply into the hills. Then they ran out of petrol or got bogged in the river they inevitably felt compelled to cross.

'This is the country, you idiot,' muttered Halley, divining petrol shortage from his expression. They'd give him a lift into town, but he could sort out his own way of getting back, she decreed. He had the engine of his bike idling, though, she realised, a big shiny grey thing parked in front of the neighbour's. Whatever. If he'd wanted something he would have approached them by now. She had customers to serve. She accelerated, shifting the car crunchingly into third gear with a satisfying spray of pebbles and lifting her arm in an airy country wave as she flew past. In the rearview mirror she saw him turning again to keep looking after her.

'When are we going to travel?' persisted Matt, once they'd crossed the creek and she'd settled into fifth gear, trees and fields and cows swiftly gliding past.

'When will we have the money? You're the one who ...' She stopped herself.

'The one who what?'

Too late. Matt knew what she had been going to say and they could have that whole argument without her needing to say another word.

'The one whose fault it is that we need more staff, is that it?'

'We decided together,' she muttered, unwilling to do this with Benny in the back seat. But also aware that with every silent kilometre they covered the ill-feeling between them would grow.

They had bought the cafe to give themselves both jobs – hard things to find up here in 'Paradise', as people, both tourists and residents, called it, and without any irony that Halley could detect. After all, no one comes to Paradise for a job. This resulted in a lot of people in their little town being short of employment and short of money. Not too little for a coffee or a meal though, and the cafe had turned out pretty well. People congregated there, under the jacaranda trees where most of the tables and chairs were placed. They spent hours typing on their laptops or reading from the pile of outdated surf and fashion magazines which sat next to the water dispenser, just inside the door.

Halley pulled up in front of the cafe and Benny walked off towards school without kissing her goodbye. Matt began dumping the boxes of the chutneys they'd made on the weekend onto the road beside the car. A young woman wearing tiny denim shorts, a black singlet and Doc Marten boots emerged from the cafe. It was their new waitress. Halley had high hopes for her.

'Hi Lisa.' Halley picked up a box and pressed it into her arms. At least she and Matt couldn't go on with this conversation. Matt would be stewing on it all morning, though, and it would make him even slower, even more forgetful and absent-minded, so that if they made it through until lunch without a complaint or a misplaced order it would be a miracle.

Halley started taking orders at the cash register while Matt got things moving at the espresso machine. Most of the customers had been coming in for years, but when she looked up to take the next order a stocky, middle-aged man she didn't recognise was standing in front of her, with sandy red hair and nice blue eyes.

'You after coffee or a meal?' She smiled and took her pencil from behind her ear and held it over the order pad, waiting.

'Megan.'

Halley felt a surge, her heart flowering or tipping over.

'It's me.'

Her hand opened, change falling out of it into the drawer of the cash register.

He was holding a bike helmet. He was the man who'd been outside her house this morning, she realised, and anxiety flooded her. This wasn't a coincidence. 'Aidan? Is it you? Is everything all right?' What a stupid question. Of course it wasn't. He'd been looking for her. 'Are you okay? Where have you come from?'

'From London. I arrived yesterday. I'm fine.'

Her hand resting on the till recollected her, and for something to do she began neatening the twenty-dollar bills.

'Listen, we can't talk now,' she said, looking over his shoulder to nod at the woman standing behind him in the queue, and doing a quick scan of the cafe. No one was looking at them, but still.

He took a step back, as if she had physically repelled him, and Halley regretted her tone.

'We're busy,' she said more gently.

He stepped forward again. 'I'm not.' His voice was rough.

'Excuse me,' she said to the next customer in line. 'Lisa, will you fill in here for a second?'

She beckoned Aidan over to the bank of fridges that lined one wall, modulating her voice below their mechanical hum. 'You can't just walk in here and start talking to me.'

'Why not?'

Because I might fall over, she thought. Because I might cry. 'This isn't a good time.'

'When is?'

'You can meet me tonight at six thirty, after closing. Wait for me outside the Commonwealth Bank round the corner. We can decide where to go after that.'

Halley watched him walk out of the cafe, wishing he'd ordered something to make their transaction look more normal. Matt didn't seem to have noticed anything, though, seemingly fully absorbed pushing levers and filling cups at the espresso machine. Halley motioned for Lisa to keep taking orders, and she went over to the ovens where she could work with her back to the cafe.

People had walked into the cafe over the years and recognised her – of course they had: Mullumbimby wasn't that far from Sydney, after all – but she had toughed it out, pretending not to know who they were talking about and nodding in polite agreement at how similar a person could look to someone else. She'd stopped dreading it, because even though her heart would hammer and her palms would sweat, she was so good at hiding it that no one looking at her would know that she was feeling anything more intense than feigned interest. Today, though, as she measured spices and sifted flours, the familiar movements and routines failed to calm her, and all day as she worked she thought about how to evade him, and all day she kept concluding that she couldn't. Aidan would find her again if he wanted to, or somebody else would. He was in a position to insist, and she was in no position to refuse. And this was what she'd been expecting, wasn't it? All along. They don't let you go so easily. They never let you go.

'What do you want?' she asked him as soon as he climbed into her car. She'd beeped her horn and beckoned him over from where he was waiting outside the bank, motioning that he should get in.

'Yeah, I'm well, thanks. How have you been?'

'I'll take us to a place I know. No one will be there at this time.'

They drove in silence through the quiet streets and a few minutes later she turned the car onto a dirt track and brought it to a stop beside a boat ramp, facing a wide, slow-moving river. Dusk was falling, and the towering gums on the opposite bank were already in shadow. A pair of ducks burst into flight as she wound down the car window, but otherwise the water was still and empty. She unbuckled her seatbelt and leaned her head against the headrest.

He knew he had all the power in this situation. She must know it too. And yet if it bothered her she didn't show it. It pulled the rug out from under him. He'd imagined he'd have to keep her from running, or calm her down or … something. That it would be difficult to find a way to simply sit and talk. Yet here they were sitting side by side in a silence that was going on way too long to be comfortable and she was acting as if she was in control, not him.

'How did you find me?' she said at last.

'Luck.'

'Come on.'

'A lot of people come here for a holiday.'

'You better tell me.'

'Someone told me, all right? Someone … it's not luck.'

'Of course it's not. Christ.'

A metre away from her he felt the heat of her glare.

'I just want to talk.'

'You came to the other side of the world, to my cafe, just to talk?'

'Of all the cafes in the world ...' Aidan mused.

'Oh please shut up,' Halley snapped, and Aidan felt oddly warmly towards her, as if she was the sister he'd never had.

'How did you find me?'

'My brother.'

'Liam knew I'd be here? Liam's in prison, isn't he? Liam knows where I am?'

Now she definitely seemed frightened.

'No. Dom.'

That took the wind out of her sails.

'Years ago, he told me. If you ever disappeared this was where you'd choose to disappear to.'

'That's true.' Her face crumpled and she turned away.

'We were always talking about it. He used to dream about that a lot when we first moved out here, did he tell you? About disappearing.'

'I thought you'd already disappeared,' she said, still turned away from him. 'When you came out from Belfast to Australia. I thought that was your mother's plan. How is your mother?'

'She passed away five years ago.'

Her shoulders began shaking, and he put a hand on her back, resting it for a moment on the soft cotton of her long-sleeved top.

'I came here because I need to talk to you about Dom,' he said softly.

'What about ... Dom?' She spoke his name hesitantly, as if she wasn't used to it.

'I need to know why.'

'Why what?'

'You know what. Don't make me say.'

She wiped her eyes and blew her nose on a tissue she pulled out from her bra. She turned back towards him and their eyes met, and between them there passed a warmth, a transference of energy, something heating and melting and healing, Aidan fancied, because she relaxed then, leaning back into the car seat and taking her hand away from the door. Aidan relaxed too, relieved, yet still nervous. He wouldn't put it past her to read his thoughts. To bore into his brain. To divine that he was lying.

CHAPTER THREE

Halley checked her watch as she ran up the stairs. Their house was a Queenslander, a wooden house built on stilts in the 1930s, rising above flooding rivers and deadly snakes, sitting in the way of cooling breezes – although these last few summers they'd had too few of those. It was 8pm. Not so late, but too late to help with dinner, and too late not to have called to say she'd been delayed.

'It's not just me,' Matt pointed out, standing lank and relaxed in the doorway like a ground vine bending up around a frame.

'You think Benny was worried about me?'

She walked to his bedroom door, which this far into his adolescence he still kept open when he was home. He was sitting at his desk, staring into his computer.

'Hi Mum.'

'Sorry, I should have …' She stopped herself. Why was she apologising to Benny when it was Matt who was angry with her? 'Are you hungry?' she asked. The only question from his childhood that she still had left. That was still relevant.

'I already ate.'

'Sorry if I worried you,' she mumbled, leaning over him at the desk, nuzzling her cheek against his for the second she allowed herself – stole, really – before stepping back to ruffle his hair. 'I got held up at work.' It was easier to lie to Benny for some reason than to Matt.

'I wasn't worried.'

'Sorry,' she said to Matt, who was standing in the middle of the kitchen on the old kilim rug, but she didn't mean it anymore. That hot prickly feeling of the rainforest closing in on the house descended on her like a dusty blanket. 'I'm only an hour late,' she added.

'I thought you might have had a flat tyre, or an accident, and your mobile went straight to message bank. I was about to come out looking for you.'

The kitchen was lit by the lowest wattage light bulbs Matt had been able to find, giving the room an almost candle-lit feeling. The wooden venetian blinds on both windows were closed against the chill of the early spring night. A bowl of pasta and another of salad sat on the table, next to a bottle of wine.

She walked over and kissed him. 'I'm sorry,' she said again, with real warmth this time. 'I took longer than I realised. I should have called.'

He put his arms around her shoulders and pulled her close to him for a second before letting her go.

'You okay?'

'Just tired.'

'Sit. Eat. I'll do the chores.'

She waited until the screen door banged behind him and then sank into a chair.

For the last eight hours, ever since Aidan walked into the cafe, her thoughts had been racing, her armpits sweating and her palms clammy, clothing her, she assumed, in a stench of fear. Now she felt her tension easing. Aidan's story made sense. Dom was his brother, after all. But saying his name had sent a message through her veins, confusing her, and clouding the relief she felt that Liam was not involved. It was a message of alarm. A message of something sharp. Something blooming in her chest, like hope. And fading, like a sigh. It shocked her, the impact just saying his name had on her. She hadn't known that it could, because it had been so long since she had said it, even though she could remember their first proper meeting on the steps of her childhood home in Sydney twenty years ago, as vividly as if it had happened yesterday.

Sydney, 1989

She was heading up the stairs to her bedroom when the doorbell rang.

'Freddie!' her mother called.

They had Freddie now, who was six foot seven and from Tonga, and spent his days standing next to their front door.

'Where's Freddie?' said her father, coming to the living room door.

'I'll get it,' said Megan, hoping it would be a journalist so she could spit on them. Or see them, at least, this invisible enemy stalking her father, surrounding them, so that he couldn't even leave the house until dark. When she opened the door, though, it was the leader of the youth group at their church.

'Dom? What are you doing here?'

Glancing over her shoulder she glimpsed her father retreating into the living room.

Dom was at university, which made him a grown-up in her book. He wouldn't be helping someone looking for a story, would he? The moment she thought that she was surprised at herself – something like that wouldn't have occurred to her a week ago. But her family hadn't been in the headlines a week ago, either.

'We've all been thinking of you,' he explained, as she showed him up to her room. It was the first time she'd ever had a boy in there, and although it was messy she was surprised at how relaxed she felt. But she usually felt relaxed with Dom. In the few small instances of time they had been alone together she had been unselfconscious, answering his questions about school and church with an openness that surprised her. The youth group leaders were trained for this, or selected on the basis of it, she supposed. Being good with people, and putting them at ease.

He sat on the floor, his back against the bed, his long legs stretched out in front of him. Her bedroom was a hexagon, a little tower built at the top of the house as an afterthought. Megan's father had thought he might use it for a study at one point, and for a while her mother had come up here to practise yoga. Once she turned thirteen it became Megan's domain. Too small for a bedroom really, it was crammed with her bed, her desk, her chair and her Persian carpet.

'Are you not going to sit down?' His accent was Irish, Megan remembered. Father John had told her.

'I'm fine,' said Megan, standing next to the bed.

He stared at his hands for a while and then at his outstretched feet. Megan stared at him. He was dressed in blue jeans and a blue T-shirt, with *Sydney University* written on it in letters of faded gold.

'I'm sorry this is happening to you,' he said at last.

'It's not happening to me, it's happening to my dad.'

He looked as though he was about to contradict her, but must have thought better of it.

'I like your view,' he said, after another extended pause.

Megan shrugged. Of course he did. That's why the house had cost so much – as if in stunned wonder, her father had kept repeating the price for weeks after they'd moved in, and that was just the starting amount before her mother renovated it from top to bottom.

'Must be nice, waking up to this every morning.'

'To tell you the truth I hardly notice it. You get used to it. Just like you get used to anything ... I suppose.' Dom had come from Northern Ireland to live here when he was thirteen, she remembered – Father John had told her mother in a whisper – because his father had been murdered.

'Come here and sit next to me.' He patted the carpet.

Relenting, she took her place next to him on the floor. The harbour looked bigger from here, sea and sky and horizon filling all that she could see.

'Megan. I ... I think I know what you're going through.'

She stared at him. All of this was so unexpected, so unusual, that she couldn't even guess what he was about to say.

'My father was a lawyer, back in Belfast. He was a barrister, like your dad.'

Dom's eyes were brown and his hair was black. Sitting this close to him his face seemed almost familiar. He wasn't handsome – or she hadn't thought so – but now she reassessed. His face wore a gentle, hurt expression, and his cheeks were a little jowly. But his skin was pale, almost white, his lips a bitten cherry red. She raised her eyes. He was holding himself rigid, leaning away from her.

'He was a bit famous too.'

Deliberately, as though she knew what she was doing, she put her hand over his hand where it supported his weight on the floor.

'A bit notorious even, like your dad ...'

She leaned forward and placed her mouth on the lips she had just been staring at.

For long seconds he didn't move. Megan was waiting. She didn't feel scared. She felt calm and, surprisingly for a girl who had never kissed a boy before, in control. She held her lips there, breathing him in. His mouth was soft and dry. Then with a lurch he shifted his weight towards her and for a moment he pressed his mouth against hers. Megan closed her eyes. Her head swam. He eased back and lowered his head, and she dropped hers also, so now just their foreheads were lightly touching. She could hear the two of them breathing and feel the warmth of his breath against her skin. She could see the tiny crucifix he wore swinging on its chain beneath his collarbone, his cheek planing away from her like the infinite curve of a planet. Dizzy, she reached for his shoulder to steady herself.

'I just came to see if you were all right,' he said, drawing away.

He looked shaken, or frightened maybe, thought Megan.

'Thank you,' she said. Were they going to pretend nothing had just happened, then?

'I'm too old for you, Megan. I'm almost twenty-one.'

She liked him for saying that. She felt relaxed again. 'I'm almost seventeen.'

'Right.' He laughed a short humourless laugh and stood up, brushing the carpet fluff on his hands onto the thighs of his jeans. 'Your parents wouldn't be too thrilled.'

'They wouldn't mind.' It wasn't true, but two flights of stairs down in the living room her parents and their problems suddenly seemed wonderfully far away.

'Well I do,' he said, his expression miserable.

'You'd better go,' she said abruptly, taking pity on him. Stopping herself. From what? She wasn't sure. But he was still a person, she reminded herself, even though for a moment she had become a character in a play.

The stained-glass window above the front door cast a pool of light on the marble floor of the hallway, which they stood in as they said goodbye.

'So you'll come to the youth group tomorrow night?' said Dom, in a social tone, as though this is what they had been discussing all along. As though her parents might be listening, thought Megan.

She felt embarrassed, in quite a different way than she had with him at first in her room. She and her friends went to films together, and the occasional party. They drank espressos at Maisie's Cafe on Military Road, or sneaked into the bar at the Oaks, sipping Cokes up the back and trying to look eighteen. No one she knew socialised at church on a Saturday night. But that meant she wouldn't run into anyone she knew, she realised. No one would try to talk to her about her father.

'Okay.' She was staring at his mouth again. It was as though her body was telling her to lean forward and kiss it.

He reared back as though he felt it too, opening the door and pausing for a moment on the white stone steps. She could see the crowd of reporters staring at them through the bars of the closed gates across their driveway.

'You know why they're picking on him, don't you?'

'My dad?'

'Of course. It's because he's Irish Catholic. Patrick Cooney's the first Irish Catholic appointed to the Supreme Court. Your dad's his friend, and the highest-ranking Irish Catholic barrister in New South Wales. It's a born-again Christian, you know, who's taking him down.'

It was quaint to her, the way he seemed to think this was about religion. Maybe that's how things were back in Northern Ireland, but not here.

'They wouldn't be on this witch-hunt if he was a part of the Protestant establishment, that's for sure.'

Once he left she went back to her room, to sit on the floor again and look out at the harbour from this unaccustomed viewing point. They were privileged, she knew that much. Her mother's BMW and her father's vintage Mercedes sat parked in the gravel driveway that led from their elaborate wrought-iron gates around to the front door; their speedboat lay tethered to their private jetty, which jutted out into the harbour next to their pool – silent witnesses to the wealth her father, the son of a lab assistant and a teacher's aide, had created for them. But now her parents spent their days locked in the living room with a crowd of lawyers she'd never met before, speaking in low voices and staring miserably at the phone. It was strange to imagine they were being picked on.

There had been a telephone conversation between Megan's father and Justice Cooney a month ago, back when all of this began. Her father asked the judge how a party had gone the night before. 'Got too tired,' he had reportedly replied.

The conversation had been illegally recorded by the police, and then illegally leaked to one of Australia's leading newspapers, which had illegally published a transcript of it last week. Since then it had been repeated everywhere, including on the radio which they still listened to every morning, so that Megan would brace herself for the piercing beep that would cut across the reporter's words about to come.

'Ate too much. Drank too much. *Bleep* everyone.'

At first she'd thought the bleep noise was covering the word 'fuck', and Megan sympathised. As though Paddy, which is what they called Justice Cooney at her house, was dismissing it all. 'Ate too much. Drank too much. Fuck everyone!' A feeling she was becoming familiar with as the weight of her father's problems settled on her family. But then she saw it in print one day, even though they took pains to treat the newspapers as offhandedly as possible in her house these days, letting them mount up in the hall for the lawyers to cast their eyes over in the morning and dumping them in the garbage bin each night. But that day she couldn't help looking, as though her eyes needed proof of what the judge, their family friend, had said.

'James O'Dea, QC: 'And how do you think it went?'

Justice Cooney: 'Got too tired. Ate too much. Drank too much. F***ed everyone.'

And that changed everything. Fucked who? Megan wondered, despite herself. That arthritic old man who showed up at their table for Friday dinner, fucking? She couldn't imagine it. But then she couldn't imagine any of this, and it was actually happening.

'Meggie, my little darling. How about a squeezy-up?' Paddy asked her just as usual when he came to dinner that night.

With the vague hauteur of a teenager Megan thought of that time when she used to sit on his knee and cuddle him as aeons ago, lost in the mists of antiquity. It seemed almost foolishly sentimental to mention it. But Paddy always did. Just as he always said what a beautiful young lady she was growing up to be, and what wonderful things he was hearing about her from her father. Megan took all of this in her stride, his adoration a pleasant echo of her father's, simply a matter of course.

'He's acting like everything is normal!' hissed Megan to her mother in the kitchen, where she was adding dobs of thick whipped cream to the chocolate mousse.

'We're very lucky he's here.'

'What do you mean?' said Megan. They weren't the ones who had fucked everyone. He was. Those words – they had never even been said in this house.

'He's standing by us.' Her mother's blonde hair swung in its neat bob as she measured peppermint tea into the thermos that would be parked for the rest of the evening next to Paddy's arm.

'We're standing by him, too.'

'You don't get it, do you?'

For a moment Megan saw the surface of her mother's prettiness crack, and a fifty-five-year-old woman with thin shoulders and a wrinkled brow stared back at her.

'They're picking on us, Megan. They're looking for a whipping boy and your father is it.'

'Isn't Paddy it, too?' Megan said quickly. That's what Dom had said. She didn't want them to be 'it' alone.

'He's a judge of the Supreme Court. That makes him almost untouchable. He's also an old man at the end of his career. He doesn't have a future, or a family, or ...' Her mother's glance took in the Swarovski crystal chandelier and the white Carrara marble benchtops, '... all this to keep up.'

'You mean we might lose it?' Megan felt a kick in her stomach, of fear.

'Your father has enemies. People out to get him.'

'But why? Why us?'

Megan's mother shook her head, and they both watched silently as she finished laying out the tray.

That night they were eating in the dining room instead of the kitchen. It was a bare room, filled with the grand panorama of Sydney Harbour, which by night shimmered like velvet, surrounded by pinpricks of light from the houses – mansions like theirs, mostly – arranged around the point. When she was younger, Megan liked to sit perched on the windowsill and stare at them. Strangely, they mostly seemed empty. Vast places ready for a grand life, and yet almost nothing moved. A housekeeper occasionally could be seen in the daytime, or a gardener, but children, friends, parents, where were they? Megan wondered, searching the rooms with a pair of binoculars that her mother used for the ballet. It made Megan feel lonely sometimes just to look at them. Did her house look like this from across that expanse of water? If you looked at her house from a boat or a ferry – people often did, you could see them pointing – would they think they were looking at a mausoleum? Or would they think, What a beautiful home for a lucky family? Until a few weeks ago Megan had assumed the latter. Their house had buzzed with life on the weekends. But in the last few weeks no friends had come, and their house tingled with a silent cool anxiety. Doors were closed with a quiet click, the phone picked up on the second ring, as if the security guard stationed out the front was keeping all signs of their old warmth and happiness at bay. When he left them it would all come flooding back again, Megan was sure.

When Paddy left, Megan walked through the French doors onto the patio. There was no moon tonight, and the harbour was quiet, the lights from ferries and boats moving like stars across the water.

'It's always been this way, Meggie,' said her father, tapping his cigar against the balcony railing. 'For over eight hundred years, and counting. The English hate the Irish, and it's just the same the other way.'

'I don't hate them.'

He shrugged and ashed his cigar again, little red specks like cinders landing on the surface of the pool.

'I don't even know who was originally from England and who was from Ireland here,' said Megan.

'How many people who aren't Catholic do you know?'

That was easy. She had gone to the local Catholic parish playgroup and preschool, and then on to the convent school she attended now. They went to dances and staged musicals with the Jesuit boys' school down the road, and at the train station they flirted with the boys from the Marist college further north. Brothers of girls she knew from school boarded at St Joseph's, a couple of suburbs away, and she was friends with girls from two other harbour-front Catholic schools in the eastern suburbs, across the bridge.

'No one.'

'Well, generally, Catholics are the Irish and the English are the other way.'

Protestants, he meant. Megan thought of the snooty girls on the train who went to the Ladies' College further up the line, their accents bizarrely slurring, as though they came from another, slightly better, country. They were usually brilliant at the flute or French or something equally decorative; the uselessness of it as much a source of pride to their parents as their accomplishment. 'She'll never have to work,' Megan once overheard her father saying to her mother after a party. 'That's what they're really saying. She'll never have to lift a finger to support herself.' Her mother had said something in a softening murmur, which made her father laugh. 'Megan, you're a worker,' he turned to her to say, and she had been filled with pride. She'd had a Saturday morning job in a newsagents from the age of twelve. She'd just started training to work the cash register when her father's scandal broke. She was taking a break, she had told the manager last Saturday, until she was less busy. What she meant was, until life returned to normal.

'So don't tell me you don't know who's Protestant and who's Catholic,' said her father. 'That's all over, or so they say. But all of this is ours just as much as it's theirs, Megan, and I won't give it up without a fight.'

He gestured widely with both hands out to the harbour, and Megan was reminded of the crucifix she'd seen around Dom's neck – that face wracked with suffering, and those arms outstretched. She thought of every martyr and hero who had ever tried to break free.

'I love you, Daddy.'

'My darling girl,' he said, his voice thick with emotion. 'I love you too.'

The next evening Megan walked into the basement of their church. Children and teenagers sat in a loose semicircle on faded green corduroy beanbags and discoloured orange chairs. Dom sat cross-legged on the floor in front of them, a guitar propped on one knee.

'Your worst nightmare, right?' he called across the room. 'Guitar. Beanbags. I've even got the Christian songbook.'

The others all turned to look at her as she walked across that endless-seeming floor.

'Hi,' she sang out bravely.

'Hi,' they sang out in return.

Their ages ranged from nine to nineteen. Dom was the oldest, she learned. The oldest at the Saturday night meetings of the youth group, anyway. Other couples his age attended the camps they all went to in the school holidays, each couple acting as an honorary mum and dad for the children until they went home, and for some of these children, more of a mum and a dad than any they had ever known.

Although Megan's church was in a wealthy suburb, many poor people lived in the area too, Megan realised, that evening and over the following weeks. That's why Dom had volunteered for this parish, he explained to her, even though he lived across the harbour, a train and a bus ride away. This was where there was the most unmet need, Father John had told him – precisely because people assumed that everyone who lived on the lower North Shore these days must be rich. But it hadn't always been that way, and in the workers' cottages in the steep streets rising up from the harbour and the giant blocks of flats lining the highway, there were still pockets of desperate poverty.

'Let's pray.' Dom's voice was earnest, but compelling.

Megan closed her eyes. The first few minutes of praying at school and at Mass always felt stagey to her. Hands clasped, an unnatural silence settling over them all. She used the moments to catch her breath. To find a comfortable position to sit in. To ease herself into the quiet.

'Our Father, who art in Heaven, hallowed be Thy name.'

And that prayer – it eased her. She supposed it worked like a mantra, just as the rosary did. Over the next weeks and months Megan began regularly using the silver and pearl one her parents had given her for Confirmation.

'Thy Kingdom come. Thy will be done.'

Dom sometimes asked the youth group what they thought the Kingdom of Heaven would be like. One of the children wanted to be a current affairs journalist there. 'There'll still be things that happen!' he cried, hurt by their gentle laughter. 'People will still want to be kept up to date!'

'Jesus said to love others as you love yourself,' Dom told them. 'That means that you must love yourself, just as much as you love other people. What would that mean? To love yourself?'

'To go to school every day,' said one. 'To ask for prescription glasses,' said another. 'To have breakfast.' 'To ask for extra blankets.'

The contrast between their lives and hers made Megan feel like crying.

'I want to do something,' she'd say fiercely when she got home.

'Do well at school. Go to university and change things.' Her father would say it like a chant. He made it sound so simple. It seemed so simple to Megan, at that time, too.

CHAPTER FOUR

Aidan sat on his bike, idling, debating whether to park it here outside the cafe or across the road, in the shade. A man paused next to him and mouthed something. Aidan took off his helmet and turned off the engine.

'Huh?'

The man jerked his thumb over his shoulder and Aidan realised this was Megan's husband, the man who'd been sitting beside her in the car the other day. He hadn't recognised him in that apron and with a bandanna in his hair.

'Can I help you?'

'I don't know. Can you?' Aidan rested his weight against the bike, curious about what was going to happen next. Ready to wait here in silence for minutes, if necessary, to find out, which was a skill he'd learned at work. In Legal Aid no one is ever very keen to see you. Turning up at offices and government departments, ready to argue for some poor – and that was usually the case, literally – person's rights. He liked to relax in these situations. Let the tension rise. Let the cards fall where they may.

'What's going on?' Megan appeared next to them, her arms filled with plates and cups and saucers.

'Nothing,' said Matt and Aidan in unison, as if caught out somehow, and guilty.

'Aidan, this is Matt, my partner. Matt, this is Aidan. We were kids together. In Sydney.'

That wasn't quite accurate, thought Aidan, but he nodded anyway.

'He's here on holiday,' continued Megan, turning to Matt. 'Wandered in here by chance the other day.'

'You didn't say anything about it to me.'

'Because there wasn't anything to say.' Her voice rising. 'I'll come out soon, when I can, okay, Aidan?' she said, dismissing him. 'Matt, listen, we're already falling behind.'

Matt gave Aidan another long, considering stare before following Megan back inside.

Aidan chose a seat outside, where he could watch her wait on the customers without being too obvious about it. Coffee, eggs and muffins were the way to go, he learned. Finally she walked over to him.

'You can't just turn up here whenever you want, okay? I don't want people wondering about you. And you can't call me Megan, either. My name is Halley.'

'Okay, Halley. Where can we talk?'

'Again? Now?'

'When else?'

He watched her go back behind the counter and say something to Matt, who nodded without looking up from his work. She peeled off her apron and picked up her bag.

'I don't have long,' she said, and walked on, not pausing to see if he followed. They walked around the corner to a bend in the river, sitting down on the grassy bank in a spot well protected from passers-by.

'It's funny to think how different it all is now, isn't it?' said Aidan, plucking at a dandelion stalk. 'From when we were kids, I mean.'

'Wrinkles and grey hair and all that, you mean?'

Aidan lowered the stalk. 'No. I mean how back in the nineties, if you said you were Irish Catholic, people automatically thought you must have an opinion about Northern Ireland. And then September 11 changed everything.'

'Sometimes there are leeches around here.' Halley pulled the hem of her skirt tightly around her ankles, drawing her legs up under her and casting an eye over the ground around them. 'Especially when it's rained.'

'So where were you when it happened?'

'When what happened?'

'When the Twin Towers fell.' He couldn't believe she wasn't already well versed in this conversation. This century's equivalent of, 'Where were you when you heard JFK had been killed?' Or in this country, he reminded himself, 'Where were you when Gough Whitlam was sacked?' Megan had explained it to him a long time ago, when she was at university. He remembered her clearly from then. Her outrage. Her purple top and purple skirt flowing out over her ankles. Her sexy platform peep-toe shoes. The uneasy mixture of assertion and caution in her manner that he learned to associate with intelligent young women. That was all gone, though. Not her face, or her figure. They were youthful still. Perhaps all that cafe work. Or perhaps her bizarre quarantining from history – from any consequences, or even thoughts, it would appear – had kept her young. They said the Virgin Mary never aged. Her manner, though, was unassuming. Without those startling bursts of animation she used to have, she gave nothing away. He was disappointed. That Megan he had known – it didn't seem possible that this is what she had become. All that flowering – for this?

Perhaps she felt something of what he was thinking, because she climbed to her feet, brushing down her skirt with rough gestures. 'I have to go.'

'Already?' Now that she was leaving he needed more than ever to talk. 'You're telling me you don't remember where you were on September 11?'

'My life isn't like yours, Aidan. I don't go anywhere. I do the same thing every day. Why would I remember? I would have been in the cafe or at home. I would have been working or it would have been my day off. There's nothing to remember.'

'Jesus.'

'I heard it on the radio. But I didn't realise what I was hearing. No one did. I think I saw it for the first time at the pub. It's the only place in town with a flat screen TV.' She shrugged, smiling at him. 'It looked like a film, didn't it? I couldn't believe it was real.'

'And that's it?'

'What do you want from me, Aidan? What are you getting at?'

He sat up, throwing the dandelion stalk away. He would keep the conversation general for the moment, he decided.

'I've seen genuine 1970s Kombi vans parked at the supermarket. The paper is full of the dangers of wi-fi and vaccination and fluoride in the water. Does the outside world, or even this century, penetrate this town at all?'

'Call me next time and make an appointment if you want to see me, okay? Here's my number.' She scribbled on a piece of paper from her bag and dropped it into his lap. 'I have to go.'

He watched her walking away, admiring the way her bottom hugged the thin cotton of her skirt. She was in good shape for a woman of thirty-seven – he had worked it out. Better than him.

Just this morning he'd looked in the bathroom mirror at his motel and despaired of ever being a handsome man. His red hair and fair skin freckled in the sun and developed a rash when it rained. He looked mouldy, he'd decided, peering at himself, the sink digging into his stomach as he leaned forward. His face, once okay-looking, was sagging into a pudding shape. An unremarkable red-faced, red-haired pudding-man, that was him. At least he still had his hair. He smoothed it back. He wore it short, but sometimes wondered about letting it grow. He was also considering a soul patch, the little postage stamp of hair some men grew on the very tip of their chinny-chin-chin. No. Not even that would make any difference. He hadn't been born beautiful and it looked like it wasn't about to happen now.

He lay back on the grass. He had been in London, on September 11, with Anne.

'But I haven't brought my lunch,' she objected, when he hustled them out of their building.

'We'll buy it, for once. Let's go for a walk and then sit down somewhere.'

The temperature was crisp, the sun shining, and he was glad to be out of the office. The world felt bigger out here, the people walking briskly past creating a feeling of privacy and anonymity that had been impossible in their open plan office.

'I can't. I'm meeting with the board this afternoon. I have to prepare.'

'You can't break up with me and work.'

'I'm not breaking up with you.' She hunched her shoulders. She was wearing her old brown cardigan over her crisp white blouse and grey wool work trousers. 'Can we please go back inside?'

'Everything is better with a good airing. But aren't you cold? Why don't you have your coat? Your little hands!'

She prised her hands out of his and glanced down the street. 'I thought we were just popping out.'

'Wear my scarf, at least.'

'If we're going to go, let's go.'

They walked past the house with the sunken front garden that they had been keeping a close eye on since it was first planted three years earlier, but Anne didn't look at it. Wordlessly they passed the double-fronted Victorian that was just the kind of thing they'd like to own one day, and the tightly luxurious little mews that always had some new, absurdly pretentious flourish they liked to laugh over, but Anne's gaze remained fixed on the footpath in front of her, and so Aidan pushed his hands into his pockets and focused on silently keeping up with her.

'What are we doing?' she said, after four blocks.

'Putting off the inevitable, I suppose.'

She stopped and stared at him, her blue eyes watery. 'Inevitable? Why then, in God's name, did we ever start going out?'

'That's not what I mean.' He cast his eyes up to heaven, wishing he believed there was someone up there who could help him. 'I mean talking about Liam is inevitable. And us walking in silence has been putting it off.'

'Then let's talk.'

'I know you don't like me going to visit him in prison, and you don't like me going to his hearings. That's why I haven't talked about it.'

'But you're going to visit this weekend. I saw the paperwork on your desk. And this morning I took that message for you from ... who is Knowles?'

'That's his court-appointed representative. He's very good. You'd like him. He's fair.'

'That's not the point.'

They were standing on a corner so bleak it was as if they were on a different planet from the street they worked in, thought Aidan. Identical tower blocks of orange-brick flats loomed on every corner, only protected from the thick streams of traffic by low walls like the one they were standing next to.

'You've always known about Liam,' pleaded Aidan.

'This last time has got me thinking: this is never going to change, is it? You said it wasn't always going to be like this. After the Belfast Agreement you said there would be progress, and that's three years ago already.'

Aidan swallowed and looked around, as though this conversation might not have to happen at all, if only he could put it off for a little longer. Brakes squealed as traffic slowed and then accelerated around the corner. Across the road a children's party supplies shop punctuated the line of boarded-up windows. 'Mr Squeaky's Palace of Fun' was written in white cursive across the shopfront, and a bunch of blue foil balloons in a bucket of sand at the doorway wavered and snapped in the breeze, so false in its cheer on this barren grey corner that it seemed as though it might be a lure into a trap.

'Liam said there would be progress,' he said finally. 'He said things would change. I don't understand why they haven't. I thought he would be released by now.'

'I can't hold him responsible for that,' said Anne. 'But I thought that you meant *he* might change. And I just wonder what he would be doing if he wasn't in prison. And I don't think he'd be supporting the peace agreement.'

'You don't even know what he did.'

'No one knows what he did.'

'And whose fault is that?' said Aidan, his voice rising. 'Who started with the secret trials? Who put the ban on news reporting about any of it in this country? The Brits!'

'Your brother is in a prison for terrorists, Aidan.'

'Some people would say that's a cultural construct. Some people would say Liam's a civil rights activist, a freedom fighter.'

Anne laughed, a chuckle so cynical bubbling out of her it shocked Aidan.

'Some of them are in parliament,' he said.

'They say today's terrorist is tomorrow's minister for education,' said Anne, gathering her hair into a ponytail and skillfully tying it with a rubber band she kept on her wrist for that purpose.

'The British called Ghandi a terrorist, once,' muttered Aidan. 'In any case, where Liam is he can't be doing any harm.'

'You're being willfully naive. He can organise all kinds of things from prison. If I know that, how can you not?'

Aidan did know, and when he visited Liam it was one of the things he couldn't stop thinking about.

'I can't stand this. I think I can, and then visiting time comes around again, or a letter or a phone call, and I have to admit to myself that you support him.'

'I don't support him! He's my brother, that's all!'

'That's not all!'

'Stop.' He didn't think of Liam like that. It wasn't like that. But somehow, somewhere between his world and Anne's, the labels were pasted on, and the blame was laid, and the past with its secrets and its riddles settled between them like a raven into its nest. 'You see poverty as political, right?' He nodded at the tower blocks around them. 'You don't blame the people who live here for its ugliness, do you? Or for what they have to go through?'

'You know I don't.'

'And shit happens here.'

Just last week they'd been sitting in a café around the corner and someone had come running past and snatched a woman's bag right off her table. 'It's the kids from the estates,' said the waiter. 'Happens all the time.'

'Don't.' Anne put up her hand. 'Don't compare. It's cheap.'

Was it? wondered Aidan. He didn't know. He was just searching for reasons, using whatever came to hand to find arguments for something he couldn't argue rationally because his decision to stand by Liam wasn't rational. He and Liam were from the same place, that was all. They'd been through the same thing, and how Liam had ended up where he was and Aidan had ended up here was a mystery he could never get to the bottom of.

'Can we go inside somewhere please?' said Anne. 'I'm freezing.'

'The Bat and Ball is around the corner.'

Anne cringed, but he took her hand and they walked there anyway.

The patrons of the Bat and Ball wore thick gold watches and loafers with tassels. The women put their phones on the table next to their glasses of wine. Not their type of people, and not their type of pub, and that was precisely what made it a good venue for today, thought Aidan. They wouldn't be tempted to return. Aidan had learned the hard way that a place could be ruined by sadness, so that even if a place had been your favourite, your heart's home, the associations would render it forever a radioactive zone. The way he felt about Belfast. The way he felt about Sydney.

They walked in and the blaring TVs put them off immediately. They were set to extra loud, it seemed, and everyone was staring up at them, as though stunned. Aidan thought of asking for the one in the corner to be turned down, but something about the fact that no one else seemed to be talking put him off the idea. Later he remembered how a group of men had turned to look at him with what he thought at the time was suspicion, and realised it had been a longing to share the bad news. A childish apprehension of doom. Of wanting to be the first ones to tell. To see their own reactions when they'd first heard the news written on Aidan's and Anne's faces so that they could watch this time, and perhaps better understand what was happening. At the time, though, Aidan thought they were averse to strangers coming into their local and, sick of them already, walked out.

'What's wrong?' asked Anne, joining him outside.

'I can't face the wankers.'

Anne stepped close to him, grasping the lapels of his duffel coat and pulling him close. 'I need some time away from you,' she said gently. 'To think about things.'

'I knew you were breaking up with me.'

They walked home, and Aidan packed an overnight bag while Anne emailed work to tell them she was sick, and that neither she nor Aidan would be coming back to work that day.

'I'll see you later, then,' said Aidan, once he had his coat on and was ready to leave.

'Where will you go?' Her face was white and her hair seemed even finer than usual, tendrils floating around her head like a halo.

'I'll go to Tom's.' Tom wouldn't be home, but his cat would be, and Aidan knew where he kept his spare key.

'Call me later.' She rose on her toes to give him a quick kiss and pat on the shoulder, as though this were any normal day.

He was at the end of their street, about to disappear into the crowds on the Edgware Road, misery overtaking him, when he heard her footsteps pounding up the street behind him, as if reminding him that sadness could be outrun. By Anne, at any rate.

'Stop! You can't go on the Underground. Come home.'

'What are you talking about?' Hope filled him again, as suddenly as it had ebbed away.

'Come and see.'

They walked swiftly back to their flat and opened the door to the blaring of their own TV. A talking head gave way to a shot of the New York skyline, and a building spewing smoke from a hole in its side.

It had saved them, temporarily. Given them room for hope. He hadn't left her side that evening or for a day after. Instead they sat on their sofa, watching the Twin Towers falling, over and over again.

In the days and weeks following he'd felt the ending of something. Like a final wave that takes the last of the sandcastle out with it to the sea, he felt the era of Northern Ireland's Troubles – and his own troubles along with them – fading. This was a whole new ballgame – the players, the terror, the politics of it all as unfamiliar to him as they were to Anne. It was a nice feeling, that. Suddenly to have a world-view that the two of them could share. He thought of Liam, in his prison cell, and wondered if he felt it, too. The tide sweeping out and leaving him stranded on a forgotten, irrelevant shore. There would be no more attention given by the United States, and the world, to the problems in Northern Ireland anymore, nor to Liam and the others like him. No one outside that tiny little place would even care.

It was over.

He was wrong, of course. It would never be over, and not just for the victims on both sides. A year after the IRA announced it would begin to disarm, Liam joined the Real IRA, a splinter faction that insisted on carrying on with the fighting, and the respite that had been offered, to Aidan and to Anne as much as to anybody else, ended.

He'd felt lonely then. Unable to share with Anne his thoughts and apprehensions. The shaky state of their relationship underlining his orphaned state. That was the first time he'd thought of Megan and seriously wondered where she was, and decided that he would look for her one day. He wanted to talk with someone who'd known his family. He wanted to talk to someone for whom the past was as real as it was to him.

CHAPTER FIVE

Halley swung the steering wheel to take the bends in the road. Go slow, the sign said. As if. She felt like singing. From here, up on the ridge of McAuleys Lane, she could see the flat flood plain of Mullumbimby laid out below. Macadamia orchards, dairy farms and the sinuous curve of the Brunswick River almost hidden by greenery. Here, above it all, she could slam her foot down on the accelerator and sing.

Her voice cracked a few lines into a Dolly Parton song. It wasn't a particularly good voice, she knew. She thought she deserved to sound like smokey honey, crushed velvet and mulled wine. To her own ears she sounded young and rather sweet, but Benny said she sounded like a man singing in falsetto.

The car rattled over the wooden bridge made a century ago, perched over a ravine that the disused railway ran through. There was something inviting about the way the narrow hillsides closed in on each other to form a narrow V. She slowed the car and looked to the right where the train track ran out from the ravine onto the plain. The escarpment rose straight up from the flat land, as if a green-forested curtain had been pulled across the sky. As she finished with the bridge and hit bitumen, she floored it again, reaching one hundred kilometres an hour on the straight.

She had just made love with Sug at his cabin in the hills. It was so easy, so pleasant, and all the uneasiness stirred up by Aidan's reappearance in her life had left her, temporarily at least. He had even offered her wine.

'I couldn't,' said Halley, lounging on his beaten-up old sofa.

They had already kissed and broken apart, him pulling away and walking to the battered fridge on the other side of the crowded room.

'You don't drink in the day?'

'Exactly.'

Sug poured himself a glass. 'I had no idea I was with such a good girl.'

'Don't call me that.'

'What?' He paused by the open fridge door. 'You don't like me calling you a girl?'

'No ... Forget it,' she muttered. She wanted to get out of there, then. Her gaze slid sideways to the door.

'Hey.' He came over and kissed her. 'Tell me what you like and don't like, okay? I want you to stay.'

That had been the only sour note. All the rest was good. His body was beautiful, which was no big deal. A lot of men's around here, Matt's included, were. It was all that physical labour, all that surfing and sun. On top of his beauty he was kind, she discovered. He was playful. He was free.

'Sug as in Sugar,' he'd told her the other night in the Middle B. Halley hadn't asked what kind of a stupid made-up name that was. Living here she'd learned not to. Long stories about ashrams and spirit guides too often intruded into the conversation when you did. But Sug offered, anyway. 'That's what my mother called me.'

They'd been sitting on one of the old sofas in the Middle B's lounge, wedged in between the piano and the bar. The pub was crowded, and a woman sat jammed on the other side of Halley, so no one would have thought that she and Sug were together to look at them. Others sat up at the counters lining the windows, open to the street outside where smokers stood nursing their drinks on the sill. It was dusk, and noisy fleets of birds were swooping around the palm trees. The sky was a mackerel pink, racing over Mount Chincogan, which stood like a friendly ogre to the northwest of town, looking down its thickly-treed crinkled green hide at them all.

'Because you're as sweet as?' she'd asked, tempering the come-on of her words with a close-lipped, downward-turning smile. Let him take it as he chose.

'Try me.'

She had nodded, smiling into his eyes. He was hers. She could feel it. It was only a matter of time.

'So. Tuesday afternoons?' she asked, when she was zipping up her jeans. He lay on the bed, surrounded by violently orange pillows.

'Hmm?'

He was dreamy, only just managing to stay awake. Halley was sorry to leave him, but they'd lingered over the preliminaries.

'For our ...' she paused, balancing on one leg as she pulled on a boot, searching for a suitably delicate euphemism '... date.'

'You want to schedule a regular time?' said Sug, shaking his silver grey head, his dark eyes bleary.

So seductive, thought Halley, still with the feeling of him inside her, and the weight of him on top of her.

'I have a husband. And a child,' said Halley, hopping around on one foot while she struggled with the other boot.

'I'm aware of that,' said Sug.

He'd said he'd first noticed her six months ago, when they'd had dinner in his restaurant where Benny was working – it was a pizza joint next to the roundabout on the way out of town. 'I was sorry,' said Sug, 'when I realised you were Benny's mother.' She'd come in on her own while Matt went to the bottle shop. She'd been wearing a red floaty dress that she'd bought for four dollars from the op shop next to the cafe. 'I was sorry,' he said, 'when I realised you weren't free.' 'You're sweet,' Halley had replied, it not even occurring to her for a minute to believe him.

'I have a business,' she said now.

'Yes,' said Sug. He was awake again, looking at her with sad, level eyes. His face was more defined than Matt's, thought Halley, his every expression more intense.

'So we need to make a time.' Halley squatted down and cupped his face with her hand. 'Otherwise I'll never see you.'

'I'm just dazed by the speed we're going at, that's all,' said Sug. 'But sure. Tuesday afternoons.'

They kissed, just the kind of kiss Halley wanted. Warm. Loving. His tongue in her mouth producing an instant feeling of relaxation in her. It was erotic, and ... there was that word again. That was what this was all about really, thought Halley. Free.

When she walked into the café she could see from the number of customers sitting at tables with no food on them that Matt was buckling under the pressure. Don't snap, don't push, she told herself, as she made her way to the kitchen. But Matt was sometimes so achingly slow, she thought, as she watched him. From stove to preparation bench to the sack of mixed salad on the floor and back to the preparation bench again, he seemed to move through an ever-thickening glue.

'Order out.'

'Is everything under control?'

'Where have you been?'

'Pilates. I told you. Do you need ...' She checked herself. 'Can I give you a hand?'

He shook his head, lowering it so that his mop of curling blond hair fell forward, hiding his face from her. They stood at the bench side by side, wordlessly watching his slow-moving hands.

They were what had attracted her, she remembered, when they first met. They'd worked side by side when she was hired as a sous-chef at a cafe in Belongil, the beach next to Byron Bay. Matt was the dessert chef, and his slow, mindful way of working, so consistently and steadily, each movement so considered, had calmed her when she was feeling frantic. He made coffees when his desserts were done, and his way of looking out at the surf while he worked calmed her, too. Making her look out at the empty beach and horizon from time to time, reminding her of how beautiful this place was, and how removed. He was friendly, but distant, with everyone, and that had attracted her, too. He was never curious. He was never loud. He didn't startle her with sudden movements or announcements, except when he proposed, just three months after they'd started going out. 'Because I love you,' he'd said, standing in the sand in front of the cafe one night after closing. 'But why?' Halley had asked him, honestly questioning. He'd crinkled his eyes in amusement. 'Because you don't want to talk after we make love. Because even though you're quiet, you're warm.'

Halley nodded. By those criteria she loved Matt, too, and the years since then had only given her more reason. He was a wonderful father, and a good person, helpful to everyone he came across, friendly and calm. But still slow. And still withdrawn, quiet to the point of being uncommunicative. Months could go by when she would have no clue what he might be thinking. Or, sometimes, if he even was. She suspected surfers like Matt existed in a zen-haze of exercise-induced dopamine at times, their bodies recreating the feeling of surfing when they concentrated hard enough, so they would be reliving a great wave when they were meant to be talking to their partner, or running a cafe, like now.

'We could give Lisa more responsibility, let you just do coffees and the till,' she said on the way home. She'd meant to broach it slowly, but now they were in the car she was too tired. First Aidan, and then Sug, and then all afternoon in the cafe and cleaning up afterwards had just about done her in.

'And give her a pay rise, you mean? No.'

Belatedly she touched his shoulder. He pulled away.

'No. I don't need ...'

Go on, thought Halley. Get angry. Swear. She wanted him to.

'... help.' He subsided.

And that was it. They were at loggerheads again. If loggerheads could be spiky on one side, fuzzy on the other.

When they got home he mowed his way through the evening chores, Benny's as well as his own.

'You shouldn't be doing the chickens,' she said.

He'd been crashing around the yard, swearing and swooping for the last fifteen minutes before bringing one of them inside. It was Mabel, their red bantam, with a sore wing. He shouldered past her into the house, the work boots he wore muddy on her freshly swept carpet and wooden floors.

'Shouldn't?' His lip curled.

'No. You shouldn't,' said Halley, as her fingers explored the joint under Mabel's wing. 'Benny will never learn responsibility if you shield him all the time.'

'Shield him from what, Halley? From you, you mean?'

Benny could be slow, too, like Matt. Muddling through, forgetful, scattered.

'He has to learn.' She arched her back, her eye unwillingly clocking a patch of new mould up near the ceiling.

'Learn what?' he said, as Mabel clucked enquiringly, her beady-eyed gaze fixed on the doorstop of bread he was slathering with peanut butter and honey right next to her at the table. Using the same knife for both jars, noticed Halley.

And that's how it was. Somehow she had become the enemy the two of them conspired against. The stand-in for school and the world. They helped each other in the tiny contributions she asked of them. They conspired together in avoiding her too, she sometimes thought. Always the other one, the one she wasn't looking for, in possession of the mobile phone. And, like school and work and the world, she resented them in return.

It's funny how we get caught in these patterns, thought Halley, as she smoothed Mabel's feathers and tickled her neck. Their lack of interest in her rosters and strategies and schemes for getting all the work done. Their barely concealed boredom when she wanted them to stop playing trap cricket in the back yard and go somewhere and do something together as a family, for a change. Were schools jealous of the pupils who didn't care? Were workplaces resentful of those who wouldn't take them seriously? All those meetings with Benny's teachers, over the years. The perennial concern that he wasn't living up to his potential. Were they really just disgruntled that he seemed to be so happy and complete already? And when they used to say he might have a learning difficulty – was that just another way of punishing him for not being interested in what they wanted him to learn? Benny had taught himself to surf by watching Matt, it seemed. The first time he'd gone into the water with a board at Brunswick Heads it had been a matter of minutes before he was riding a wave, standing nonchalantly on his board, all the way in to the shore.

'I don't know,' she sighed. She wouldn't have dinner tonight, she decided. She was too tired. And after all, she shouldn't be impatient with Matt for being uncommunicative. If anyone kept too much to themselves, it was her. Matt had never been anything but open with her about his past, whereas he knew nothing of her previous life.

'Know what?' Matt gave her a half smile. He put his hand over hers, which still cradled Mabel's warm breast. 'You're good with her. Look how calm she is.'

Halley looked down at their entwined fingers, closing her eyes and lingering for a moment on the warmth. But then she thought of how abruptly he'd moved away from her the other night.

She got up, thrusting the chicken into his startled grasp, and left the room.

CHAPTER SIX

For Aidan it was the smells that triggered his memories of living in Australia as a child, and the sea. He rented a holiday flat at Brunswick Heads, the little seaside town fifteen minutes drive from Mullumbimby, and every morning he woke to that clean-scrubbed smell. As though the air itself had been washed and wrung and laid out to dry in the sun. And the food smells. Hot chips and frying. Barbecues on the weekend and fresh-cut grass. Then the sounds. Dogs barking. Magpies calling. Yet a pervasive quietness. There just weren't the quantities of people and cars and shops here that there were in England. Everything was sparser, emptier, more raw. In the restaurants on the strip where he'd started buying his dinner most nights, the very air hurt his ears. Chairs scraping painfully over the concrete flooring, cutlery clashing and voices ringing harshly against the bare walls.

And the ants still had it in for him. He remembered that, too. Sitting on a soft patch of grass, cool breeze, dappled shade under a swaying palm tree and – wham! A stinging bite. Jumping up, like a drug it was, he could feel the poison coursing through his veins. Ants didn't bite you like that in England, or in Ireland for that matter.

And food didn't taste like this, either. Salty strong flavours coming at him with so many memories attached. He ate lunch at the pub in the lovely beer garden opposite the river. Wooden tables and chairs set out under the poinciana trees and kids running everywhere. He had the salad and chips, and longed for the steak. He didn't in London. It was easy to be vegetarian there. But here people walked past him with their hunks of dead animal laid out all fresh and dripping on their plates. In triumph, he thought, as though they'd just hunted it down and slaughtered it themselves. For the first few days he stuck to the Greek salad and the tofu satay, but then on Sunday he succumbed. You paid your money and they gave you a buzzer that went off when your food was ready. He had 'The Works'. Fried onions, a slab of grilled steak done rare and a beer. It was first class, and if Anne had been there with him it would have been up there as one of the nicest meals he'd ever eaten. And that was it. After twenty years of being vegetarian he took to meat as if he'd never been away. Breakfasts at the cafe along the river – bacon and avocado and an egg splitting open, oozing yellow on the white yummy bun. Roast chicken sandwiches and spaghetti bolognese. 'You're getting fat,' he told himself in the mirror of his little flat. His leather jacket didn't zip up so easily anymore. 'You're getting fat and old and past it.' He rubbed his stomach as you would a Buddha's. Perhaps it would bring him luck.

'You have to help me get out of here,' Liam said, the last time Aidan had visited him in prison.

Aidan had endured a difficult week at work and visiting Liam was the last thing he felt like doing. Liam was leaning forward across the table, whispering. He was in with the general population this time, and the whole room was filled with people, all talking so loudly it was hard to hear even when you practically shouted. Aidan also had to lean forward to make out what Liam was saying, no doubt attracting attention they would never have attracted if they'd just kept speaking in a normal tone.

'What?'

'You have to help get me out of here.'

Aidan sat back.

'What are you talking about?'

He'd never been up for anything with Liam. From the beginning, he never wanted to help with any of his schemes. None of it interested him in the slightest. As though he'd been born not trusting him.

'Shhhh,' said Liam.

'Shhh your fucking self. I don't need to whisper.'

'Asshole.'

'Crumb bucket.'

'Don't you mean scum bucket, you fool?'

'Shithead shitkicking shitstirrer.'

They smiled.

'Okay,' shrugged Liam. 'Don't help.'

'It's not that I don't want to help.'

'Oh, then what is it? You don't want to get involved in any way. You don't want to do anything at all out of the ordinary or anything that might upset your little lady ...'

'Shut up, Liam.' Aidan hadn't told Liam that he and Anne had broken up. In fact he hadn't told anyone. Preferring to give vague excuses at social events. Glossing over the fact, when invitations were proffered, that she would never be coming anywhere with him again. 'I don't have to visit, you know.'

'I know.'

Aidan knew Liam didn't receive many visitors anymore. None of the women who used to flock to him. None of the journalists or the brothers in the movement. None of the old ladies, either, seeing in Liam some version of their fathers or brothers, sons or grandsons. All of that had faded away. Was it Liam who had become less interesting? wondered Aidan. Or was it the world that had become less interested in Liam?

He wasn't as good-looking anymore. That unshaven charisma he used to exude, that sexual power, had run to fat. In his blue overalls and faded blue T-shirt he looked comfortable and pudgy. Heavy smoking had turned his nails dark, but his glasses still gave him the look of a learned man. He claimed he read philosophy inside, Nietzsche and Marx, but Aidan wondered. All he ever asked for were detective novels and the occasional girlie magazine. You weren't supposed to, but the guards never seemed to notice when you handed them straight over the table as Aidan had just done.

'You still working out?' Aidan asked.

'Sometimes.'

Liam's arms were flabby, and his hands seemed small in proportion to the weight of his forearms. They used to be ropey with muscle. He slumped comfortably in his chair whereas he used to have the coiled energy of a panther. Aidan smiled at the memory of him standing on the back verandah of their house in Balmain, framed by the lush tropical garden, back when he was beautiful, performing for them.

'What are you smiling at?'

'Remember that audition piece you did for drama school? The Woody Allen?'

It had been one of Liam's party pieces. He recited it beautifully, making all of them laugh, making his mother fall in love with him all over again, and any other woman watching, remembered Aidan.

Liam looked up at the low ceiling striped with fluorescent lighting. Bits of concrete rotted off occasionally and dropped fragments in the cardboard cups of tea that you could get from the machine. He raised his eyebrows, inhaling through his nose as though he was smelling that long-ago tropical garden in Sydney, thought Aidan. A rich, verdant, fertile smell. Liam dropped his head, looking into his lap, and started, his voice low, even and spell-binding as he recited his monologue.

Until he faltered. 'Uh ... no. Let me start this over.'

'You're going great,' said Aidan. He really was. The woman at the next seat along was glancing at him, obviously more interested in what Liam had to say than her boyfriend sitting opposite.

'It's part of the script, you numbskull. Shut up and listen.'

Liam glanced at the woman, somehow aware of her interest although up until then he'd been staring into his lap. An actor could sense these things, Aidan guessed, and in his mind Liam was, always would be, an actor.

Liam didn't try to sound like Woody Allen as he recited the rest of it. He didn't sound neurotic or unsure or indecisive. He sounded passionate, with a tinge of irony. He sounded like himself. It was the Irish way, said Nuala, when Liam did it on that balcony overlooking the garden in Balmain. He made it his own.

When he finished the sound of clapping startled Aidan out of his reverie. The woman was clapping Liam, gold bracelets flashing and dreadlocks swinging.

'That was brilliant,' she said in her lilting Jamaican accent. 'Brilliant! Did you write that?'

Liam looked confused, thought Aidan. Frowning and shaking his head, hunching his shoulders as though he didn't want to draw attention. The woman's boyfriend nodded at him. Not smiling, but not annoyed either. 'That was good, man. Enjoyed it.'

'It's from a movie,' said Aidan, when he realised Liam wasn't going to say anything, or to explain, although once he would have been a fountain of words on the topic. 'A Woody Allen movie.'

The woman shook her head.

'Manhattan.'

'That's the movie?'

'Yeah.'

'Don't know it. I loved that, though. Loved it. You should be an actor.' She smiled at Liam and turned her attention back to her boyfriend.

'I can't believe you remember every word,' said Aidan.

'I can't either,' said Liam.

'They should have let you into acting school,' said Aidan.

'What are you talking about? They did.'

Now Aidan dimly recalled the excited phone call late at night, his mother's eyes shining as she relayed the news.

'They even let me defer two years running, but ...' Liam looked around. 'I was needed, for this.'

But but but, thought Aidan. He didn't want to hear it. Whatever Liam's string of excuses today would turn out to be. Whatever line of 'and then's and 'would you believe it?'s and 'no one's fault really's that their conversations here so often devolved into.

'I forgot,' said Aidan, cutting him off. 'I forgot you got in.'

'Yeah.'

Liam didn't say anything more, to Aidan's relief. They weren't going to go down that road this time.

The woman next to him stood up to leave. Her bum was packed tightly into the thin denim, a roll of coffee-coloured flesh exposed between the blue cotton of her T-shirt and the waistband of her jeans. Her red-taloned fingertips delicately brushed the fingertips of the man still seated opposite.

'See ya,' she said to them as she turned away.

Liam and Aidan both nodded. Her boyfriend stood, scraping his chair loudly against the concrete flooring, and loped away.

'Shit,' said Liam.

'What?'

'I shouldn't have attracted his attention.'

'What? Him?' Liam nodded. 'I thought he enjoyed it.'

'Yeah.' Liam's eyes darted from side to side, the professional glance of someone who can map a whole room without turning their head.

Aidan felt disconcerted. He smelled fear on Liam, and caution. His big brother, the star, the adored one, acted small in here. His light slowly fading, his mane of hair thinning, his body melting, his face creasing. Aidan was glad their mother hadn't lived to see this.

'Okay, Liam. All right,' he relented. 'What help do you need?'

'Talk to her, find out everything she remembers. Find out what she knows. If I have to turn her in to get me out of here, I need to know what she understands.'

CHAPTER SEVEN

Halley was catering for a dance party being held in the community hall out past Main Arm, a scattering of communes and farms and a corner shop, deep in the bush twenty minutes drive west of town. She went early in the station wagon, filling the boot with the rice balls and nori rolls she and Matt had made that day. She'd wanted to hire staff to help with serving, but the people organising the event said they would help her. Which meant, no doubt, another night of doing everything single-handedly, thought Halley on the way there, tired already at the prospect.

When she arrived the DJ was practising, and a loop of cartoons was being silently projected against one wall. The hall itself was a beautiful thing, made twenty years ago of local red box and cedars in a hexagon, the windows and platforms and a stage arranged around the sunken dance floor. Whatever theory it was they'd been trying of stepping down into a sacred space, it meant something here. Deep into the night these events could become magical. Hearts would open, a feeling of joy and love would permeate this hall full of strangers, and Halley would believe in the goodness of people again for a little while. That's why she still signed on for these things. That and the money, of course. Five dollars for a rice ball was a good deal whichever way you looked at it.

Three hours later as she cleaned a broken bottle out of the sink in the toilets she was reconsidering. Benny was here, drinking and throwing up into the bushes, part of the crowd of teenagers, unwilling to pay the entry fee yet drawn like children to see what the adults were up to. They were having their own party, complete with bonfire, just outside. A girl was crying, huddled against the wall of the toilets; another girl had her arm around her, murmuring to her as she hiccupped and sobbed. A woman in one of the cubicles was talking loudly about how these children were spoiling our dance parties and our community. What community? wondered Halley, as she swept up the broken glass.

'Benny?' she called, standing tentatively at the edge of the group gathered around the fire. 'Benny ...'

He turned to look at her. 'Mum?'

He frowned at her, appalled, thought Halley. She scuttled back to the kitchen, peering out the window to look for him from time to time.

The young people were gathered around bottles and piles of stones, the girls barely dressed, the boys likewise, their smooth hairless torsos extending up like sculpted marble, pillars of youthful masculine energy. Old men planned wars to deal with young men like these, thought Halley, her eye drawn unwillingly down the muscled back of a boy who looked about seventeen, his jeans riding so low that the hills of his buttocks rose above his leather belt, the grooves of muscle on his lower stomach drawing her gaze downward as he turned. She started as his eyes met hers. She looked away to the other side of the campfire where figures were silhouetted against the flames. Like cavemen. Like people at the end of the world. The music swirled up like the woodsmoke into the moonlit sky. Tonight was the spring equinox.

A girl was dancing out there to the music blasting from the speakers inside. She had the expressive, adorable cuteness of a 1930s comedienne, droll expressions flitting across her face at lightning speed as she mimed the words to the song. 'The dog went – growl. I went – ahhh!' She moved loosely, coordinated in the way few people are, talent oozing from her fingertips, her body seeming to say things with just a twitch or angle of a hand or leg. And so quick. With each phrase of music her limbs told a different story. Sexy, funny, innocent, sensual. She wore a loose-fitting white dress, cloudy with lace, and cowboy boots. Halley noticed with a start that one of the boys staring at her was Benny.

'Benny, don't,' she pleaded in her heart. That girl was a heartbreaker. But she was looking right back at him as she told her story and sang her song, Halley realised, dread dragging at her.

'It's statutory rape.'

Halley turned back to the counter. A woman stood there. Halley was not even sure if this woman was talking to her. Psychological problems merged into mobile phone conversations merged into drugged states merged into one-sided conversations with aliens around here. You never could tell.

Halley smiled professionally. 'Rice ball?'

'I said if your son touches my daughter it's statutory rape.'

Halley stared. The woman had short, well-styled grey hair and wore a loose tunic made of expensively rumpled linen. She spoke with a slight German accent.

'If you want to talk to me you can come around the side,' said Halley.

The woman disappeared.

'You all right if I leave you here for a minute?' Halley said to the girl working alongside her, the one volunteer helping this evening.

'I'll be fine. What about you?'

'I'll let you know,' said Halley, wiping her hands on her jeans as she approached the side window where the woman was waiting.

'I don't understand what you're talking about.' Halley's mind flashed on the boy she'd involuntarily ogled a few moments ago, and she thought of Benny. That word, rape. It was so frightening, always.

'Oh come on. I've heard of slack mothers but this is ridiculous. He's outside there staring, you know, your son.'

This woman was daring to call her slack. This woman, whose daughter was out there too, after all.

'I ...' Oh God. 'I don't ...' Halley shook her head, trying to clear her mind. It was 2am and the music was thumping. She and the woman were leaning towards each other to be heard, too intimately close to one another to effectively attack and defend.

'What are you talking about?' She gave up. She would have had the words, once, to put this woman in her place. To assert her own membership in the class this woman evidently came from. What had happened? Too many rice balls. Too early in the morning. Too many arguments and days spent cleaning. She longed for Sug. She longed for bed. She longed for a cigarette, staring into the rainforest, sitting on her front verandah. But this was about Benny. She roused herself.

'Who are you?'

'My name is Anna Muller, and that's my daughter, Gretchen. She's fourteen.'

Halley turned to look where the woman's finger was pointing at the dancing girl.

'She looks at least eighteen. And quite beautiful,' added Halley.

You'd think this might have softened any mother's heart, but not this one.

'I have great hopes for Gretchen,' continued Anna Muller, unmoved. 'I don't see why she's messing around with your son.'

'Honestly, I don't see what I'm supposed to do,' said Halley, shocked into frankness by this woman's own. 'I didn't even know she existed until five minutes ago.'

'Talk to your son.' Anna Muller looked outraged. 'You're his mother. He must listen to you. Tell him she is too young for a relationship. Tell him to stay away from Gretchen.'

Maybe it worked that way in other countries, thought Halley, defeated, as she carried boxes and supplies out to the car. Maybe for Anna Muller, a tiger among mothers, an empress, it worked that way. Or maybe it worked that way for the mother of daughters. But then she remembered herself at that age. She was only sixteen when she met Dom. It certainly hadn't worked that way for Halley's mother, and it didn't work that way for her.

It was almost afternoon when Benny walked into the kitchen, yawning. 'Morning, Mum.' He was wearing just a pair of black jeans and white tennis socks, even though it had been cold enough earlier to leave a frost on the grass. He walked past her into the living room and sprawled on the couch, reaching for a bowl of left-over spaghetti bolognese that he must have left there after he got home from the party.

Halley climbed stiffly to her feet. She had been going through the cupboards on her hands and knees with a dustpan and broom, sweeping for weevil eggs and cockroach droppings. She kept all her groceries that didn't come in tins in plastic containers, yet that didn't stop insects of all descriptions nesting in the kitchen.

'We need to talk, Benny. About Gretchen.'

'I love her, Mum.'

Halley's hand, reaching out to stroke his curls, froze in mid air. She jumped back, her fingers splayed, as though she'd just touched a fence that turned out to be electrified.

'Love?' She couldn't stop herself. She couldn't help herself. Her face must have shown her feelings.

'Yes.' Benny put the bowl down and jumped to his feet defiantly. 'Love!'

'Benny.' Halley stalled for time. 'Benny.' She needed to hold him there, to keep him here until she could work out what to say. 'Sit down, would you. Please?'

'Her mother's upset because she doesn't know me. She thinks I'm just after sex. But I'm not. Gretchen knows I'm not.'

Halley smiled, unwisely allowing herself to express her relief. 'That's not what I'm worried about.'

'You're not?'

That took the wind out of his sails. He collapsed back into the couch. Had he grown taller lately? wondered Halley. When he sat like that, his knees almost reached his shoulders. She could still remember him perched there, holding up a book for her to read to him, the couch seeming huge and comforting, enveloping her little boy.

'No.' She sat down next to him, carefully, as if he were an animal that might get up and bolt.

'I saw her mum having a go at you out there last night.' Benny snorted. '*Ja Kommandant!* Statutory rape!'

Halley smiled, ashamed, yet pleased to be complicit, even in this off-colour joke, with him.

'You know it would be, though, don't you?' she said tentatively.

'Statutory rape? I would *never* rape.'

He was such a lovely person, thought Halley, always. In any circumstance he had such a sweetness to him. Always in trouble as a child, and still somehow so often upsetting the adults around him, he nevertheless never became hardened or cold. He never was anything but this eternally optimistic, loving person. Even when he messed up so badly you thought it could never be made right, he believed it could be. He knew you would forgive him. He knew it would all be okay. She remembered once crying when they left an expensive gift shop in Byron Bay where he had somehow managed to bring down a whole shelf of glassware. She didn't understand how. She had looked away, it seemed to her, for a millisecond. He had taken her hands and brushed away her tears. 'It will be all right, Mummy darling. It will be all right.' That was the term he used for her as soon as he started talking, and had used for her right up until he was about … oh. She couldn't remember when it had ended. 'Don't cry, Mummy darling. It will be okay.' And it had been. Somehow Benny's mischief always came with a dose of Benny's magic. The store manager called and told her they would say it was an accident and claim the damages on insurance.

'I would never rape,' said Benny again, lightly, as if the whole idea of it was simply too ridiculous.

'That's not what she meant. It's a legal definition. It's to do with having sex when you're under-age.'

'I'm under-age?'

'No darling, she is.'

'You can say her name.'

'Gretchen. Gretchen is under-age.'

'She's the one who wants to have sex.'

Ha! I knew it! Something in Halley crowed. Little trollop. Precocious little ... And then her invective, silent though it was, trailed away. This girl existed in a whole different dimension, thought Halley, of childhood. The idea of combining that with sex, even in conversation, made her nauseous.

'Do you intend to?'

'I love her, Mum, and she loves me.'

He made it all sound so simple, thought Halley, looking at her like that with that oh so Matt-ish transparent regard.

'Benny.' She put her hand on his arm. How could she explain about this? 'Sometimes the idea of sex can be ... overpowering.' She remembered her first time alone with Dom, the way she had pressed her mouth against his. That first jolt of knowing, it was electrifying. That foretaste, that discovery of the power she had over him. Like stumbling onto an unknown continent. How could a girl stop herself from wanting to explore it when she found herself there? What rich resources might she stumble upon? What as yet untapped reserves of wealth and opportunity might unfold?

'But sometimes a girl might ... say and feel something different than what's actually the best thing for her.'

'Oh spare me,' said Benny, pulling himself just a fraction, just a few millimetres, but oh so telling, away. 'She said you'd say this.'

'Who?'

'She said you'd laugh and try to say it was all some ... some kind of a hoax or something.'

'Gretchen said I'd say this? She's never even met me.'

'She said you'd try to say it doesn't exist or it's not real, but it is and it does and whatever you say it doesn't make any difference, Mum, because it is. It just is.'

'Why would she say that about me?' It was bewildering to Halley how much this hurt.

'Because ...' Benny bit his lip and looked at the door.

He was choosing his words, realised Halley. Somewhere, somehow, when she wasn't looking, he had become an adult. Just as she had done at his age, and it was far too young. Her father had done it to her. Who or what had done it to Benny? Or Gretchen for that matter?

'Because of how things are with you and Dad.'

'What?' It was like a wash or a tide that came over her. A flood. Of blood. Of feeling.

'Hey.' Benny grabbed her hand, resting on the black vinyl of the old settee. 'Are you all right?'

'I'm fine.' Halley forced herself not to gasp as she spoke. 'I'm fine.'

Benny squatted in front of her, looking up into her face so that she was forced to meet his eyes.

'Gretchen says people like you and her mum just don't remember what being in love is really like.'

He has no idea of his cruelty, thought Halley, as he rose up on his skinny legs and stalked away.

CHAPTER EIGHT

Sydney, 1989

'This is wrong,' said Dom, pushing Megan away from him, breathless from kissing. 'You know I don't believe in sex before marriage.'

They were parked on the street outside her house in the youth group van. That day they had taken a bunch of children out on a bush walk in the national park and then to McDonald's for dinner. The last child dropped off home, this was their first chance to be alone together all day.

'But I really like you,' said Megan, stroking his hair.

His fingers gripped the steering wheel as he looked straight ahead. 'I like you, too.'

'And it's only a four-year difference. They say girls mature faster, anyway.'

'So they say.' He laughed. A reluctant laugh like a grunt dragged up out of his chest. 'Megan, I have to go away tomorrow, on that field trip.'

'I know,' said Megan. That's why she was extra keen to have this time together. She didn't want to waste it talking.

'I don't want to break up with you, but I think we'd better.'

He wouldn't look at her even though she was looking at him. He stared at his hands. And then it swooped in like a storm front, hitting her with a blast force, the furnace heat of rejection. The shame of what they had been doing. Without him wanting to be with her, what was it? What was she?

'I can't believe you're doing this to me.'

All safety left her. It flew out the window and past her house where there was no safety anymore and past the jetty and the boat to the horizon, where it hovered, out of reach. Her hands grappled with the handle of the door.

'Megan, wait!'

Her fingers found the latch and she jumped down, her white tennis shoe hitting a stone and turning her ankle over her foot. It hurt. She hobbled to the gate, jamming her finger down on the intercom and screaming into the microphone. 'Let me in! Freddie! Let me in!'

'Wait. Megan. Don't.' Dom was jumping down out of the van after her, turning back to wrench the key out of the ignition.

The gates began whirring open and Megan hit the button again as soon as she slipped inside. He could have come through after her, but instead he just stood there as they glided closed in front of him. They looked at each other through the heavy wrought-iron bars.

'I don't want it to be like this.'

'Don't worry about it,' she said, her feet already turning, taking her away from him down the drive.

As if in tune with her feelings a late rainy season began, pouring down over Sydney, blanketing the harbour in misty greys. She lay in bed all the next day, convincing her mother she was too sick to go to school, sobbing with a strength that was almost orgiastic in its intensity. It was as if all the upset of the last six months was washing out of her, rising and falling in waves, leaving her huddled and drained on the bed.

'Is it Dom, darling? What's happened?' Her mother hovered in the doorway, soft and neat and worried. Megan longed to be cuddled by her, but instead she flapped her arm in dismissal, murmuring something unintelligible before rolling over to face the wall.

'Did he hurt you?' asked her father, she didn't know how much later.

'Yes!' She sat up, glaring at him, curious to know what he was going to do about it.

'What's he done to you?' His voice was low. The past six months had made him more serious. His mouth was pulled down, his eyes narrowed.

'Nothing, really,' muttered Megan, backing away, her instinct telling her to shield Dom from what her father might do.

'You're just a young girl, Megan, and you shouldn't be expected to cope with all this.' His voice was calm, yet she could feel his fury. 'He's old enough to know he has no right to put you through anything more.'

'He hasn't, really.' She sniffed luxuriously. Whether it was her father's protectiveness or the memory of Dom's reluctance in the van, forgotten in the awfulness of what it was he had to say, she felt safe again.

'Good. Because ...' He scratched his ear, and loosened his tie. Lately he'd been wearing his work suits again and going out for the day, to meetings in town, and to attend to business at his chambers. He covered his eyes with his hand and sank down to sit on the end of her bed.

'Dadda?' She put a hand out, and rested it on his leg. She was wearing his old grey sailing sweater, thickly ribbed and moth-eaten that he'd put out for the rag collection last year. She'd rescued it from the green bin bag and carried it back to her room. She liked to think that it still smelled of him, the scratchy feel of the wool like the scratchy feel of the whiskers on his chin.

'Meggs.'

Was he crying? Megan took her hand away, shocked. 'Dadda, what's wrong?'

'It's not something an innocent young girl like you or a wonderful woman like your mother should ever have to go through. I'm sorry, Meggie.' He swept her up in a hug, his arms as strong as a bear's around her. He was crying, Megan realised, her face pressed into the buttons of his shirt.

'I'm sorry, my little pony,' he said. He hadn't called her that for years.

'Dadda, what for?'

He didn't answer, and she kept hugging him tightly, her arms locked around his neck.

'Megan?' Her mother called up the stairs the next morning. 'It's for you.'

She emerged from her room, still in her father's old jumper. Bored and hungry, yet still too lethargic to go back to school.

'It's Dom, I think.' Her mother's voice could be like a glass of water sometimes, so clear and neutral.

'Hi.' Megan's own voice sounded wan as she spoke into the phone. She was pleased with it.

'I've been thinking about you.'

'Have you?'

'Worrying about you.'

Worrying? How awful. He knew how awful she'd been feeling about him, then. That was even more humiliating. She decided to tough it out.

'We were just fooling around, I know that,' she got in first. Let him be the one to try to pin a feeling on her. Let her be the one to deny everything.

'What? Well no. I wasn't. And I hope you weren't.'

'I wasn't really,' she said in a rush. She felt so raw, unable to hold things back, to be that cool, hard person she wanted to be.

'No, but ... I'm phoning about your father. I've been worrying about you and your mother and your father.'

It felt to Megan as if her whole body went quiet and flat and still, cells and organs, veins and arteries all arrested. 'What about my father?'

It was all over the news. Her mother came up to her room with a lunch tray once she was off the phone, and told her. It took her a few attempts before Megan could understand.

'I got too tired. Ate too much. Drank too much. Fucked everyone' – it wasn't Paddy who said that after all. This was all coming out in her father's appeal. The dialogue in the transcript had been misattributed. A simple error, Paddy was saying, but everyone knew he had been trying to take the fall for his friend. The person who said it was her father. He had gone to a party, drunk too much and eaten too much and fucked everyone, and then talked about it to his friend Justice Cooney in a series of questionable phone conversations late at night. Whether or not the police had the right to record him in the first place was a moot point. Whether or not the papers had the right to publish the recordings was being forgotten. Whether or not he had engaged in corruption faded into insignificance next to these revelations about the way her father had talked to his – to their – family friend. It was disgusting, thought Megan. She thought she might be sick from the shame of it. It was unbearable. There must be something that could be done.

Megan burst into the living room, her mother closely following, trying to take her arm. Megan shook her off violently. 'How could you?' she screamed.

'There are some things you don't understand,' said her father. He was collapsed into an armchair. The room, for once, was empty of lawyers. Even the phone was silent. A cigarette lay on the ashtray on the table in front of him, its plume of smoke melting up into the blue brocade French curtains.

She'd never seen anyone smoke inside, before. Her mother didn't allow it. Not even Paddy, who liked a cigar with a glass of port after dinner. He smoked it outside on the balcony, in wet weather and in cold. She'd never even seen her father smoke before.

'I believed in you!' screamed Megan, trying again. This should be her mother screaming like this. This should be her mother forcing justice out of this situation, and sense. Instead she just stood there. Megan didn't know which of them she felt more angry with.

'I shouldn't have done it. I probably shouldn't have talked about it on the phone with my friend. But it doesn't change the facts,' said her father.

Next to him on the coffee table was heaped a pile of newspapers. '*A father's shame*,' said the headline.

'What facts?' said Megan.

'That I did not try to swing any cases, just because Paddy is my friend. I did not conspire to corrupt the law.'

His words faded into meaninglessness as Megan thought of the girls at school. Their fathers. Even worse, their mothers. She thought of youth group. Of Dom. She thought of Jesus and Bobby Sands. They wouldn't have gone to a party and drunk everything and got too tired and …

'Who did you fuck?'

She rushed to the pile of newspapers stacked beside the phone and skimmed the columns of newsprint. 'Distinguished career … scandal involving call girls …' The words seemed to leap from the page at her. '… paid cash to hire prostitutes …'

'That's enough,' said her mother, pulling her away.

The world of Friday night dinner with Paddy, and Megan perched on her father's lap and safe always in the triangle, the holy trinity of her and her mother and her father, was collapsing around her, and still they were being so calm about it.

'How could you?'

'Megan, we're very sorry about how this must be affecting you,' said her mother. 'Even though you've coped so well.'

'You've been so brave. We're proud of you,' echoed her father, but their kindness could scarcely register. Megan was sure they must all die of this shame.

'None of this has been easy,' her mother was saying, 'and we've decided to end it.'

Megan began to cry, collapsing onto the carpet. She felt like a child of twelve again, when all around her, it seemed, her friends' families began falling apart. It had been her nightmare then. She knew intimately the way it went. They sat you down. They told you that they loved you, that they would always love you. That it wasn't your fault. And then they dropped the bomb.

'You mean you're getting a divorce?'

'Who said anything about divorce?' said her father, his face quizzical, almost smiling.

'We're not getting a divorce,' said her mother. 'I meant the appeal. We're dropping it.'

'It's enough,' said her father, making a washing-up motion with his hands. 'We can't take it. I can't take it. Your mother shouldn't have to take it. I'm not going to practise as a barrister anymore. Whatever they decide.'

'But what will you do?' said Megan.

'I'm off to the races,' said her father. 'I'm going to bet on the horses, professionally.'

'But you can't give up! It will look as if you're admitting that you're guilty.'

'This is enough for all of us,' said her mother and Megan saw that beneath her calm facade she was humiliated. This shame had ended it for her. 'We're not going to keep on with the appeal.'

'You'll understand when you're older,' said her father, as if that was some kind of reassurance.

'You'll understand when you're older,' echoed her mother, like a curse.

The injustice was something they were going to accept, Megan realised, as she fled back up the stairs to her room. Well, not me, decided Megan, throwing herself onto her bed. Never me.

Dom phoned her again later that day, and every day after for the duration of his trip. He phoned from public telephone boxes and people's houses. He was struggling financially, yet he always had an endless supply of coins to feed into the payphones to talk to her, asking how she was and genuinely wanting to listen. Genuinely wanting to know. He was on a mission up north to catch cane toads; he and some friends from uni had been planning this for months – days spent sweating in swamps, he said, nights camping and paddling at the beach. But not for a moment did Megan feel left out or jealous. They were beyond that. Somehow with him breaking up with her he had demonstrated his superiority, or his dominance, or something ... her mind faltered at these words. She didn't have the power that she had been so enjoying, after all. She didn't own him by owning sex – he didn't even want that. And yet he phoned and kept phoning. He kept writing. Short letters, generally an illustration or two taking up most of the page. By breaking up with her he had ended something deeper between them. A tension, she supposed later, when she was old enough to analyse these things. The question of who was boss. It was answered. And it wasn't who Megan had been expecting.

'I miss you,' he'd say at some point in their conversations, the silence between them humming with unexpressed emotion. She would wait for his phone calls and then race up to talk to him in her room kneeling on the floor, bending over the phone like a penitent.

'I miss you,' she would finally reply, when she could breathe again. Colour would rise in her cheeks, an ache spread across her chest, a warmth down into her groin. They couldn't talk any more, it seemed. All that joking and chatting and laughter had gone, and now it was like this. Deadly serious. Painful almost, and real. Megan would hunt desperately under the bed for a magazine as he talked, dredging up details of his day, trying to distract herself from the urge to tell him that she loved him. That she loved him more than anyone. That he should come home. That they needed to get married right now.

'You still there?'

'Still here,' she'd reply. Breathing deeply. Amazed at herself, and at a world where this could happen to someone. No one had ever loved anyone like this.

CHAPTER NINE

'Don't go.' Aidan rolled over and squinted at the late afternoon sun. He'd never get over his jetlag if he kept falling asleep in the day. His plan for this afternoon had been to meet up with Megan somewhere near the cafe and ask her the questions Liam had prepared for him. Instead he flopped back onto the mattress, his hands shielding his eyes from the light. 'Don't go,' said the voice in his head. It was Anne's voice. It was what she used to say on all those weekend mornings when he would haul himself out of bed to visit Liam. 'Don't go.'

It seemed always to be winter in his memories of their time together. Grey and damp outside, lamplit and golden within. She liked to wear his pyjamas around their little flat. When he pictured her he saw her in a shirt two sizes too large for her, his pants rolled over around her waist so she could walk without tripping, her fine blonde hair trailing across her face. 'Don't go,' she would have said, if she were here, holidaying with him in Australia. But that made no sense. She left him, finally, because he always did go. To Liam's parole hearings. To his defence councils. To his support meetings. To his prison visits – in Maghaberry for the last few years but all over the place, in London and Manchester, before that. To see him once a month when he was transferred back to Northern Ireland, every first Saturday morning.

He looked around at his holiday let, the beige curtains and carpet, the neat kitchen area and little table. It wasn't that different to his London flat, actually. 'Don't go.' Her soft voice reverberated in his memory. But the left-hand side of his bed was empty today, as it had been for the last three years. He got up, leaving the mess of sheets and pillows as they were. No one would be seeing any of this anyway, until he got back. He ate some toast and drank some tea, leaving the dirty dishes in the sink. They would smell by the time he got back, cockroaches be damned. He picked up his keys and backed out of the flat, locking the door behind him. Bounding down the stairs, over the pile of mail spilling onto the floor in the entry hall and out into the blasting sun.

He sighed, struck by the calm beauty of the scene in front of him. He sat down on the front step of his building to take it all in, the green mountains rising in the distance in the haze, the river sparkling in front of him, the caravan park, the kids playing on the sand, a dog sprawling at their feet, begging for left-over ice-cream, thinking of an afternoon in Belfast with Liam, thirty years ago.

Belfast, 1979

'Do you want to do something a bit different this afternoon?' Liam stood in front of Aidan in the teeming corridor. He was surprised to see Liam here, in the littlies part of the school.

'Is something wrong?'

Dom usually walked him home, but he'd gone with their nanny, Dearie, to get a dental plate today.

'Everything's grand,' said Liam. 'But on the way home do you want to do something? It will be a good laugh, I promise you.'

'No.' Aidan longed for his bedroom, and the chocolate biscuits Dearie had promised would be waiting for him in the fridge. He'd been thinking about them all day. He'd only been at school for the last three weeks and his mum said he was finding it difficult to adjust. 'I want to go home.'

'We will, but first we're going to do something exciting on the way.'

'I don't want to.'

'I thought you might be excited, you wee rascal. I thought it might cheer you up. I can see you from the other playground you know, Mr Miserable, walking around with the long face.'

'I like school,' said Aidan valiantly.

'Liam!' someone called. 'Get your skinny arse over here.'

'Coming!' he shouted over his shoulder. 'How did I end up with a softie like you as my little brother?' He gave Aidan a punch on the arm, that was meant to show it was a joke, but to Aidan it didn't sound like a joke. And lunch was even longer than usual and the afternoon dragged even more slowly as they practised reading and learning about animals in the animal kingdom. If the lion was king who was queen? he wondered, and did they have a pope in the animal kingdom, and would that be the elephant? But he knew better than to ask. Mum and Dad and Dearie liked his questions, but the teacher didn't. She sighed when she looked at him and so he stayed quiet up the back, and squeezed his eyes and opened them and squeezed them again when he felt like crying.

I have to be brave, he kept telling himself. I have to show Liam why I'm his brother. Don't cry. Don't think about the chocolate biscuits. They would still be there waiting after he went out with Liam, and in the meantime he would have to be brave just a little bit longer, the way he was on the second day of school. On the first day he'd been excited, but the second day he'd known what he was in for, the long hours siting at a table or swimming in a sea of little boys. No one was mean, but it wasn't like being at home, which, he realised, had been paradise.

'Why can't I stay at home with you and Mummy and Dearie?' he'd asked his father last night after dinner, when he was sitting on his lap in the kitchen. 'Why do I have to go to school?'

'Because we want you to go to the university,' said his father. 'To get a good job and make a contribution to society.'

It sounded impossible to Aidan.

'Because I think you're going to enjoy it after a little while,' said his father, pulling him close and nuzzling him with his whiskery chin. 'You're going to make friends with some of the other boys, and you're going to start being interested in what they teach you in lessons.'

'I like being home with you.'

Aidan let his eyes wander over his dad's long face, his big glasses with rims that looked as if they'd been made from a tortoise's shell, his fine fair hair, which Aidan liked playing with when he sat on his lap late at night like this. He liked twisting it while he sucked his thumb and let his mind wander.

'We'd get boring after a while, I promise you.'

You wouldn't, thought Aidan, but he was too sleepy to argue, and lay back dreaming in his father's arms.

Liam was waiting for him under the oak tree in the big kids' playground. He looked older than his classmates, to Aidan, his blazer worn more stylishly, his maroon tie already stuffed into his bag, his school shirt open a few extra buttons, his muscular legs in their pulled-up grey socks with the blue band around them spick and span. Aidan's left sock had collapsed. Dearie had sewn him elastic garters but he'd somehow lost another one of them today.

'How do you lose a garter?' asked Liam. 'Never mind,' he said, as Aidan was about to try to explain. 'Now where are the others?'

Aidan looked around. Liam's friends were the loud boys who threw balls too hard and smashed the stained-glass window of the school auditorium last week. No one had been hurt, but he didn't like to think what they would do without teachers or parents there.

'The huffy poofters. They've abandoned us,' said Liam. 'Not to worry. We'll do it on our own.'

'Do what on our own?' Aidan's voice sounded even more babyish than usual in his ears. He felt both relief and alarm that the other boys hadn't shown up. Maybe it would be over faster.

'You'll have to be my right-hand man.'

'What's a righthandman?'

'The one who is there when your poofter friends don't show,' said Liam, walking off down the street ahead of him.

'Are we going to the football?' asked Aidan, delighted, as they came to a stop in front of the fence that, he knew from when his dad took him with his brothers in the season, led around to the main entrance, where they had flashed passes and gone through the gates in a horde of people smiling and shoving good-naturedly. They'd eaten chips and had Cokes all round, and even when their team lost Aidan still had a wonderful time.

'It's not on today.' Liam kept looking behind them and then at the fence and then behind them again as they walked slowly beside the palings. Aidan looked behind too, trying to see what Liam was looking at. Big houses, like their house, lined both sides of the street, which came to an end here in a cul-de-sac. He could hear water splashing – someone had a fountain, he guessed. The house closest to them had a high green hedge and wrought-iron fence, with an elaborately tiled front path and an imposing front door like their own. He liked this street, Aidan decided. It was peaceful.

Liam jumped up and grabbed at the top of a wooden paling, pulling it down with him as he landed on the ground, crumpling on top of his bag with the paling falling beside him.

'Mum and Dad will make you pay for that,' cried Aidan. 'Like the auditorium window.'

'Ah shite,' moaned Liam, prodding at one of his ankles with bleeding fingers.

'Have you broken it?' asked Aidan hopefully. He could go up to one of the houses and ring on the doorbell – he felt quite confident about that. He could explain what had happened and ask them to telephone his father for help. He even knew his number. But no one was at home, he reminded himself, his hope fading. That's why he was with Liam. Not until tea.

'I need you to do something for me.'

'Okay,' said Aidan. He could ring on a doorbell anyway. Maybe they'd have a car and give them a lift home. It was only a few blocks away.

'Throw our bags in.' Liam nodded at the gap in the fence.

'In there?' Aidan looked through the fence. He could see rocks and grass, and away in the distance the seats they'd sat on, in metal rows, and the stands where they'd bought the chips and the Cokes at half time. It looked strange today, like a stage set. Huger than it had when there were thousands of people inside, the field empty, and inviting. Like the time they went to the Black Mountain and there had been a sheet of snow left over from winter. Aidan remembered the way his footprints had made a path in it, cracking the crispy edge of the ice with a satisfying crunch, like stepping on a Jacob's cracker.

'Wake up!' Aidan felt a punch on his shoulder. It wasn't gentle. 'I need you to throw our bags through the gap, okay? Good.' Liam stood up gingerly, holding on to the fence for support, and eased himself through. 'Now pick up the paling and prop it back up against the fence.'

'But why?'

'So no one will notice and wonder who's in here, you eejit,' said Liam.

Once the paling had been rearranged to his satisfaction he straightened up and began hobbling down the rocks and the steep side of the hill to the stands, Aidan scrambling after him, a little bit excited. By the time they got down to the tarmac Liam was walking almost normally. They weaved their way through the metal rows of seats, making a bee-line for the other side of the grounds. If anyone were to check they would see the two of them quite clearly, thought Aidan, but Liam didn't seem to care. They got to the end of a row and Liam slowed down a little to climb the wide, shallow stairs.

'Where are we going?' asked Aidan, more to break the strange silence than because he thought Liam might explain to him. They were up near the gates, where they'd all come in for the game that day. Men had stood taking bets, holding tickets and money in their hands, and Liam had wanted to take one, Aidan remembered, but his father had brushed him off, saying he was too young. Liam kept talking about the odds, though, and when they came out of the ground later, the crowd so changed and disappointed, he talked all the way home about about how much money he would have won if he'd been allowed to place a bet. They reached a row of stands, decorated to look like festive tents, but empty now, that had been selling food and drink during the game. Aidan recognised the Coca Cola sign on one stand and knew others sold hot dogs and chips. A hot dog was a sausage in a bun, Dom had told Aidan, but they'd had tea before they came out, so he hadn't ever tasted one.

Liam was searching for something, his gaze travelling over the different stands until he nodded in satisfaction, and began walking purposefully. 'It's that one.'

'What one?'

Aidan felt almost lighthearted. If they were just going to hang around here all afternoon he didn't mind. It felt special, as though he'd been given a pass into a magical kingdom, to be here on their own. Liam squatted down next to the concession stand. He thrust his hand inside the gap where the sides of the red paper tent didn't quite meet, his face blank as his hand searched for something and then lighting up into a crooked smile.

'What is it? What have you found?'

'Shush, will ya?'

Liam pulled out a bottle of washing detergent. It was yellow, with *Spark washes all your stains away* written on it in white. Aidan was surprised that, just as his father had promised him, he was learning to read. He wouldn't have been able to do that a few weeks ago. Or maybe Dearie had told him what it said on the bottle, he thought, his spirits sinking. Liam had taken the top off the bottle and was splashing it all over the stand.

'Step back.'

Aidan felt his heart small in his chest, like a cherry pit, but heavy and hurting as he watched Liam pull a silver cigarette lighter out of his blazer pocket.

'That's Dad's!' Aidan cried out. It had the engraving of a mermaid on the front of it, and he had been looking for it last night.

'Shut up.' Liam's fingers were flicking at the lighter, and there was the flame. He held it to the corner of the red paper tent, which began burning like the kindling in the fireplace at home.

'Let's go,' said Liam.

The flames were moving along the frilly edge where it hung down over the plywood to the ground, like a skirt. Aidan knew enough to know this was very wrong. He ran after Liam, who was hobbling fast, almost running. They were about to start back down the stairs, the way they'd come, when Liam stopped so fast Aidan bashed into him.

'What's that sound?'

An alarm was ringing. Distantly. Aidan wouldn't even have heard it if Liam hadn't said.

'Oh fuck,' Liam muttered. 'They've seen us.'

'Liam!' No one ever was allowed to say that word.

'We'll have to go out the front way.'

Liam turned around and began hobbling back in the direction they'd just come. The stand was blazing merrily, like a carnival, thought Aidan, except eerie and weird in the pervasive quiet. It was creepy in here, actually. As if something could jump out at you, or fall down on you at any moment.

'Liam, I'm scared,' said Aidan. Normally he would never have admitted this to Liam, not in a million years, but this felt like important information, like a clue about what might be going to happen next.

'There's no time for that,' cried Liam. He was rushing towards the turnstiles that they'd passed through to get in that other time. He ducked under them and turned back for Aidan, who was stuck to the ground, his muscles paralysed. The alarm was ringing again, and he couldn't understand how before he hadn't heard it. It was loud enough to wake the dead, as Dearie would say, reverberating and echoing around the grounds.

'If you don't come this instant I'll leave you here. I promise you on Granny's grave.'

'You wouldn't.' He was too scared to cry.

'I would.'

Aidan could force himself to move, he found to his surprise. Even though his feet didn't want to he could make them, just like he could stop himself crying, which was something he hadn't known he could do until he started school. He discovered he could make himself run, too, and stand against the wall, not breathing, when Liam instructed him to. He could creep back around the fence and slip through the gap in the palings and get their bags. It was the bravest thing he had ever done. There were cars with flashing lights at the concession stand, which was a charred, collapsing thing, the gay red bunting gone, and just the plywood left. He could duck when someone pointed his way, and wait for them to turn away before scrambling back out to Liam and saying, 'They saw the gap. They're coming.'

They took a shortcut down the stairs to Fairway Drive, and when they got to the bottom Liam made him pull up his socks and smooth back his hair. Liam did up the buttons of his own shirt and put on his tie. He did up the buttons on his blazer and straightened Aidan's cap.

'There,' he said, grinning, as the cars roared past them, their alarms blaring.

'Shouldn't we leave here?' said Aidan.

'No, why? Schoolboys are allowed to be interested. It would be weirder if we weren't a little bit curious.'

But Aidan felt sick, and Liam believed him when he told him. Aidan did a great line in thick vomit, their mother said, and so they went home. Liam offered him an ice-lolly from the shop on the corner, but Aidan's stomach was roiling, and even when they got to the front door and Dearie and Dom were waiting for them in the hall – Dearie saying where have the two of you been? We were starting to worry about you – he had to go straight up stairs and lock himself in the bathroom, where he began shaking. Even after he'd gone to the toilet and washed his hands and face he couldn't stop.

That night his dad was surprised to find his lighter. 'I could have sworn I checked those pockets,' he said, when Liam handed it to him.

'You must have missed it,' said Liam.

Aidan was unusually quiet over supper, and he said no to ice-cream, which his mother exclaimed over. 'Liam says you were a helpful good boy this afternoon,' she said. 'How about if I let you have some Ice Magic on top?'

His shaking had stopped – no one had even noticed – but his stomach still felt tight like a knot.

'I can't,' he whispered, his heart breaking for the way the chocolate syrup would splurt over the fresh white mounds of ice-cream, and then harden – yes, like magic! – into rock. Like the snow they had walked on at Black Mountain, he thought, as he watched Liam and Dom do it. Like the way he'd felt when they were walking through the football grounds this afternoon. Before he'd realised what Liam was going to do.

'Why can't you?' his mother asked.

'Liam set a Coke stand on fire today.' He didn't think about it or he would never have said anything so stupid. He knew what kind of person grassed on their brother. He knew the contempt his family and everyone else held for a tout. But the words just came out of his mouth, and they wouldn't stop. 'He set it on fire with Dad's lighter.'

His father put down his spoon. 'Is this true?'

Liam rolled his eyes and kept spooning ice-cream into his mouth.

'Liam?'

He ate another spoonful of ice-cream before his father reached over and pushed the bowl away.

'Answer me.'

'You fucking grass,' said Liam to Aidan.

His mother stood up, leaned over the table and hit Liam across the cheek, a smashing blow that jerked his head back.

'Steady on,' said his father.

Aidan couldn't believe his mother could hit anyone like that. She had only ever tapped him lightly on the bottom.

Liam was cradling his cheek, glaring at her. From the other side of the table Aidan could hear his heavy breathing. Everyone else sat silent and motionless, as if they were waiting.

'I'll hit you like that only harder if I ever hear you speak that way again in this house,' said their mum.

They all stood up and cleared the table, and his mum and dad talked in quiet voices in the living room and then his mother picked up the phone. Aidan tried to talk to Liam a few times, once when he was in the bath and later when he was in his room. He wanted to explain how the words had just come out of his mouth without him deciding for them to, but Liam wouldn't even look at him, and it made the explanations dry up and evaporate in Aidan's mouth. But hadn't he been a great help to him before that? Aidan kept telling himself, as he submitted to having his hair washed by Dearie. No one seemed to want to talk to him, except Dom, who came into the bathroom as he was brushing his teeth. 'You did the right thing,' he said, putting his hand on Aidan's shoulder for a moment before leaving the room. His parents were still saying things to each other that he was too far away to fully catch. Words like 'explanation' and 'payment' and, 'That would be a mistake at this delicate time'. What was a delicate time? he wondered when he was in his father's lap later that evening, playing with his buttons.

'You know it's not your fault, don't you?' said his dad, but Aidan was too tired to make sense of it. Like those games where you follow the numbers with your pen and it turns into a giraffe, even though at the beginning it just looked like a mess of dots. Everything that had happened that afternoon still looked like a mess of dots to him. 'You know Liam should never have involved you in anything like that.'

'I wanted to,' said Aidan, thinking of how it had felt when he'd looked out over the arena, the field and the concession stands and seats empty and waiting, like fresh snow.

It was years later when Aidan finally learned the reason why. He and Dom were talking one day about Dearie, when out of nowhere, Aidan remembered it.

'It was so random,' he said. 'Why set that stand out of all the others on fire?'

'You didn't know?' said Dom.

'Wasn't it because Liam was a ...' What had they called it when the police came round and gave his father a ticket? Liam had to work all that summer in the garden, paying off the fine. 'A juvenile delinquent?'

'No,' said Dom, shaking his head, surprised – although Aidan wasn't – by his ignorance. 'That day, when we went to the football with Dad, do you remember it? Glentoran played Linfield and Glentoran won.'

'I remember,' said Aidan. It was one of his best memories – how relaxed his father had been, the four of them together, enjoying themselves. It was a taste of their future as a family, which they had never got to. It was a way of being that spelled happiness.

'When Liam went to buy the Cokes with Dad and you and me, the owner called Dad a turncoat.'

'What did Dad say back to the man, then?'

'Nothing. He just gleamed at him. Remember how he'd do that?'

Aidan remembered. His gaze grew keener. His face became more pointy. He focused on you as if he was piercing you with his intelligence, like Luke Skywalker pointing at you with a lightsaber, is how Aidan used to think of it.

'That's how Dad knew the minute you said something that Liam did it. Apart from you and me and Liam, no one else could have known about that.'

'Huh,' said Aidan, thinking of the determined way Liam had walked past all the other concession stands to get to that one. The way he'd reached under the red paper skirt so confidently for the Spark bottle that he must have nicked from home and on another occasion stored there.

'It wasn't personal,' said Dom. 'It's just the stupid petty shite jealous people say. Dad told me that. It was no reason for Liam to take revenge.'

After that night, when Liam called him a fucking grass, he'd never mentioned it. Aidan had tried again over the following weeks a few times to apologise, and to explain it, but Liam had brushed him off each time, as though it was unimportant. As though he didn't care. Even when he was working in the garden every morning, and Aidan tried to help him, feeling that he should be bearing some of the burden, he wouldn't accept it.

'It's okay,' he said, suddenly, one day. It had stormed the night before, and Liam was raking leaves and branches and heaping them into a pile at the back of the garden. School would be starting the next week. 'You were a help to me. It would have been much worse for me if I'd been caught by the peelers without you there. You were my cover.'

'I never meant to say anything. I just couldn't help it,' said Aidan, in his familiar refrain.

'I know you couldn't,' said Liam. 'In your own way, Aidan, you're a good lad. Don't let me or anyone ever tell you different.'

Aidan sighed, shifting uncomfortably on the hard stone step of his apartment building. A pelican was landing in the water in front of him, its huge feet creating a wave like a surf ski.

Liam had phoned him before dawn that morning. To check on him, he'd said, as though that made it okay. No one else would phone him at that time, thought Aidan, before he was even fully awake. It could only be Liam, and his heart had started hammering, as it always did when Liam phoned.

'You get used to it, I suppose,' he'd told Halley. 'You get used to the tension, to the point where you forget that there's anything different.'

He walked around the back of the building to where his bike was parked in the area reserved for him. Mullumbimby and Megan's cafe lay to the south. He pulled on his helmet, started up the bike, and headed along the riverfront in the opposite direction. This is what his mother had wanted for him, he thought as he rode slowly, meandering up and down the streets in front of the beach – this atmosphere. So sunny and untroubled and free.

CHAPTER TEN

Halley stood at the stainless steel workbench in the cafe, creaming the dressing for the Caesar salad. If her father were here he'd order every-thing on the menu to show how proud he was of her, she thought. Her mother would order coffee, black, no sugar, and make it last an hour. They would both be full of admiration and eager to let the customers know of their relationship with her. 'And this is my daughter,' her father used to say, as if in triumph. 'My Black Beauty,' he used to say, as if he knew the impor-tance of a father's affirmation of his daughter.

'Too bad about his sexual conduct,' muttered Halley, washing the beater with savage efficiency.

'Huh?' Matt was leaning against the counter, flipping through a surfing magazine, waiting for her.

'My father was unfaithful to my mother,' she was about to say, but then she pulled herself up. After all, only the blameless should cast the first stone, as Dom would have reminded her. 'My father made some … mistakes, shall we say.'

'Ah,' said Matt, going back to his magazine, spectacularly tactful or incurious, thought Halley; she could never tell.

She'd told him when they first met that she was estranged from her family, and he never pressed her further. But he hugged her sympathetically if he came upon her crying sometimes, and last year at Christmas he stroked her arm when she said straight up as soon as Benny was out of the room, 'I miss my mum and dad.' Sometimes she wondered what it might be like to tell him about them. But if she spilled – the perfect word – then what else might come haemorrhaging through that gap? She started as she caught sight of herself in the gleaming stainless steel of the stove top she'd just wiped clear of smudges. In the reflection she could have been eighteen again, her hair framing her face as it had then, her features wiped clear of any traces of age.

'You know, I was beautiful,' said Halley, coming to stand in front of Matt, 'when I was eighteen.'

'You're beautiful full stop. And anyway, what eighteen-year-old girl isn't?'

'I can think of plenty,' snorted Halley, recalling the heavy-set girls who crowded around the school bus stop when she dropped off Benny. For some girls it was when they were at their plainest, and looked their oldest, thought Halley, weighed down by their changing bodies, and the impossible, contradictory expectations the world had of them.

The cakes cabinet next to the cash register looked good, she thought, as she picked up her handbag and walked around to the front of the cafe. No. Grand as her father would say. It was a Saturday and so there were just a few slices of each cake left on the set of matching plastic strawberry platters she'd bought from one of those two-dollar variety stores. 'If you stopped buying this crap you'd bankrupt the Chinese economy,' Benny said, when she'd brought them out to the car. They looked beautiful, though, framing the last of the flourless chocolate torte, the cheesecake and the ricotta and honey cakes that she would replenish on Monday. Each slice was a little piece of paradise, thought Halley. A work of art, a still life of how perfect a thing could be.

Once she'd locked up the cafe they drove to the beach at New Brighton, where Matt changed into his wetsuit while Halley changed out of her stained black work shirt into a white shirtwaist dress and swapped her sensible black shoes for strappy platform sandals. She watched Matt trot across the parking lot towards the beach. He turned to wave and then hurried toward the surf, lost to the world for the next few hours. She climbed into the car. Benny was at Sug's restaurant, cutting mushrooms and whipping egg yolks. The afternoon was all hers.

On Saturday afternoons, while Matt surfed, Halley indulged her weekend passion of looking through the houses for sale, open for inspection, that were dotted throughout the countryside, satisfying her curiosity about properties that were usually so impenetrable, sitting secretly behind their gates and winding driveways, and luring tourists who came up for the weekend and would be going back to Sydney or Melbourne having bought a house and changed their lives.

Over the years she'd looked through Queenslanders and bungalows, newly built sandstone castles and red-brick ranch houses. Every house told a different story and she would begin speculating from the moment she walked in. Those wedding photos – blended family. The bad finish in the bedrooms? Ran out of money halfway through. The German tiles? The French showerheads? Loaded and then they lost it in the crash.

People came here to build their dream homes, where they would live out their dream lives. Houses that would never make back their investment value. Houses built by hand for no money out of found objects – those could be depressing affairs. Houses built on a lifetime's savings and never lived in – sparkling sterile palaces. Houses built in celebration of late second marriage – a French Provincial farmhouse; a concrete and glass tribute to Frank Lloyd Wright. These were the houses of lifelong fantasy. Meditation towers, Feng Shui alignments and Chinese herb rooms that must never be seen by the sun. Sweeping staircases, built-in dressing rooms and Olympic-sized swimming pools. The owners spared no expense or effort. But interestingly, to Halley, they so rarely settled in their new homes. After building their paradise they didn't feel up to inhabiting it, and would put it on the market soon afterwards.

This house was one Halley could have imagined buying, she thought, entering that afternoon's selection, if her life had turned out differently, the way her parents must have hoped it would. Built in 1901, it was the first house in this particular valley, and was placed in the most beautiful spot. Nestled in the foothills of the mountains, an old orchard shielded it from the road. Old steps, worn from a century's worth of feet going back and forth, took her up to a generous verandah. It was a place for mint juleps and flirting, thought Halley, but the owner said that had never happened when she was here. They usually ended up drinking wine or vodka tonics out the back, she told Halley, where she could keep an eye on her kids in the pool. But the kids were gone, to university in Sydney and working overseas, and the house was too big for just her. A lawnmower puttered from another property some distance away. The rooms were half empty – her husband had moved out two months ago, the woman said, taking a lot of the furniture with him.

'It's all so beautiful,' sighed Halley, sinking into a sofa in the dining area, when she had finished looking. The woman had gone to greet some new people, who from the look of it, thought Halley, might actually have some money.

Would I like to live somewhere like this? Halley wondered momentarily. No, she answered herself instantly. All this excess, even the idea of it, frightened her, and she reverted to her usual self-denial in the face of it. There was nothing here she truly wanted, that's what she told herself. Nothing here – nothing anywhere could satisfy her. Not now.

Sydney, 1989

When Dom came home from that trip catching cane toads Megan had turned seventeen, and everything was different.

She didn't want any part of her old life – she wanted a new life, and that's what Dom promised her. Love healed, said Dom. After the death of his father he had thought he would die. Instead he was saved, and look where he was now. The key was to forgive. 'Leave your family and follow me,' Jesus said to his disciples. That meant you didn't have to abide by established rules, said Dom. You were free, every single moment, to start again. But it was also to do with politics, the way Dom explained it. It was to do with justice and direct action. Jesus was a revolutionary, said Dom. You could change the way the world worked on the outside by asking God to change you from within.

Sex with Dom was different too. Well, not sex – but everything Dom would let them do, that he considered not-quite-sex. Feeling like this about a man made you vulnerable, Megan was realising. She yearned to pour herself into him and disappear completely, to vanish into love. Just the touch of his hand holding hers made her happy. Lying down with him, his body pressed against hers, his mouth pressed against her neck, must be the closest you could get to heaven without dying. She knew what it meant in the sappy romance novels when a woman talked about 'giving yourself away'. She didn't cringe any more when the nuns at school talked about keeping yourself whole. She was just managing to keep herself in solid form, knowing that, the day she made love with Dom she would melt away, and merge with him, forever. She would belong to him completely.

'You wouldn't want to marry me,' he said one day, six months after he returned from his trip. He had deferred his postgraduate studies in economics and dropped down to part-time hours working for a stockbroker in the city, so he could start a youth refuge in a working class area on the other side of town. 'I'll never make any real money,' he said, watching her carefully.

'I don't care.'

'Your parents do.'

'They worship the ground you walk on! They think you're a living saint. We can get married today if you want to. I bet you they would agree.'

'We should wait until you're twenty-one.'

'That's three years away,' she groaned.

She truly did think that if she asked her parents if she could marry Dom immediately they would agree. Perhaps if they hadn't trusted him so much they wouldn't have made it so easy for Megan to leave them, substituting the broken man of her father for the better one of Dom. It made it easier for Megan to gloss over what had happened between them. It wasn't until years later that she thought perhaps it had made it easier for them as well.

'We don't see your friends anymore,' her mother sometimes complained, and then Megan would make sure to have a brunch, or invite her old friends around for pre-dinner drinks. That was their idea. Megan would no more have thought of having a pre-dinner drink than a session at a day spa, but some time in their final year of school her friends had become sophisticated.

'It's the other girls' mothers,' said her mother wistfully one day. 'They're bringing their girls up to be ladies.'

'And what are you bringing me up to be?' Megan asked.

'I don't need to bring you up to be anything, darling. Look at you.' Megan shifted uncomfortably. She was wearing jeans and a T-shirt, ready to go out with Dom. 'You're your father's girl.'

'No, I'm not.'

Megan felt insulted, but she also felt, obscurely, relieved. She loved her mother, but the last thing she wanted was to be like her, so stoic and passive in the face of insult and betrayal.

'Your father worked day and night to give us all this, Meggie,' said her mother, as if guessing her thoughts. 'The best of everything. He had to fight the whole way to give you the opportunities you enjoy. If he'd had to he would have sacrificed everything.'

Fucked everything, Megan silently corrected her. And she didn't want all this anyway. The thousand-dollar sheet sets and the perfect place settings. Trying to prove something that should never have to be proven. To right wrongs that could never be healed.

That night at youth group she was unusually boisterous, unusually inspiring as she talked about the children in Palestine. She decided they should have a slide show about Nelson Mandela at their next weekend retreat, and a walkathon to send money for the famine in Ethiopia. Dom agreed with everything she said, his eyes dark with pride as he looked at her.

When she started university she moved out of home to live in a share-house on a traffic-choked street nearer town. Somehow, she felt like an orphan, the money deposited by her parents in her bank account every fortnight like a kiss-off. She knew it was unreasonable to feel this way, when it was she who avoided them; who somehow could only rarely find the time to see them, agreeing at the last minute to accompany her mother to the ballet, or to drop in on her father's birthday dinner at home, staying for as short a time as possible before making her excuses and slipping away.

'I worry about you,' her mother said to her once in the hall after Sunday lunch, helping her pull her scarf around her throat.

'What is there to worry about?'

'I miss you.'

'How can you miss me? I live just a few miles away.'

'We never see you.'

She spoke so mildly, it took Halley years to even imagine what pain it must have cost her to say those words.

'I'm proud of you,' her father said, when she passed her first year law exams with distinction. They took her and Dom out to dinner at a famous restaurant in Paddington, and presented her with a cheque for a holiday overseas.

'You shouldn't be,' said Megan.

'What do you mean?' asked her mother.

'Because I'm not like you,' she wanted to say, but they were the ones paying for all this, she reminded herself, and so she just muttered that it was a stupid course.

CHAPTER ELEVEN

When Megan met Liam she was halfway through her law degree, and had been going out with Dom for nearly three years.

'Hi,' she called out automatically as she knocked and then walked through Nuala's open front door.

'The summer's flower is to the summer sweet,' someone was saying, so loudly she could hear it clearly from the hall. *'Although to itself it only live and die.'*

A duffel bag lay splayed open like a corpse at the foot of the stairs, the legs of pants and arms of jumpers spilling out like entrails.

Megan paused in the doorway of the living room. Aidan, Nuala and Dom were sitting facing her on the couch, transfixed by the man standing in front of them. From the back he looked like a woman, thought Megan. Long black hair rippled past his shoulders and thick bracelets clanked down his arms.

'We're in the middle of something,' he said, turning to her.

A large silver buckle sat square below his navel on his low-slung belt. A silver necklace nestled among the black hairs of his pale chest. His eyes were rimmed with kohl, their intense blue matching the flowers on his shirt. He had Dom's dramatic colouring and Aidan's delicacy of features combined, thought Megan: the face of a sulky angel.

'I said, we're in the middle of something.'

She had been expecting a smile, or an introduction, but they all simply stared at her. Even Dom, his face more hangdog than usual, glanced at her wearily.

'Sorry.' She scuttled over to squeeze in between Dom and Nuala on the couch.

Liam took a deep breath and began again.

'They that have power to hurt and will do none,
That do not do the thing they most do show,
Who, moving others are themselves as stone
Unmoved, cold and to temptation slow.'

It was his accent, thought Megan, with that delightful Irish lilt. It was his way of standing, with all his weight on one hip. It was his way of looking at them, eyes lowered before glancing up at them frankly for a moment before lowering them again. And then the purity of that blue-eyed gaze restored, as he looked out over their heads towards the back windows. What was he thinking of? wondered Megan as he stood in front of them, inhabiting all his beauty. Who?

'For sweetest things turn sourest by their deeds;
Lilies that fester smell far worse than weeds.'

He swept his arms out, stepping back on one foot and flinging his head down in a low bow, his hair falling forward to touch the carpet.

'You never told me your brother could act!' said Megan, punching Dom lightly on the arm.

'You didn't tell her I can act?'

Liam was eating peanut butter toast, his bum propped against the kitchen counter.

'He can act,' said Dom, wiping his hand over his face, dragging at his features wearily. As always he looked rumpled and shaggy, as if he'd been up drinking and smoking all night. A few minutes later, Megan was surprised to learn that he had been.

'Late flight,' said Liam.

He put himself at the centre of every interaction: Megan noticed it even then. Claiming the praise or the blame.

'Three times!' he yelled, throwing his plate into the sink and leaving the room.

'Three times what?' asked Megan, bewildered by the general change in the household. Nuala, for once, was happy, and that wasn't hard to understand. All her boys were home. Dom was withdrawn. He'd hardly said a word since she'd arrived. Aidan was the only one behaving even vaguely normally – watchful and anxious to please. He jumped to her rescue.

'Three times he was called back for an audition at RADA this year. He's waiting to hear if he got in.'

'RADA?' Megan looked to Dom for explanation but he was staring at the table.

'Royal Academy of Dramatic Art, in London,' said Aidan. 'It's one of the best acting schools in the world.'

'I've never heard of it,' said Megan.

'Oh, well, it mustn't be all that good then,' said Dom.

Megan flinched. He had never spoken to her like this before. 'I know nothing about acting.'

'Clearly,' said Dom.

She felt as if he'd slapped her.

'Being called back is a wonderful honour,' said Nuala.

'What no one seems to mention is that he hasn't actually gotten in,' said Dom.

'Dom's annoyed because he doesn't see how Liam can make a living acting,' said Nuala confidingly to Megan. 'But he's doing all right in the meantime. Picking up odd jobs. Helping out his uncle on this trip.'

'If that's what you want to call it,' said Dom.

Megan had never seen him like this before, and although she was appalled, she was also fascinated. Dom had shrunk, his arms folded, his face turned inward. Where was his usual humour? His universal love and warmth?

'Oh Dom,' said Nuala, 'there's nothing wrong with it.'

'Oh Mum, how can you be so naive?'

'I may be a lot of things, but I am not naive,' said Nuala.

The kitchen felt freighted with silence, bearing down on them.

'Pardon?' said Nuala, as Dom muttered something. 'I didn't catch that.'

'Sorry Ma.'

She smiled, forgiving him with a nod of her head.

'We're raising money for the families of political prisoners, is what we're doing,' said Liam genially, coming back into the room and rejoining the conversation as though nothing had happened. 'It's an association for people all over the world wanting to find a solution to the Troubles in Northern Ireland. It's called Progress, Megan; Dom, I'm sorry you don't want to get more involved.'

'By asking our uncles for a job?' said Dom, his tone withering.

'It's hard work,' said Liam steadily. 'I'm the handler for Kevin Kennedy,' he said, turning to Megan. 'He was imprisoned for more than seven years in

London for a bombing he had nothing to do with. He was just a builder's labourer and they fingered him for being IRA.'

'How long will you be on the tour?' asked Aidan.

Megan had forgotten he was there until he piped up. Liam walked over to where he was perched on a stool at the kitchen counter and hooked his arm around his neck, looking straight at Megan all the while.

'We're doing a seven-city fundraising tour in Australia, starting and ending here in Sydney.'

Megan shifted uncomfortably under the pressure of his attention.

'Then we're going onto Canada and the USA.'

'Raising awareness about the Troubles?' asked Megan, pleased with herself for using the proper name.

'Raising money,' said Dom, with a harsh laugh. 'There's something so romantic about the Irish once they've left Ireland, the way they think giving money will help.'

'And money,' conceded Liam, shrugging. 'Finding a peaceful solution to the centuries of oppression the Catholics have endured in Northern Ireland is something a lot of Irish everywhere care about, and yes, it does take money.'

'I care about it,' said Megan, surprising herself as much as Dom, who stared at her with frank incredulity.

'Since when?'

'Since just now,' said Megan, half cowed and half defiant. Since forever, she thought. Since her father was picked on by the Protestant establishment, and his infidelity to her mother revealed to all the world.

'Looks like you've made a convert,' said Dom to Liam, his face and his voice hard in a way Megan had never encountered before.

Nuala stood up from the table and began banging around in the cupboards. 'I just want to enjoy having all my sons around me for the first time in years. I just want to enjoy your company.'

Dom stood up too and grabbed a pack of cigarettes from the kitchen counter, which Megan had assumed were Liam's. She'd never seen him smoke before.

'I'll get out of your faces then,' he said, slamming out of the kitchen.

Megan was about to follow him when she felt Nuala put her hand on her arm.

'Give him a minute.'

Megan was happy to comply. What was going on here was something out of her league, and the change it made in Dom frightened her.

'Why don't you and Liam go sit on the back verandah?' Nuala suggested.

'That poem was Shakespeare, right?' said Megan, once Nuala had installed them outside with glasses of lemonade and chips in a wooden bowl.

'It was a sonnet. And yes.'

'Do you know a lot of him by heart?' Megan felt shy with Liam, and young, as if she might say or do something inappropriate or immature at any moment.

'I know all of him by heart.'

'All?'

'Wait a sec.' He stood up and went inside, reappearing a moment later holding a thick volume, and handed it to her. 'Read me any bit, any section of any speech, anything. I'll tell you exactly where it's from.'

'You happen to have *The Complete Works of Shakespeare* on hand?'

'It belonged to my dad. Shakespeare belongs to everyone, he used to say.'

Megan looked down at the book and saw that it was old, and well thumbed; the dust jacket with Shakespeare's portrait on the cover meticulously mended with transparent tape in the many places it had been torn.

'You must miss him.'

He put his hand on hers where it was resting on the arm of her chair. 'Constantly.'

The two of them exchanged a glance of – thought Megan – pure and complete understanding. She had never seen a man look so vulnerable.

'I'm so sorry.'

'And I'm sorry about what they did to yours.'

Megan pulled her hand away, her cheeks reddening.

'It was a dirty business,' said Liam, shaking his head, oblivious, it seemed, to Megan's discomfort.

She quickly learned that Liam always went for the jugular. Coming out of nowhere with a comment or action so personal, delivering it so intimately, that she felt mugged, or groped.

'He always does that,' said Dom that afternoon when he drove her home. 'Stay away from him, Megan. For me.'

But she had already volunteered to go with Liam to a meeting of the local chapter of Progress, the association Liam was working for.

'I'm begging you, Megan,' said Dom. 'Don't go.'

'No.'

'I don't want you involved with him.' Dom said it again, robotically this time, as if already hopeless.

'And I don't want you telling me what to do!'

It wasn't just because Liam had said they desperately needed the support of clever young people like her that she refused Dom. Or because of that moment she and Liam had shared, when he had touched her hand, before he had almost ruined it. It was because of something between her and Dom. Their struggles had worsened in the last few months. Their stalemate expanding, so that it wasn't just about no-sex before marriage anymore.

Give sexual attraction long enough to die and you'd never marry anybody, thought Halley, arriving late at the cafe. She and Dom had had all the responsibilities of marriage with none of the benefits. Even though she lived in the rundown terrace house in Redfern while Dom lived with two other young men in a modern flat in Glebe, they always knew what the other one was doing, whereas members of her constantly shifting roster of housemates would go out for a drink and disappear for days. It's quite possible no one knew what they were up to.

'They were sleeping on someone's couch and watching music videos all day,' Dom said, when she tried to explain the appeal of this way of living to him. 'It's not exactly exciting.'

Dom was critical of the casual woundings and split-second relationships that surrounded them at university, and the unfathomable hostility with which young men and women treated each other.

'But even so,' she would petulantly reply, 'they get to be irresponsible.'

She and Dom got to negotiate. Plans. Dreams. Everything had to be discussed and agreed. Megan began wondering if the future would ever get here, or would it always be retreating from them, even as she and Dom planned for it.

'Let's take a break,' they would agree. But a break wasn't what they needed, they would agree, back together again a few weeks later, unable to breathe or feel even physically normal without the oxygen provided by the other.

'I don't want to go to youth group anymore,' Megan said, the day she met Liam, staring out the windscreen so she wouldn't have to look at Dom.

'I thought you believed in it.'

'I do,' said Megan. 'But not for me.'

She'd begun to feel frustrated with the children at youth group. To find it hard to believe that anything she or Dom did for them would make a difference in the long run, and that their families weren't somehow more responsible for their situations than Dom gave them credit for. She felt frustrated at university, too. Studying torts and contract law seemed to have nothing to do with human rights and justice, and she wondered if they ever would.

'Youth group is something that we share,' said Dom.

'Then we have to find something else we can share. Oh God, those sausages!' she exclaimed, fleeing into something light.

'You love sausages.'

'Not every Sunday on a slice of white bread I don't. I know! I know it's shallow of me, but there it is. I don't know why you love me. I really don't.'

'Don't you?' His expression was sad as he looked at her.

'Is it because you think you can save me?' she asked, emboldened by the way she'd heard Liam talking to Dom that day. 'Because you're sorry for me, with what happened to my dad? Why did you come around to my house that day, anyway?' she pressed. 'Is it because you wanted to rescue me and be a good boy for Father John?'

'Maybe before I met you. Not after the first ten minutes.'

'But Liam's the bad boy and you're the good boy, isn't that right?'

'No.'

She bit her lip, staring out the window into the darkness that had fallen while they were speaking. Something about meeting Liam was giving her the courage to say the things she'd been thinking about for a while now, but hadn't dared say.

'Next time at confession tell the priest that we've decided to do things our own way. That it's not all about just what you believe, that it's about what I believe, too.'

'No.'

'Well then it can't be up to you anymore what I choose to do and not do.'

He looked sad as he started up the van, his bag filled with pictures for the children to colour in and riddles and puzzles about that week's Bible reading next to him.

'I don't deserve you,' she said, as the van disappeared around the corner.

Everything turns to shit if you give it long enough, thought Halley, eyeing the rotten lettuce leaves that had been left at the bottom of the crisper.

'Who the fuck left these here?' she snapped, wheeling around to face the kitchen. Four startled faces all stared back at her.

'Well who?' Now that she'd started, she had the stagey feeling of having to keep it up. Of having to justify her outburst in the first place.

They all just kept staring. Lisa, the new waitress had a gleam in her eye, noticed Halley, as if in some part of her she was entertained. Matt was the worst. Gormless, blank, waiting.

'Oh fuck it.' Halley threw the lettuce leaf she was brandishing to the floor and picked up a plate from the stack on the shelf that separated the stoves from the preparation area.

'You going to throw that too, boss?' asked Drummond, their apprentice chef. This would bring them all closer to each other, thought Halley, uniting them against her.

'No, I'm going to put a big fat piece of chocolate cake on it.' She smiled and, relieved, they all smiled back. 'Don't mind me,' she said over her shoulder as she squatted down in front of the cake cabinet. 'Just a touch of PMT.' 'Or menopause,' she muttered to herself as she dolloped cream onto the side of her plate and went to sit outside. She felt like crying.

'What was that about?' asked Matt, pulling out the chair opposite her and sitting down. She'd purposely chosen a small table so no one would feel welcome to join her, but Matt didn't bother with nuance.

'Nothing. Sorry.'

'You don't usually swear at work.'

'Well now I do.' The tears that had been damming up behind her eyes all morning were trickling down her cheeks.

'Who did this?' Matt was leaning forward, staring at her.

'What?' She couldn't be bothered to wipe her tears away and she didn't let them stop her eating, either, so she was spooning up salty chocolate icing and cream.

'This. Who did it to you, Halley? Tell me and I'll ... I'll kill him.'

Carefully, deliberately, Halley put her fork down. She picked up a cloth napkin that a customer had left lying on a chair and wiped her eyes. Blew her nose. She kept her eyes lowered. He had shocked her. Predictable Matt had managed to genuinely surprise her during a rare lull in customers on a Tuesday morning. Exactly how much, she wondered, did Matt know?

He was still looking at her. For want of something to do she picked up her fork again, but she couldn't eat any more.

'Halley?'

What was interesting about this, thought Halley, blowing her nose again and playing for time, was that Matt assumed this someone was a he, and that what was upsetting her was something he had done to her, instead of the other way around.

He reached forward and grabbed her hand. She dropped the fork, clattering it onto her plate, and held his tightly. Their fingers, all food stained and work roughened gripped each other's.

She took a deep breath. 'When I work it out I'll tell you.'

'All right.' His brown heavy-lidded eyes glanced shyly into hers and then away, back to the kitchen.

No one was looking at them, noticed Halley, and that was the giveaway. They were all studiously minding their own business, but probably trying to lip-read every time Halley and Matt spoke.

'Better get back,' said Matt.

'Okay.' Halley's chair shrieked on the bricks as she stood.

'Back to the fucking lettuce,' Matt muttered, so low that only Halley could hear. She whipped at him with her snotty napkin as she followed him back to the kitchen.

CHAPTER TWELVE

Sydney, 1992

'Now *this* is something real,' thought Megan, when Liam took her to her first fundraising barbecue. They stood in Amanda's back yard – she was the Sydney convener for the group – and ate sausages wrapped in sliced white bread. But they drank beer instead of lemonade, and talked about politics instead of God.

'Something real, Megan?' said Dom, when she told him about it that evening. They were sitting in the living room of her share-house on Cleveland Street. Beer bottles and stinking ashtrays crowded the coffee table in front of them, and traffic honked and roared six feet away on the road, but he'd refused when she'd invited him upstairs to the sanctuary of her room. 'And what we do at the youth refuge is not real?'

It had expanded in the last year, and they had received funding to employ staff, and keep it open full-time. Dom was being paid now to spend his afternoons on a skateboard and his evenings playing pool. He'd taken in another flatmate, so he could get by on his shrinking salary.

'This is urgent,' she said gently, taking his hand.

'And a child without breakfast this morning isn't urgent?'

'There's a real chance we can get the British government to the negotiating table this time.'

'A real chance you can bomb the British government to the negotiating table, you mean.'

Megan winced. The IRA had claimed responsibility for a nail bomb that had exploded in a London nightclub and killed three people and injured hundreds the week before.

'You know that Progress is not the IRA. We support the political process, not the violence.'

'They're the same thing, Megan. When will you get that through your head? Two arms of the same creature.'

'This moment in history is the greatest chance for peace in Northern Ireland yet,' said Megan carefully. She had rehearsed this today at their meeting. 'We have to keep up the pressure.'

'It's America's support that really counts.'

'That's not true. Australians sent half a million dollars over last year, collected from the parishes alone.'

'Imagine if they had chosen to spend that money on the children in their own parishes, here in Australia, instead.'

'Those kids have to go out into the world one day and it's not just hunger that will hurt them. It's about knowing that they're worth something. It's about saying to the British government, and anyone else who would try, that you can't keep trampling on people. That we won't be defeated.'

'But we *are* defeated!' Dom burst out. 'We were defeated centuries ago and every Irish person living overseas knows it. That's why they left. Or their ancestors did. That's why it hurts so much, don't you see? But it's over, Megan. It's done.'

'I believe Ireland can be reunified,' said Megan steadily. 'And I believe we're closer to victory than we have ever been.'

'We? You're Australian.'

'I used to think I was,' said Megan. 'Until it turned out some Australians are different to other Australians.'

'I knew this was about your father.' He shook his head and blew the air out of his cheeks.

'And are you trying to tell me that going around saving fatherless kids has nothing to do with yours? This is about justice.'

'It's a quagmire over there, Megan, believe me. Nothing you do is going to make a difference.'

'Liam says it can.'

Two months later, Megan stood at the back of Paddington Town Hall, her legs trembling and her heart pounding. Her hair was pulled into a high ponytail and she'd applied mascara for once. She wore a denim skirt and black leggings, her backpack slung over her shoulder, stuffed with her clipboard and pens and the pager that Liam had given her as soon as she'd taken on the job of organising the event.

The crowd stirred and Megan once again checked her watch.

'It looks good, don't you think?' she whispered, without turning her head or taking her eyes off the empty stage.

'It looks great,' Dom's voice whispered in her ear, and a moment later she felt his arms around her waist. 'I'm proud of you.'

She leaned back against him, a thrill of happiness flooding through her that was partly the excitement of the crowd, partly anticipation of the evening to come and partly the still and always-there delight in being physically close to Dom.

And the stage did look good. Banners in green and white and gold were hanging along the back of it. *Sinn Fein* read one. *Ireland + Australia* read another. She'd had them made up by an activist printing press in Haymarket, convincing them to give her a discount on the no gloss, with an extra colour thrown in for the Cause. The guy she'd been bargaining with had asked her if she was Irish, and she'd said, 'Yes, if it will get me a better deal.' He'd laughed, and she'd felt that same feeling she was feeling tonight. That maybe she was good at this. That maybe she belonged. *Provisional IRA,* another banner had been going to read, but it had caused such a fuss and a fight at the last meeting that at the last minute Liam had nixed it. It wasn't worth the trouble it would cause, he said. He'd just come back from touring the rest of Australia, and would be leaving for the US in the next few days. The speaker tonight wouldn't have liked it either, Amanda had said, 'considering he's just been exonerated from a false conviction of being in the IRA, Susan,' she'd added, her voice dripping with scorn. Susan had shrugged. She was more militant than a lot of them, convinced of the importance of the armed struggle. They all had a position on the violence: the bombings, the assassinations and torture carried out by the Provisional IRA, the armed wing of the movement – good manners at their meetings demanded it. Most of them, Megan included, were against it.

Four drab green metal chairs were arranged at the front of the stage, filled with portent. Megan checked her watch again. She was just starting to worry when Liam and Amanda walked out from the wings. They smiled modestly and Liam took his seat as Amanda walked up to the lectern.

'This man.'

The crowd hushed.

'This man was imprisoned for the crime of being Irish on the night of the Kilburn bombings. This man was sent to prison for the crime of being Irish in London at the wrong time.'

The crowd booed softly.

'This man endured appeal after appeal in prison.'

She paused, waiting this time, and the crowd obediently booed again.

She'd done something to her hair, thought Megan, it looked silkier, and – was it possible? – it looked as if she also might have put on lipstick for this special night.

'This man was convicted of a political crime, yet he was given none of the rights of a political prisoner. In March this year, seven years after the British government incarcerated him, this man and his friends were finally freed. The British justice system could not keep them down. It could not keep the truth from being free. And this man ... this man ...'

The anticipation in the crowd rose. Megan could feel her own pulse quickening.

'This man is here!'

The crowd erupted, clapping and cheering. A skinny creature in designer denim jeans and a black – could it be? Megan stared – ACDC T-shirt came jogging onto the stage, his fists raised above his head in victory. He beamed at the crowd and they beamed back at him. They kept on clapping. Finally he moved over to the lectern.

'It was horrible being in prison, I tell you.'

Everyone laughed, as though he'd made the most hysterically funny joke.

'And it's heaven being outside, I'll tell you that, too.'

Amanda was looking up at him from where she sat on her green metal chair. For the whole time he was speaking her gaze didn't waver. If the rumours were true he would have his pick of the women here tonight, thought Megan. His reputation had preceded him to Sydney. In a part of her, in a funny way, she wanted to make love with him too. As though she might be able to take a tiny part of the pain and the injustice he had endured into herself, and heal it somehow.

'Let's get married,' Dom whispered into her ear.

'Huh?' It was all going perfectly, thought Megan, just as she had planned.

'Let's get married.'

Megan glanced over her shoulder, sure she had misheard, but he was frowning slightly and smiling at the same time, as if waiting for an answer.

A few seconds later they were standing next to a telephone booth underneath the vestibule stairs. She was still near enough to the hall's entrance to hear if anything in there went wrong.

'What about finishing uni? What about getting the refuge up and running?' said Megan, her eyes searching his face. This is it! a little voice inside her sang, happiness breaking through like sunshine into her heart. This was her real life beginning, at last.

'It doesn't matter.'

When they were married they would be together, all the time, the little voice inside her sang. When they were married they would make love.

'But ...' Megan glanced at the hall door. 'Liam's asked me to go to London, to help him organise some of the events over there.'

'I know he has.'

Doubt stopped her. A cloud blocked out the sunshine and a chill dampness spread.

'Is that why you're asking me?'

'I just think it's time.'

'But why now?' she insisted. 'Is it because of Liam?' She hated this. She hated to even say words like this.

'No. It's because in a few months you won't be a teenager anymore.'

'But why do you get to decide?' It may have been childish but it bugged her, as though he had changed his mind on a whim.

'I'm asking you, Megan.'

This is it, Megan reminded herself. Dom was finally saying what she had been waiting so long to hear.

'I'm not saying no,' said Megan slowly. This was all wrong: it was not what you wanted to remember on the day your true love proposed.

'What are you saying then?' His face was blank. That lilt in his voice the only giveaway that he was feeling anything but calm.

Megan glanced behind them, at the hall, where a thundering roll of applause was building. She could feel the rising excitement of the crowd, like a storm front approaching.

'Look, go to London first then,' he said quickly. 'If you have to.'

'I want to.'

'If you want to, then. How long is it for anyway? Six weeks. And then you can decide.'

She stepped closer to him, sheltering in the lee of the telephone box. 'Do you mean it?' More than anything she wanted to say yes.

'It's a feeling I have,' said Dom. 'Like a calling or something. An intuition. From God.'

'You have a calling from God to marry me?'

'Something like that.' He grimaced, embarrassed.

'I think I have a calling from God to help with this, too.'

'Megan?'

They jumped, turning around to see Liam behind them. How much of their conversation had he just overheard? wondered Megan.

'We need you.'

Dom scowled at him.

'Something to do with the lights,' said Liam.

'Oh, for sure,' said Megan, smoothing her hair.

'Sorry to interrupt,' said Liam to Dom.

The look the two brothers exchanged was cold.

'We need your woman inside.'

PART TWO

CHAPTER THIRTEEN

Dear Anne, Aidan wrote in fine black pen on the off-white card. What else could he write? he wondered. A description of the scenery?

He'd spent the afternoon at the beach. A pretty beach a twenty-minute bike ride from his flat in Brunswick Heads. He'd gone there bored, looking for something to do. Unless you were a child, it seemed, you wouldn't find it. He had walked around for a while and wound up sitting in the beer garden of the pub. More kids – Halley had told him that all people did around here was breed – played on the sound stage, and people stood in line to buy their meals. Aidan had made do with a beer and a packet of chips. He'd found this postcard at the newsagents, a landscape image of the place. The twin peaks of Chincogan rising above the river, snaking, like a golden path inland to Mullumbimby, sitting at the foot of the mountain.

Dear Anne, he tried again. *Unlike most places you see on a postcard this is even more beautiful in real life. In a funny way it reminds me of India, and it reminds me of you.* But everything did, and he didn't want to write that. He put it in the inside pocket of his jacket, next to his heart. He'd think of what to say, the exact words, another time.

South India, 2005

'And are you making the sex?'

The young man who seated himself next to Aidan on the train to Madurai seemed like a welcome piece of luck at first. Travelling in a couple, people had told him, meant you tended not to meet anyone, and so far that had proved to be true. That's why Aidan had chosen to go second class, as well.

'You'll meet interesting people and I'll have a lovely rest,' Anne had predicted when she said goodbye to him that morning, in that clear, simple way he loved her for. She felt none of the angst Aidan was feeling about separating, even for just three days, on their holiday.

Aidan could never see things simply. It was a gift and a curse. He couldn't write people off, but he couldn't place them easily in their proper context, either. At work, for example, he was famous for his sympathy. Always seeing the client's side. Always falling hook, line and sinker for their story. This was all very well until they ended up in court with a week's worth of Aidan's time down the drain when it turned out the client in question was a serial liar and a cheat. Anne wrote people off too quickly, she acknowledged that. On the other hand it kept her time outside work nice and free for loving him. Although far above him in responsibility and pay grade at the Legal Aid office where they had met and both still worked, she was always the first one home.

'And are you making the sex, I'm asking?'

The first time the young man asked him this question Aidan pretended not to hear. They were travelling through flat dry country, scrubby low bush and dirt as far as the eye could see. The sky hurled him into a depth charge of blue, so dazzling and pure was its light.

'Excuse me my good friend? Aidan?'

His name was Nandan, and they'd had a good hour's conversation already. Religion, income, work, family, and India compared to Australia compared to England had all been covered.

'Yes,' said Aidan.

Give him a break, he told himself. Young people were sheltered in this country, and it was not likely, unless he could afford a prostitute and was willing to see one, that Nandan would have any sexual experience until he married. Although Aidan wasn't the type, normally, to hand out sex advice on public trains, he would look at it as a form of education, he decided. An act of goodwill and charity.

'Um. I have a fiancée,' he added. He really wasn't the type to talk about sex at all, racking his brains for a time that he ever had. Never with his brothers growing up, and they would have been the likely suspects. Dom was too good, and Liam was never there. Liam would have loved to give him advice, Aidan felt sure, but he didn't want the *Kama Sutra* mixed with the world's worst pick-up lines that only Liam could carry off falling on his head. Aidan had made his own way and he had found Anne, hadn't he? It hadn't been too bad.

'I would like to make the sex.'

Nandan was fine-boned and slim. He wore immaculate white trousers and an off-white button-down long-sleeved shirt that looked as if he'd just put it on. No mean achievement in this dusty country and this packed train carriage, sweltering already despite the whirling ceiling fans. Aidan hadn't realised until he got on that second class meant no air conditioning.

'Well, it's good,' said Aidan, smiling, and turning to look out the window again. This was where, he decided, the sex part of the conversation would end.

'And have you made sex with the man?'

Aidan stared out of the window extra hard, craning his neck, as they passed some brightly painted wooden animals grouped on the outskirts of a village.

'Excuse me, Aidan, my good friend, I said—'

'I heard.' It was different here, he reminded himself. This country, so open in some respects, so much less uptight than the UK, was much more stitched up in others. 'And no. My answer to you is no.'

'I am wondering why?'

It was ridiculous, but Aidan was sweating. Even more than he had been a few minutes ago.

'Because I'm not ...' He shook his head, unable to remember if Indians used this word. 'Gay.'

Nandan laughed, a joyful, flashing-toothed laugh. 'You're funny, my friend. It's a good joke.'

The heat. This young man. Aidan noticed suddenly that Nandan's hand was resting on his white-clad thigh, alarmingly close to Aidan's. The rocking motion of the train. The strong smell of sweets mixed with sewage that he'd been flinching from ever since he got on the train.

'Oh God,' he moaned.

'Give him air!' a woman was saying, her voice loud and bright. It sounded instantly cheerful to Aidan. 'Give him air!'

Aidan opened his eyes to the white flag flapping of a hankie.

'What happened?' he mumbled. His eyes felt fuzzy, his head groggy.

'You fainted.'

A smooth brown face and neat grey hair, a pair of round wire-rimmed glasses appeared in front of Aidan. He pushed himself up. He was still in his seat. The woman looked at him with satisfaction.

'The heat,' she added.

She has a beautiful voice, thought Aidan. And he liked her accent. 'The heeet.'

He yawned. People were staring, gathered in a clump around them. He gave them a little wave and a smile, as if to thank them for their concern. As if they'd been concerned, he told himself. They would have been curious, probably, a Westerner fainting on their train. A moment's diversion from their real concerns. Now that he was conscious again, alive and kicking, perhaps disappointingly so, they faded away. Turning to stare out the window, or moving back to their books and papers, or dozing as they stood, leaning against the back of the person next to them.

'Where's ...' Aidan looked around. Nandan was nowhere to be seen.

'He took fright when you fainted. I swapped seats with him. I heard his impertinent questions. So you won't have him for a neighbour anymore. You'll have me.'

Aidan closed his eyes and let his body go with the rocking of the train. When he opened them again she had folded her hands in her lap and was staring into the middle distance. She looked peaceful. He was happy to be sitting next to her.

Her name was Mrs Sharma, and she was the only person he had ever met who could understand.

Her family had been living in a big apartment in New Delhi in 1984, she told him. Aidan's family had been living in a big house in Belfast in 1969. In both cases it was a charitable description to call what happened to them a riot. More like a pogrom, said Mrs Sharma. Organised persecution, his father had called it, remembered Aidan.

Aidan helped Mrs Sharma with her bags and parcels onto the platform and then over the bridge and onto their next train. They were both going to Madurai. She was a slight woman and in her bright yellow sari resembled a canary, thought Aidan – her tilted head, her bright eyes, the melodious way she spoke her elaborate, cultivated English. Indians were like the Irish in the way they caressed the language and loved it, he decided, the way they chose their words and charmed you with the delivery as much as the meaning.

She sank gracefully into a window seat while he bustled around, stacking her collection of string bags and her suitcase in the rack above their heads, and yet her expression showed that the responsibility for this journey was all hers. 'That one, that one, if you would be so kind,' she said, indicating one of her bundles. He lifted down a string bag stuffed full of tightly wrapped paper parcels. She picked carefully through it as he sorted out his backpack and collapsed into his seat, mopping his face with his handkerchief. 'Here. Please.' She handed one of the parcels to him.

It wasn't yet lunchtime and he'd eaten the packed breakfast the hotel had prepared for him only an hour before, but Mrs Sharma was imperious, so he peered inside. Golden brown pakoras nestled there, wrapped in paper translucent with oil. 'Eat, eat,' she commanded.

'They look good,' he said cautiously. *Never eat the street food,* he'd read in a tourist guide, and he hadn't been sick once so far.

'They will not harm you,' she chided him, reading his mind. 'I made them myself.' She splayed her fingers over the bag with pride.

For who? he wondered.

All through their journey – five hours through the fields and raw dry plains of Tamil Nadu, they chatted. His fingers became wet with grease and orange with turmeric, his mouth a party of spices, his stomach groaning, but in the replete after-a-kid's party kind of way. Happy, stuffed, a spoiled little boy.

'My son's in Australia,' she told him finally, when they were nearing their destination.

He hadn't wanted to ask her directly about her family, and so they talked exclusively about his. Which meant Aidan had lied to her for five hours. His prosperous brothers. His successful father. His tranquil mother. Their life of beach holidays and camping in Australia. He'd enjoyed it. Awarding his family the lives he wished they could have had. But as they neared Madurai, he noticed her eyes were filled with sadness, and he wondered if she had believed a word.

'We're Sikhs,' she told him, nodding meaningfully, and he nodded back, wondering what the significance of this might be. 'I've come on a holiday to see my own country. But it's not my country.' She shook her head, as if regretting making the journey. They were pulling into a station – not theirs – and as people piled off and on the train she looked at them, as if into a fishbowl, curious about the strange inhabitants within.

'Northern Ireland,' he'd told her, when she'd asked where his family came from. 'Catholic,' he replied to her tactfully phrased question.

'But you're all Christians, correct?' she asked and he nodded. She asked him about the Troubles and he laughed that off too, telling her not to believe everything she saw on the news.

'It's not like that for us,' she told him quietly, as if revealing something very intimate. 'I thought it was. I went to university, got my PhD. Made a good marriage. To another Sikh, of course. My son was born, and then in 1984, one night – it began. There were fires. There was burning. Whole streets of Sikhs massacred. All of us living in terror. "We are not Indians," my husband told me. "We are not welcome in our own country." We made Dev cut his hair, we were so frightened that they might kill him. We sent him to school without his turban. After that he refused to ever wear one again. "I won't be killed for something so stupid," he said to me. Yet all the same he left here. "I'm Australian, Mum," he tells me on the phone. Like you.'

Aidan wished he hadn't lied to her about his family. The fires in the night. His parents knew that story. The crowds pushing, calling for your blood.

'Twenty-four hours to get out of our home, they told us,' continued Mrs Sharma. 'We only lived because of our good neighbour who helped us. Who risked his life to take us into his home. In the same apartment block people were burned alive. Burned alive! And the people who did this were people we had to work among the next day. That we were meant to go on with as normal. Just go back to living our lives!'

Aidan knew that story, too. His father wouldn't do it. His father refused to forget it. He refused to stop talking about it. And that was why they killed him.

'As soon as Dev got his medical degree he left. "My country tried to kill me," he tells me. I'm never coming back.'

'Then you should leave,' Aidan wanted to tell her, this lonely woman sharing bags of food with a young man from another continent, instead of with her son.

He and Mrs Sharma ate together that evening and for convenience's sake – they'd made arrangements to visit some temples in the morning – Aidan had wanted to stay at the same hotel. But touchingly, hilariously, Mrs Sharma wouldn't hear of it. It would be improper, she said. Her husband was a judge and would look upon it very poorly if he thought his wife – who was on a religious pilgrimage – could be said in any way to be flirting.

And so he stayed in a different hotel. And the next day he felt slightly altered in his relationship to her. Not just a stand-in son, but something else. A protector, maybe.

'You're a good man,' she told him when she saw him off at the train station the next day. She was staying a few more days in Madurai before travelling to Kochi, where he planned to introduce her to Anne. 'A good man.'

And he supposed he was. He tried to be, anyway. Had always tried to be.

'Do you pray?' Mrs Sharma had asked him after their third temple.

'Sort of. I suppose.' He was embarrassed. Not to be talking about this, but that he didn't really know if he prayed in a way that she would count as praying. Indians spoke about religion in a way he supposed his grandmother might have understood. As if it mattered. As if it said something about you. His own thoughts about religion were personal only in that they were too confused and watery to be articulated. 'Not really,' he amended. 'I have a rosary in my luggage, though.' It had been his grandmother's. He used it like a talisman, for luck.

'That's good,' she nodded, grasping his arm tightly as they walked next to a buffalo down the teeming street.

Mrs Sharma cried that evening when they went out to dinner, holding on to his hand as they walked into the restaurant, looking to him for everything. Indian mothers, it seemed, were not so different from Irish mothers, or Australian ones for that matter.

'Dev should be living with me,' she told him when the coffee was served, skillfully wiping her eyes. She did it the way Anne did, so as not to smear her make-up, he supposed. She wore a thick stripe of black kohl on the lower and upper arch of each eye, from a distance making them look big and beautiful. Up close they looked slightly grimy, thought Aidan, although perhaps that was unfair, given the day of praying and crying that she'd had. 'Dev's wife, his children, when he has them, they should all be living with me. I should be helping them.'

What had Nuala expected? Aidan wondered. That her boys would live with her always? Somewhere inside himself that's what he had assumed he would do. After a childhood like theirs, that's what he'd wanted to do. And when his mother died, as if it wasn't cancer at all that killed her but a broken heart, he had been at a loss for a while, until he got his job at Legal Aid and met Anne. He had been living with Nuala and there had been no mention of him moving. Dom had been going to marry Megan, of course – he'd already saved up a sizeable deposit for a flat they could live in. For a long time afterwards Aidan had held on to that money, keeping it separate from his own, as if expecting Megan to turn up any day and claim it. He'd half yearned to see her again, so she could explain to him what had happened to his family, to help him through; and half hated her, blaming her for what Dom did, which from then until now he had never been able to understand.

They took everything, Mrs Sharma told him, over the coconut jelabi she ordered for dessert. Aidan was curious about the riots, he couldn't help it, and kept steering every conversation back to that night. And she talked about it confidingly, trustingly, as if divining in him a more-than-normal interest in disaster.

'They said they were angry with us Sikhs for killing Mrs Gandhi, but when it came down to it I think they just wanted our colour TV.' It wasn't very large, Mrs Sharma added, but it was one of the first in the neighbourhood.

In Belfast they'd come into Our House and taken his mother's tumble dryer. That was in 1969, five years before Aidan was born, but he'd heard all the stories of that day. They all called it Our House, as though the houses they moved to after that, on Duncairn Gardens, and then, the year after Aidan was born, Malone Avenue, were provisional. The Protestant looters had taken his grandmother's wedding rings and his grandfather's carpentry tools. But much more importantly, the deeds to Our House were never retrieved, so his family couldn't sell it, nor have any chance of claiming it back. They simply had to leave Our House on August the fifteenth, 1969, with less than ten hours notice, and never went back.

Mrs Sharma was shaking her head, the slight smile she habitually assumed giving her the face of the eternally lost, and sweet-natured, and perplexed. Aidan recognised it. It was the face of his own mother. The face of an overwhelming, bottomless grief.

It was like falling down a well, is how Nuala had described it to him once. Her fall had started the day his father was killed. She was reaching out with both arms trying to break her fall, or even just slow it down but she couldn't, and she kept falling and falling.

'When does it get better?' Aidan had whispered to her. They were lying on her double bed, fully clothed underneath the duvet, side by side.

'It doesn't.' Her eyes open wide, unblinking. 'It doesn't.'

But it had. Aidan knew that it had. They packed up and came out to Australia after his father's funeral. That sunny place where history seems like a chimera, until you realise it's you who can never let it go. His mother smiled and sang as she set up their new household. She had a manic energy about her in those days. A single mother, a widow, with no inheritance but a hefty deposit from the sale of their Malone Avenue house, a good job and three hungry sons. The better they had done, though, and the more settled they became, the more she seemed to collapse. Sometimes he thought they should have stayed where they were in Belfast. She would have kept up the fight every day, that way. To keep proving herself. To keep going. In Australia she felt too safe, so safe she could let go and drown in her grief. If they'd stayed in Belfast she could have gone to Rome for a holiday, like Mrs Sharma here in Madurai. Visiting the Vatican if she felt nostalgic – although she had never been particularly religious – and going to Mass with the Pope. For a moment Aidan imagined himself accompanying her. But Liam, Aidan reminded himself, before he got too carried away with what might have been. Nuala would never have stayed in Northern Ireland because of Liam. Even at that age – how old was he then? Fifteen? – he had been way too interested in all the goings on.

'He beats me,' Mrs Sharma said in the hotel restaurant.

Aidan had been sorting out the rest of the malai kofta, wondering if she was up for seconds of the veg jalfreezi. He assumed he'd misheard.

'Dev's father. He beats me.'

Aidan's hand came down to rest on the plastic white tablecloth.

'It's not his fault.' Mrs Sharma's bracelets clanked as she waved her hand. 'He's always sorry. But ...' She took a deep breath.

Aidan realised he was holding his own.

'If I had my son, if Dev were here.' Her gaze was trained on the tablecloth. 'I think if we were living with my son ...'

Behind her glasses Aidan saw the glinting diamond of a tear forming.

'Sorry.' Mrs Sharma dabbed a tissue delicately at her eyes.

'That's okay.' It really was. Aidan wasn't worried by a woman crying, although he knew so many men were. His mother, and in his job. And Anne very occasionally. He was used to it.

'What was I saying?' She laughed tremulously.

'That if you were living with your son ...'

'Oh yes. I think it would be different. I think my husband could relax.'

Aidan nodded, but he knew he would never have let anyone beat his mother. He would have stood up to anyone, including, definitely, his own father. And for a moment he hated Dev. If he lived with his mother he could protect her.

'It's the stress, it gets to my husband,' said Mrs Sharma. 'It never happened before the riots in 1984. It brought it all back up, you know. Partition. What happened to him in the past.'

She was staring at Aidan intently and he regretted again his crazy decision to lie to her, that happy family he'd so enjoyed manufacturing for them both on the train.

'I know,' he said. The spoon in his hand was dripping spinach all over the tablecloth and belatedly he put it back into its bowl. 'We were in a similar situation in Belfast.'

As if she knew what was coming, as if she knew they were kindred, she smiled. 'People do terrible things when they are reminded of what's hurt them,' said Mrs Sharma. 'They can't be held responsible. It's so terrible, this anger, this pain.' She shrugged. 'Some things are too hard to ever get over, and you can't blame them for it personally.'

To think of someone hurting Mrs Sharma. To think of a husband hurting his wife. The idea of it made Aidan want to lie down and cry too. To think of the damage people do.

'I know.'

CHAPTER FOURTEEN

Halley's phone rang at 10pm, startling her. She thought it must be Sug, and the pleasure she felt didn't leave her once she realised it was Aidan.

'I was wondering where you'd got to.'

'I have to talk to you.'

'Okay.'

'I have to talk to you now.'

'But I'm at home.'

'I'm out the front.'

'You can't come here.'

'I need to see you.'

He sounded drugged, thought Halley, his voice low and intense, like a dream of a desperate lover.

'I have to see you!'

'Meet me under the house, then,' she said quickly. 'But leave your bike where it is, okay? And be quiet.'

She went downstairs in her pyjamas and ugg boots, holding a washing basket against her hip as her alibi. Not that she needed one. Matt was in bed with classical music playing on the radio, book open on his chest, already half asleep, and Benny was out for the night, staying with a friend in town.

Aidan looked lonely in the half dark, dressed in his motorbike leathers, his helmet under one arm. Like an astronaut, thought Halley, just landed on some unexpected planet.

'What's wrong? What is it? Are you unwell?'

'I'm not going to let Liam turn you in.'

Halley's stomach heaved and she almost dropped the washing basket as she stooped to place it on the ground.

'Turn me in?' Her voice trembled and she made herself stop speaking for a moment before it gave away anything more. 'You said you just came here to talk.'

'Liam asked me to come out here and find you. He wants to use you as a bargaining chip with the authorities, to help him get early release out of prison. But I won't let him, Megan. I'm not going to give him what he needs.'

'So you were lying to me?' How could she have been fooled so easily? Halley asked herself, panicking at the thought of all the other lies she might be falling for. 'And how will you stop him?' she added, talking fast, adrenaline beginning its race through her veins. 'What if you can't turn him away from this?' Her voice rose. 'What if, whatever you say to him, he still has it in for me?'

'I won't let him, Megan. I know too much for him to mess with me. He'll do what I tell him on this, I promise you, even if I am just his little brother.'

He was surprised by the resolution in his tone. It gave him confidence, and he could tell from the way Halley looked at him, with a kind of relaxation dawning in her features, that she was convinced by it, too.

'When is it going to end, Megan? Is it ever?' He covered his face in his hands. 'It's been seventeen years and I'm still not okay.'

His face was pale underneath his sunburn, his features folded in misery. He looked like Dom, thought Halley. It was something in his jowls, in the haunted expression in his eyes, his full mouth drooping in misery. She wanted to kiss him.

'You'll feel better in the morning,' she soothed, crooning the words like a lullaby, calming herself as much as him. 'Let's talk tomorrow, or the day after. After lunch, at the river. I'll come and meet you there.'

She walked him as far as the bend in the drive and then stood watching him until he disappeared from view, a little astronaut navigating his way past the gum trees trailing their white hanging branches over the road.

Matt was sitting in his pyjamas at the kitchen table when she came upstairs.

'What was he doing here?' he said.

'What are you doing up?' It was the wrong answer. She realised that as soon as the words left her mouth.

'Answer my question.'

She thought about going to the sink and doing the dishes stacked there. She thought about running down the driveway after Aidan. She was scared of Matt when he was like this. His anger was slow to start, but implacable.

Not like Halley's rages, coming down hard like summer rain, drenching them, and then abruptly ceasing, leaving a certain kind of calm clarity, for Halley at least, in their wake.

'I was planning this trip to Greece to try to save us,' he said quietly, as if to himself.

She sat down at the table opposite him and poured herself a glass of Beaujolais. It would be easier to cope with this, she decided, if she was drinking.

'You knew we were never going to Greece.'

She would work out what to tell him in good time, she told herself, taking a long sip of the wine. Just as she would work out what to do about Aidan and Liam. That was the key here, not to push anyone into getting confused and then lashing out and doing something or saying something they would all regret.

'I wanted it to work, for me, for Benny ...'

He covered his face with his hands, which were reddened and thickened by work. The nails were bitten down to the quick on all his fingers, she noticed.

'Matt?' Her voice was small. She pushed aside her wine.

'You can't see him here, Halley. Not under the house.'

'What?' Halley laughed, in confusion and relief. 'No. No! It's not ...' She shook her head. Unable to even say those words: *an affair*. They had never spoken about such things. A few times over the years she had wondered if he suspected – a few times she had been almost sure that he knew about her lovers – but even in their worst fights they had never mentioned it. For all these years they had reserved their real venom for fighting about Benny.

'Matt.' She had to get through to him. She made her voice loud and certain. 'It's not that.'

'When is it going to end, Halley? Is it ever?'

'What do you mean?' The similarity of his words to Aidan's caught her by surprise, and for a moment she thought he was talking about Dom as well.

'Oh don't. Don't!' he cried.

Halley stood up and walked around to kneel next to him at the kitchen table.

'Hey.' She peeled his fingers away from his face, claiming them and squeezing them tightly with one hand against her arm. 'I promise you we're not having an affair.'

'Don't lie to me.'

His brown eyes were red-rimmed and sore looking. Was he tired? Was he crying? wondered Halley. That had never happened before. She didn't know how they would face each other in the morning if she were to see Matt cry. He drew a hand across his face and sighed, glancing at Benny's room, an automatic reflex neither of them could get out of the habit of, even though for half the evenings this week he hadn't been home.

'You can hear everything that's said downstairs up here, you know.'

'I didn't know.' She tried to remember if she'd ever spoken to anyone like Sug on the phone downstairs. Probably.

He tightened his lips, looking at her, offering her his face straight on. She wanted to kiss it. Just as she had wanted to kiss Aidan's mouth five minutes ago, she reminded herself. It confused her, this maternal feeling. She longed to stroke Matt's face and cradle him in her arms.

'Matt ...' She had the feeling she was on the edge of the precipice of his belief in her.

'You never talk about the past, ever,' he said. 'You're the woman without a past. But here he is. Here he is and you're meeting up with him under the house in the dark and it's been eighteen years and you're sneaking off to talk to him.' He was standing up. He was turning away from her. 'I can't take this.'

'Matt ... wait, I can explain.' She was losing him, thought Halley, panicking, because when had she ever worried about that?

'And another thing ...'

'What?'

He reached into the fridge and brought out two beers. He tossed one to Halley and she reached up automatically to catch it, somehow feeling as her fingers closed around the chilled glass that she'd unwittingly just been caught out.

'Why was he calling you Megan?'

CHAPTER FIFTEEN

They sat side by side in the old armchairs on the verandah, their feet resting on the wooden railing, outsized and looming in front of Mount Chincogan, the double-peak mild and unassuming in the moonlight. The beer bottle hung from Matt's hand, trailing limply on the ground as he rocked himself back in his chair. The air was cooling, finally, the lush thick heat of the rainforest almost visible in its fetid intensity as it dissipated from the leaf canopy surrounding them.

'You're saying you were a terrorist?' said Matt, as if he'd just remembered, or was waking up, or coming to. He took a sip of his beer.

'No. That's not what we called ourselves. I was a volunteer.'

'Well, and so what did you volunteer for?'

For so long she had felt out of control. Ever since that day she had been improvising, surviving, fleeing. Going from tree to tree like a monkey through the jungle, taking hold of the next possibility that presented itself for getting however the hell away. But here on this verandah someone was asking for an account of all that, and when she looked back the foliage was so thick she could barely see.

'You better tell me, Halley.'

'I'll try.'

On the day of the bombing she was wearing a cotton dress, she remembered that much – it was cornflower blue with white daisies dotted over it, full-skirted and gathered at the waist. The soft material brushed against her legs as she moved her feet over the pedals of the van. She stole a glance at Liam, sitting next to her in the front seat. He was looking out the window. He had barely spoken to her all morning. She wondered if he was having second thoughts.

'Stop here,' he said.

Megan slowed but couldn't stop. Cars were packed tightly along the kerb. Signs with red writing on them warned against double-parking as far as she could see.

'I said stop here!' Liam barked, his face still turned away.

'Where?'

'Here, dammit.'

She slammed her foot on the brake and a chorus of car horns began tooting. The impulse came over her to open the door, jump out and run away. She could run into the bookshop opposite, she thought, or the department store down the road and hide herself in the crowds. But how could she pretend to read a book or shop, knowing Liam would be looking for her? If she jumped out she would have to run and keep on running, and somehow that seemed harder than staying and coping with Liam acting this way. If she jumped out she would free herself from this scripted day, the next twenty-four minutely planned hours, and exchange them for the unmapped, the unknown, the open future. And that also frightened her. She was tied to this, and nothing had even happened yet. They were making this unexpected stop, but soon they'd be arriving at their destination – the financial district of Canary Wharf – where the plan for the action was set. The warning phone calls were about to be made. The evacuations would soon begin. She was bound to her fate, as if to the mast of a ship, and must go down with it, or sail on, she decided, wherever it might lead.

So it was funny that minutes later she was running down the street, her dress in tatters, mute with shock and terror, freer than ever. Without Liam, without anything to link her to what had just happened.

At the Australian High Commission they established her identity quickly. They offered her counselling and someone to accompany her back to the flat for her things. She said no, of course. Liam would have killed her. She went alone and quickly stuffed her clothes and toiletries into a suitcase, crying with relief that Liam wasn't there. She returned to the High Commission in a taxi. 'I just want to go home,' she sobbed. It wasn't hard to cry. It wasn't hard to act like a woman in shock. It was incredible that she hadn't been killed, they said, in light of her proximity to the blast. It was incredible that she hadn't been injured.

The consular staff couldn't have been kinder to her as they made sure her passport was in order and took her to the airport, where TV cameras were waiting. A travel warning had been issued by the British government, and many tourists visiting London were choosing to immediately return home. She sidled into the toilets and lingered there until, peeking through the crack in the door, she saw that the cameras had gone.

'What did the reporters ask you?' she asked a fellow Australian as they waited in line to check in.

'What we were going home for,' shrugged the man.

You might have thought it would have bonded them to be fleeing a city under potential terrorist attack, but they all seemed numb and separate as they waited to be called to their flights, closed off from one another in their thoughts.

She refused all offers of food on the way home. She accepted alcohol, though – whatever was offered – and she was dazed and bleary-eyed when they arrived in Sydney. At Immigration they were sympathetic to her, like everyone else unaware of the role she'd played, she registered. During the flight she had been half expecting to be arrested on landing.

'Glad to be back in Australia, I'll bet,' said the officer who stamped her passport. Megan nodded mutely.

At the baggage carousel sniffer dogs roamed over the luggage, and she felt a rush of adrenaline flowering down her back as one paused by her bag. She backed away from the crowds and headed empty-handed for the exit doors. A mistake, she realised, as she approached Customs control, that flowering down her back a signal to think again. Who comes home from England without luggage? There was nothing incriminating in her luggage anyway, she reminded herself – Liam had taught her to be disciplined about that. She turned back to the carousel, aware of the eyes of the officials upon her. They were trained to look for signs of distress, she'd heard. They looked for sweating, and odd behaviour. She forced herself to wait. Forced herself to keep her hands at her sides when they longed to reach out and pick up any bag from the moving beltway that would allow her to be on her way. But that would be stealing. And she must make sure to declare any foodstuffs, the quarantine signs reminded her. She must never break any law again, she told herself. She must live a life without speeding tickets or parking fines, without any of the myriad risks a normal person takes every day.

'Do you have anything to declare?' asked the woman at Customs.

She'd bought a cashmere cardigan for her mother on a tourist binge in Piccadilly Circus, Megan told her. And a Brighton rock candy for her father, and a tie from Liberty, for Dom. All purchased months ago when she'd first arrived in London, before she'd had any thought of bombs. The officer waved her through. The doors slid closed behind her and she was descending a walkway where people cheered and waved and clapped the disgorged passengers as if they were models in a fashion parade. She scanned the crowd, squinting against the flash of reporters' cameras. She'd lied and told her parents she would be coming home in two days. They still had no idea she had been anywhere near the attack.

'No, no, excuse me,' she said blindly as she walked on, head down, terrified someone might have been tipped off, somehow, and come to collect her. 'I don't know,' she told a young man who asked her when the survivors of the bombing might be coming through. The man she'd stood next to at check-in at Heathrow was walking out just behind her. 'Excuse me.'

She thrust her way through the crowd to the toilets where she changed into a blue skirt and white shirt, and swapped her sneakers for thongs. She zipped the bag closed and then, hesitating, unzipped it and reached in to extract her passport. She wedged the bag in between the toilet and the wall, and having locked the toilet door, she waited until the bathroom was empty before sliding under the partition to emerge on the other side. She caught a glimpse of herself in the wall of mirrors as she left the bathroom. She looked bony and pale, thought Megan, like a visitation from the afterlife. Empty-handed, she circled the crowd clustered around the arrivals ramp, walked through the automatic glass doors and out into the glare and high blue sky of the Australian sunshine. This was it, she told herself. She had made it home.

Matt took a sip from his empty bottle and then glanced at it in surprise. He hurled it into the rainforest where it landed with a soft crash into a bank of ferns.

'I can't believe you would ever get involved in something like that. That you would hurt someone on purpose, who you didn't even know.'

'I told you, it was an accident.'

Matt stood up to stare out into the rainforest with his back to her. 'Why didn't you just leave the first time anyone ever mentioned making a bomb?'

'I almost did, a few times. I even booked my ticket once, but Liam had a sixth sense for those kind of things, and every time he'd talk me around.'

'How?' Matt was breathing deeply, his hands clutching the verandah railing tightly as if for support.

'He made it a question of commitment. Of how far I was prepared to go for what I believed,' she said slowly. 'And to prove I wasn't just some dumb rich girl, saying all the right things. I wanted to make a difference. A real difference. I wanted to do something useful with my life.'

'And did you?'

'No.' She'd realised her mistake within seconds of the explosion, the final link in the chain of confounding events that she couldn't find the beginning of, no matter how hard she tried.

'And you've been lying to everyone, to me, all this time ...'

Halley thought of her days. Her memories. Her life. Bifurcated always. Her life before and her life after. What people knew about her and what they didn't. She wanted to tell Matt that she loved him, and that he and Benny meant everything to her, and that the life they'd shared together had never been a lie, but her throat felt frozen. It was as if a spell had been cast on her and she could make only the simplest responses to Matt's question.

'Yes.'

'So what now?' he asked, turning to her, his face in the darkness like a ghost's.

'We should go to bed.'

He grabbed her arm, the fingers gripping painfully. 'No, I mean what happens to us now?'

CHAPTER SIXTEEN

London, 1992

'You don't seem like three brothers,' mused Megan, on her first after-noon in London. Liam had taken her straight to the pub from the airport, her luggage heaped on the floor next to where she was awkwardly perched on a bar stool.

'What are you talking about?' he said good-humouredly.

They each of them looked so different, thought Megan: they could have come from three different families. Dom, the classically Irish-looking one. Black hair, brown eyes, white skin. Aidan, red-haired and tender-looking, his fair skin so easily burning and flushing from embarrassment. Liam, like a rock star. Vain, pampered, a pussycat of a man. Preening, it seemed to her, despite being dressed in old jeans and a battered leather jacket. And, of course, that confidence in itself, of a man allowing himself to appear so openly vain, made him even more charismatic.

'You don't seem to particularly like each other,' she said.

'Well maybe that *is* like three brothers. That's just like my father and his brothers.'

'What were they like?' Megan was hungry for any details about Dom's past that Liam might choose to divulge.

'Well, Dad went to university and they didn't. And Dad made real money and they didn't. And Dad lived in a lovely part of Belfast and they didn't. And Dad married a beautiful, intelligent woman and had three strapping sons ...'

'And they didn't,' finished Megan.

'Right.'

'What did they do?'

Liam was quiet.

'Liam?' Had she said something wrong? wondered Megan. 'Hello?'

'Do you not know anything about it? Did Dom tell you nothing at all?'

At that moment a girl came sloping around the curve of the bar. A black-clad, black-haired girl whom Megan distrusted on sight. Slutty, trampy, her mother's voice said in her ear. Catnip to a man of course. Promised to Dom as she was, Megan discounted herself from any kind of competition in these matters. And besides, she was too sure of herself, too proud to lower herself to the level of this girl, to compete. She didn't see herself in that way.

'Will we be seeing your uncles then?' asked Megan.

'No,' said Liam, biting his lip as he looked at the girl, and frowning. 'They're in Ireland. And they're old. No. But they fought the good fight.'

'Do you mean they were in the ...?'

Megan felt like an idiot at these times. Unable to be sure she understood the code. Forced to put things into words that she knew she shouldn't.

'Yes. Shall I spell it out for you?' Liam had forgotten the girl and was smiling at her. 'That's P for Provisional. I for Irish. Then R for Republican and A for Army.'

'Shut up,' said Megan, thrusting some chips into her mouth and sloshing it all down with beer. Jetlagged and sleep-deprived, she felt sugary and strange. Later she saw it all as part of the discomfort of being with Liam. He specialised in throwing her off balance.

'Yes, that's what they were. In and out of prison and my dad set up a lucrative legal practice, thank you, defending them.'

Megan was pleased. Dom's father had defended his brothers. It said something good about the family, she thought, that despite their differences he had used his good fortune in this way.

'And then was brutally murdered for his trouble.' Liam set his glass down on the bar with a bang and covered his face with his hands.

Tentatively, Megan touched his arm. 'I'm so sorry.'

Liam shook his head, like a duck shaking off water, and grabbed her hand, squeezing it tightly and looking full into her face, his blue eyes burning. 'I know you are. And what's more you're actually doing something about it. None of us will forget it.'

Like so much of what Liam had said to her, Halley had gone over and over those first hours in the pub together. Wondering how he had managed to create that assumption, that mutual understanding that she was graduating to something bigger.

'Hiya,' he said to the girl who was loitering, it seemed to Megan, with intent. 'He's not here.'

'Who's not here?' The girl's tone, her expression, the whole way she carried herself, was as if in accusation, thought Megan. As if she was already wounded. As if Liam had already treated her badly.

'Your boyfriend.'

She bridled. 'Who said I have a boyfriend?'

Megan watched, fascinated, as Liam sat up straighter on his bar stool, regarding the girl. The girl, looking sideways up at him through tousled black hair, regarded him back. Then as if remembering himself Liam slumped, swivelling his stool back around to Megan. 'Come on. Let's get you settled in the flat.'

'Who *is* she?' another girl was shouting, a week later, when Megan came back to the flat one afternoon. The days were so short in London, it would be dark by 4pm and freezing cold. She stepped inside and softly closed the front door. Liam's flat consisted of a hallway leading from the front door to a living room at the back, with two bedrooms, a bathroom and a kitchen, all coming off one side of the hall in a row. The girl was speaking so loudly that Megan could hear her as soon as she opened the front door.

'It's none of your business, really, Sarah.'

'Don't tell me ...'

'Hello?' Megan forced herself to yell, slamming shut the door. She'd bought groceries at Sainsbury's on the way home, and the plastic handles of the bags were digging into her palms.

Silence. And then some frantic whispering and Liam appeared, leaning against the kitchen doorway, one leg loosely crossed over the other.

'Had a good day?' said Liam.

Megan bit her lip. So they were going to pretend no one else was here?

'Fine, thanks.'

She'd spent it at the British Museum, lurking in the cafe. They didn't have proper cafes in London, she'd discovered, just the greasy-spoon places like the one on the corner that Liam liked. The one in the British Museum was the closest thing to a Sydney cafe she'd been able to find, and nearly every day that week she'd made her way there on the Tube.

'Hello.' A woman appeared next to Liam in the doorway, her feet firmly planted, her arms crossed, facing Megan in the hall. 'I'm Sarah.'

She was very pretty, thought Megan. She had blonde shoulder-length hair, and wore green woollen pants and a leather bomber jacket.

'And I'm—'

'Leave it,' said Liam.

Megan shut her mouth.

'Liam says you're an event organiser.' She said it nicely, thought Megan. Straightforwardly. Appealing to her for information just the way Megan would have if she'd been in this situation. If they were given the chance maybe they could be friends, thought Megan, already, only nine days after arriving, lonely to the bone.

'That's one thing you might call it,' Liam snorted.

'But I am,' said Megan.

Liam glowered at her and she closed her mouth again.

Aren't I? she wanted to ask, as she ducked into her room to put her bag down and take her coat off before going back to the kitchen where Sarah had ordered her to come for a cup of tea.

Megan hadn't done a thing since she'd arrived. Ready to get on the phone, to fill clipboards with pages of notes, to scurry from here to there and back again just as she had in Sydney on behalf of the organising committee, she couldn't understand why, every morning when she asked Liam what she should do that day, he said, 'Nothing. Have a look around. Get your bearings. Enjoy London.'

If she was in Sydney, and someone had told her this opportunity was on offer, she would have jumped at the chance. In Sydney she could have made a list of things in London that she wanted to do and see. But the damp cold and the mouldy squalor of the flat had leached away her enthusiasm, and she couldn't remember anymore what she might have liked to do. It was a different city to the one she had come to with her parents when she was thirteen. They had stayed at the Dorchester Hotel in Mayfair, and even though it had been at the same time of year, she remembered cosy lamp-lit afternoon teas and car headlights romantically lighting up the dusk. Warm rooms and hot muffins and a quaint Englishness to everything that seemed out of a children's story. The London she inhabited now was so difficult to get around, and so expensive, she found it hard to remember it was the same city. She would make her plans over breakfast – Hampton Court, the British Library – but all enthusiasm left her the moment she stepped onto the grimy street, and she ended up spending yet another day in the cafe at the British

Museum, reading novels and the magazines they offered for free. She didn't feel she could tell Liam this, it would make her look pathetic, but she wished she could get on with the work she'd come for. If she were busy, working with a purpose, with people to meet and a list of tasks to tick off, it would all feel different, she was certain.

'So what are you doing here, exactly?' said Sarah, when Megan sat down in the kitchen.

Liam was standing with his back to her, his arms folded, staring out the kitchen window, his reflection staring at him right back. There were no blinds or curtains on any of the windows, and when the lights were turned off Megan knew the night outside would encroach on them, and make the flat seem even colder and lonelier than it already was in the day.

'Well, do you know Progress?' began Megan.

'Do I know Progress?' Sarah snorted, and Megan flinched.

What was going on? As she'd walked up the hall Megan had felt cheerful for a moment, wondering if they might be going to have a sociable evening at home, or go out somewhere to grab a bite, or even get started on something for Progress at last.

'Don't give me all that Ireland Uber Alles bullshit,' snapped Sarah.

'Cut it out, Sarah,' said Liam.

'I want to know what you're doing here, in this flat, with my boyfriend.'

'Actually, you know what?' Liam turned around, his face impassive, all business. 'You can get out.'

'Right,' said Sarah. Her pretty face had paled, noticed Megan, the colour flooding out of her as if a switch had been hit.

'You shouldn't speak to her that way,' said Megan, her voice mild, but her heart pounding.

'What, you too?'

'I'm just saying ...' Megan's voice trailed off as she watched Sarah throwing cigarettes and matches into her large sack of a handbag and coiling a thick green scarf around her throat.

'Goodbye,' she nodded at Megan. 'Good luck. Don't believe a word this bastard tells you. And you can fuck off!' she screamed at Liam, startling Megan so badly she slopped her tea. Footsteps pounded down the hallway and then the door banged so loudly in its cheap wooden frame that the window rattled.

'Phew,' said Liam.

I want to go home, thought Megan, for the first time forming the words that had been at the back of her mind from the moment she'd arrived.

'Sorry about that,' said Liam, dunking a biscuit into the cup of tea Sarah had left sitting on the table and taking a bite. 'Jealous girlfriend.'

'Why didn't you just tell her who I am? It doesn't have to be some big secret.'

Liam looked at her, chewing, a slight smile playing around his lips.

'Does it?'

'The thing is, it's sort of convenient for the moment if she thinks you're my girlfriend.'

Megan looked at her feet in their felt-lined black boots. He had something in mind for her, then. In this last week so devoid of any kind of comfort, or company, even false pretenses were something.

'Is she your girlfriend?'

'Not now. Not now that she thinks you are.'

'Do you love her?'

He stared out the window for a moment and then down into his cup of tea.

'Yes, for what it's worth, I think I do.'

So he'd sacrificed something, thought Megan. He was giving something important to himself away for the Cause. She wanted to sacrifice something too.

He ruffled her hair as he walked out of the kitchen and a moment later she heard the sound of the TV in the living room, and when Megan followed a few minutes later with a bowl of soup for her dinner he was stretched out on the couch fast asleep in front of the blaring TV.

'Good news,' said Liam the next morning, when Megan came into the kitchen. 'Tonight I'm taking you to a meeting.'

Megan kept her head bent as she poured cereal into her bowl, adding milk and sugar and putting everything carefully away before sitting down to eat.

'Aren't you pleased?' said Liam, standing at the bench and staring at her.

Megan nodded, scared to reveal the extent of her relief and pleasure. Maybe now things would be different.

The meeting was held in a room above a fish and chip shop, on a corner near Kilburn Station. It felt under-resourced and improvised compared to the thoughtful discussions and extensive minutes and reports and to-do lists distributed in Amanda's Sydney backyard. Only two other people were there that evening – an exhausted-looking man in a cheap business suit and a bored-looking woman who who looked as if she'd just climbed out of bed. At the next meeting another man joined them, but they were the only people who ever came. The people at the meetings in Sydney were articulate, and enthusiastic. The people here seemed worn down and bitter, speaking only when a nod or a shrug wouldn't cut it.

The agenda Liam rushed them through that first evening seemed pointless and irrelevant, and the other two seemed distracted anyway, answering in monosyllables and looking at their watches. Was this the *real* meeting? Megan wondered after the second meeting, held in the same room a week later, or was this the meeting after the first meeting that had happened elsewhere? By the third meeting a few days after that she was sure that must be the case. Apart from Liam they all had English accents, but they spoke in such rapid, shorthand terms that she didn't have a hope of understanding them. 'The Australian,' they called her. Sometimes that's all she could glean from an entire discussion. Where were the general arguments that had engaged everyone so forcefully back home? she wondered. The discussions for and against the use of violence and the urgency of a united Ireland? Let alone what events should be organised, how funding should be generated and what to do. There were Marxist mutterings sometimes, although she could never make head nor tail of who would nationalise what or for whom. Everything here seemed settled, so settled that the only thing left for Megan to do was agree, when, to her surprise, the others would look to her, as if waiting on her nod.

'But don't you think, all the way over there in Australia, that we're all British subjects and that we ought to put away our differences and get on?' the woman asked her one day, surprising Megan by directly addressing her.

She was short and stocky with wiry blonde hair. Megan imagined she did shift work, a nurse or a hospitality worker maybe, because she always looked so tired. There had been no introductions, and that omission on its own made Megan feel disoriented, and unsure.

'It would be ideal if we could all get along,' replied Megan carefully. 'But we can't while we live in a hierarchy of oppression. Without sovereignty there can be no dignity. Without equality there can be no peace.' She was scared of that woman, Megan realised later, in some visceral way understanding she was not like her, and yet too intimidated to admit it to herself at the time.

And if this *was* the meeting after the meeting, she wondered, then who was at the meeting before? Liam, definitely, and ridiculously, even while she knew she was being excluded and patronised, she simultaneously felt proud to be associated with him. Although they always arrived separately, they took to travelling home together afterwards, setting off arm in arm for the Tube station. Megan learned not to question him on these journeys home together, nor when they got home, either, if she didn't want to wreck the mood.

'I hate it here,' she whispered one evening when she phoned Dom from the kitchen for her usual catch-up call. Although the phone was in the living room she'd stretch the cord around to the kitchen, where she had to sit huddled against the partially closed door to have some privacy.

'Then come home,' said Dom.

Megan closed her eyes and rested her head against the doorframe, letting his familiar voice warm her. She had gone that day to the British Museum again, hiding in the cafe, coming home through grey streets under grey skies to the chilly flat where the only point of warmth to look forward to was this phone call.

'I love you.'

'Then come home,' he repeated, almost pleadingly this time.

'But I haven't done anything yet.'

'All the same. Why are you going on with this?'

'Why am I going on with what, exactly?' She hadn't told Dom about the meetings yet, afraid he might mock them, and sure he would disapprove.

'You've been there four weeks already and you still don't know?'

It was nothing specific, yet. But it was not to be a fund-raiser this time, it turned out. Or a conference, which was what Liam had been talking about back in Sydney. Circumstances had changed, he said. More pressure needed to be applied to get the British government to come to the negotiating table, although there would be no human casualties, she had been assured. She didn't know what he was getting at. Or where the two of them were going with their laughter and their camaraderie, either, fixed and growing with every meeting they swung home from.

CHAPTER SEVENTEEN

The boredom of her days somehow lulled her, changing her perception of what was and wasn't radical, or too much for to her try. In all those weeks in London she must have ventured only a handful of times out of Kilburn and South Kensington, where she went to the British Museum on a double-decker bus. The streets around the Museum always seemed empty, like a stage set waiting for a play. In Kilburn they were crowded but single-minded, filled with people hurrying to and from the Tube. There was a park she wandered around, and shops she would go into, but the rest of London seemed closed to her, everything she could think of doing either too lonely, or too expensive, or too cold to contemplate. The boredom and the claustro-phobia of her life with Liam created a kind of intensity and a readiness for action in her that otherwise she would never have found. An idea that to do anything, something, whatever was asked of her, would give it all a meaning that otherwise it wouldn't have had.

And to dispel the strange notion that Liam had built up of her. Engaged to a saint, she herself nothing but a dilettante. In Sydney she would have easily ducked these charges. Either by denying them or simply laughing in Liam's face. But in London, somehow, she was forgetting who she was. Dulled, sleepy with inaction, she became the malleable thing she supposed Liam wanted her to be. Or perhaps her depression had merely been luck, a bonus arrived at on Liam's part by default, by virtue of doing almost nothing.

'It must be so boring,' Liam said to her one morning. The sun was shining for once, and Megan was up and dressed and eager to get out into the day.

'What must be so boring?' They were sitting in the living room, waiting for a phone call before they could go out. So much of that time in Halley's memory was spent waiting. She was knitting, a long scarf in green angora.

Liam was watching her, occasionally letting his head rest briefly in her lap. She didn't know what to do at those moments he sat so close. To have objected would have been to take it too seriously, and yet she didn't want to hurt his feelings by joking about it, either. That's what Liam was so good at, she realised later. Stitching you up so that to move one way or another would be to spoil something that wasn't worth preserving in the first place.

'Being married to a saint as you are. It must be boring.'

'Dom, you mean? We're not married.'

'Ah.' He nodded.

'What do you mean, "Ah?"'

'You're not contradicting the other two statements.'

Megan had to cast back in her mind.

'Well, it's not.' The moment had passed, though. She knew she sounded unconvincing, and as she counted up her stitches she wondered. She had never thought of their relationship like that before, or of Dom. 'And anyway, he's not a saint.'

'Could have fooled me.'

And that's when Megan realised what he was getting at. He was getting at sex. And confused, as always with Liam, she didn't know which way to turn. To resist? To insist that no, Dom was a wonderful lover? Which was nothing less than the truth. But too private a thing to talk about with Liam. Or to allow Liam to think this about them? Which insulted Dom and hurt her. To protest in any direction was wrong.

'I thought we were meant to be going out,' she said, pushing him off her lap and dropping her knitting next to the couch.

Already they were too intimate, she was finding. The everyday smells and routines of another human pressing in on her. His sounds, his little ways of doing things becoming familiar, and then almost loveable, simply because she was getting to know them.

'You do know what we're talking about here, don't you?' said Liam, at their fourth meeting.

Megan's heart started thumping in her chest. She swallowed. 'You're talking about a ...' she felt their eyes on her, '... direct action.'

Karen, the woman, whose name Megan now knew, nodded, and Megan sat up straighter.

'And how would you feel about participating in that?' Karen asked.

Although she had never consciously decided that this was something she would do, the moment it came up she had no doubt that she could do it. That she would do it.

'If you got caught you would get life in prison,' said Karen, expressionlessly.

Nothing in her questioned it, and although she would like to be able to look back and say that she had, she knew she had stepped across the line without a backwards glance or thought.

'You sound happier,' said Dom on the phone that evening.

'I am. I'm having a better time.'

The weather had improved and she was getting more exercise, walking around the neighbourhood and sometimes striking up friendly conversations with strangers, which invigorated her too. And when Liam put his hand on her leg one night as they were watching television – they had fallen into a ritual of eating a bowl of soup and drinking a beer each evening in front of the TV – something in her must have been waiting for this too, because she wasn't shocked. Nor was she willing.

'Get off,' she said good-naturedly. She felt more confident. More able to take Liam on and do as she liked. Much more the real Megan, whom she didn't think Liam had ever really got to see.

After a few minutes he put his hand back on her leg again.

'Get off!'

He moved it then, and that was where he left it, that evening.

Over the next few days it became a little thing between them, his hand on her leg and her pushing it off. And then more laughing and more pushing.

'You're just a coward,' he said one evening. 'You're still a virgin, aren't you?'

'You're going to have to try harder than that.'

'Am I?'

She meant he was going to have to try harder to embarrass her, but he twisted it around and made it into something different.

'All right.' His eyebrows raised, he went back to watching the television.

The next evening he invited Megan out to dinner. It was the first time she'd been out in the evening anywhere except the pub he'd taken her to that first night when she arrived, even though in Sydney she went all over the city to see bands and meet up with friends. He took her to a restaurant around the corner that Megan hadn't realised was a viable business: it looked so run-down and deserted in the light of day. By night, though, it was transformed. A line of tables ran down the middle of the narrow room, a lit candle and a rose adorning each one.

'Very romantic,' said Megan as the maître d' seated them. 'What a shame that it's just us.'

The action was planned for Canary Wharf, Liam told her that evening over steak and chips and profiteroles. On weekdays it was Britain's, and therefore Europe's, financial centre, but it would be deserted on a Saturday night and, according to Liam, a perfect soft economic target.

'That's just money,' said Megan, relieved into expansiveness.

'Exactly,' said Liam. 'I wonder if you have any idea what it's like to run out of money?'

Megan flushed. Liam knew she came from a wealthy background. Dom had probably told him about her parents' house on the water.

'England doesn't like to lose money,' he said, as if wrapping up the conversation. 'A shitload of money,' he added, and then he laughed.

Megan laughed along with him, as ever unsure.

CHAPTER EIGHTEEN

For Halley spring was the best time to be living in Mullumbimby. The days were buoyant and breezy, the heatwaves of summer long forgotten and the bitter morning frosts of winter recent enough that you could still welcome the occasional too hot day. In town, flocks of rosellas had arrived and were getting drunk on the nectar in the palm trees planted on the street corners, shrieking at each other so loudly you couldn't have a conversation underneath them for the din. Halley was lingering outside the cafe, gathering herself before going in, when Benny appeared, standing in front of her, holding hands with the girl from the dance party.

'Hi, Mum.'

'Hello, Mrs Sorenson.'

'Please, call me Halley. It's Gretchen, isn't it?' said Halley, forcing herself to smile.

Gretchen's hair was pulled into a loose bun on top of her head, and she stood with her toes pointing out, as poised as a ballerina. She was tall for her age, thought Halley, and well-developed, her breasts full under the blue cotton of her school uniform. Benny looked like a mangy beast next to her. So rangy and messy, his hair frizzy, so loose compared to Gretchen's neat and perfect proportions.

'Benny's going to buy us a bag of mixed lollies. Do you want anything?'

'No thanks.' Halley pulled her shoulder bag around to rest on her chest in front of her. It felt like protection. Benny gave her one of his sheepish smiles as he backed through the sweetshop door.

'Sorry about my mum the other day, Mrs Sorenson,' said Gretchen, looking into Halley's face confidently.

'Oh, well.' Halley had to stop herself from saying 'No problem.'

'I guess I should feel glad she's worried about me.'

Halley raised her eyebrows.

'It shows she cares,' said Gretchen. 'But there's nothing to worry about, really.'

'Actually, I am worried, a little,' said Halley, thawing. The responsibility this girl was taking for everyone's feelings, including Halley's, was a sign, if any were needed, of how out of kilter with her age her life experience must be. Yet somewhere behind that precocious exterior, Halley told herself, there was still a young girl. A young girl who needed protection. She glanced at Benny, who was pointing at various jars, through the sweetshop window. 'You're too young for a sexual relationship, Gretchen. And I am concerned about Benny.'

He was coming out of the shop, holding a gaily striped paper bag.

'Well there's nothing to worry about there, either,' said Gretchen, as Benny took up his position again by her side.

Halley adjusted her bag, swinging it onto the other hip. Enough is enough! she told herself. She couldn't allow herself to be patronised by a fourteen-year-old!

'We'll be good for each other, Mrs Sorenson, you'll see.'

'Jesus Christ!' muttered Halley.

Benny looked alarmed, but Gretchen didn't seem to register the change in Halley's tone. It wasn't just that she was fourteen going on forty-five, thought Halley, or that her mother was the scariest thing since Prussia. It wasn't just that she was evidently well off, and sophisticated. It was that Halley still couldn't answer this fundamental question – what did a girl like this want with her son?

'I have good taste, Mrs Sorenson,' said Gretchen, as if she'd read her mind.

She was just a girl, insisted Halley to herself, resisting the temptation to simply give in to her. Her bag had *Hello Kitty* embroidered on it, for Christ's sake.

'This is a collector's item,' said Gretchen, following Halley's gaze. 'I could get you one on ebay if you'd like me to.'

'That's kind of you to offer, Gretchen, but I'd never use it.'

You're just a girl! Halley wanted to cry out, but she smiled and waved goodbye as the two of them headed off to school, hand in hand, passing the bag of lollies between them. She sank into one of the cafe's chairs, letting all the strength wash out of her in a trickle of helpless grief. She had been just a girl once. Going out with a lovely boy. And look at all the damage she had done.

London, 1992

The moment Megan stood up with Liam in the living room – as though an agreement had been reached – and walked down the hall behind him, past her own bedroom door, she became aware of the cold. It had been so warm and cosy in the living room, but as they walked down the hall they seemed to be entering an ice age.

'Hey.' His hands were cold, cradling her face, pulling her close to him for a fishy kiss. At that moment she should have stopped it. She went over this in her memory at least as often as what came after. She should have muttered some apology and fled to her room. But that sense she always had of having to set Liam straight, of having to prove something crucial about herself, held her back.

'What are you thinking?'

'About Dom,' said Megan. Liam's lips were cold, too.

Liam sighed. 'I love Dom.'

'I love Dom, too,' said Megan, and somehow that released them. Having sworn her fealty, she could go on and betray him.

Liam's body was cold, and the sheets, and the bed as hard as the ground. The linen was fine and clean though, and Megan was grateful for that. Sex turned out to be nothing like what she had been imagining all these years, but nor was she surprised. This wasn't anything to do with her and Dom. Their passionate frustration was nothing like the business being done in this cold room. This was just another test of her loyalty. Another proof of her commitment to the Cause.

'Are you okay?' said Liam, after.

'I'm fine,' said Megan. Strangely she had felt almost nothing when he entered her, even though technically she had been a virgin. But when she stood up she heard Liam swear under his breath, and glancing over to him she saw a smear of blood on the sheet.

He looked at her, surprised, and for a moment Megan felt the stinging relief of contempt.

'Happy?' she asked him.

'I didn't believe it. I thought you were ... I assumed you were ... not that.'

She shook her head at him, tears making her throat swell and unable to form words. Balling her clothes and running freezing, naked, back to her own room. Liam was solicitous. Bringing her a cup of tea and Vegemite toast the next morning, neither of them mentioning it.

She didn't answer the phone that evening when Dom called as he usually did. She listened to his voice on the answering machine and decided she would tell him what had happened with Liam when she got back to Sydney in a few weeks time. She could put it in its proper context then. She could make him understand that it was just another part of the work she was doing here, another sacrifice on her part, another part of Liam's plan.

'It will be our secret,' Liam told Megan the next time they had sex. 'We don't have to ever tell anyone.'

She supposed he was referring to Dom, and even as Liam said these things Megan felt embarrassment. Embarrassment that he would think he could so easily manipulate her. That he could so easily insinuate himself between her and Dom. Yet in the end, she told herself, he had. Like their lovemaking, which compared to the reality, was a generous word. Liam was hardly a skilful lover. Or perhaps he didn't have the inclination, supposed Megan, to waste his energy on her. Yet every night for that short time – just a few weeks – that they were sleeping together, she would roll out of his bed in the morning disgusted and discouraged. Agonised with a sort of disappointed shame. This was sex? This was the whole of it?

What she did with Liam could hardly be called fucking either, so weak was his desire. It was only his desire to control her that was strong. In bed Liam was everything he wasn't out of it. And perhaps that was another thing that kept it going between them. In some crazy way she didn't want to hurt him. Seeing his vulnerability, she went to more trouble to deceive herself so she wouldn't risk doing Liam any harm.

What a lot of trouble telling the truth would have saved, thought Halley. What if she had rolled over and told him plainly: 'Liam, you don't know what to do with me and you're a complete waste of time in bed'? But that was the thing. With another woman he would have been a better lover, that's what Megan told herself. His failure to give her pleasure somehow became her own.

The more she looked back on it, the more Halley thought there was no need for anyone else to manipulate her. She did a perfectly wonderful job on herself.

'You should ask yourself how much you want to be committed.' That was another of his lines. By nightfall, after a few drinks at the pub, they would be great mates again, and it would seem the most natural, the most right, the most political, the most correct, the most committed, the most righteous thing really, to stumble up the stairs to the flat and climb into his bed. 'You should be careful that you don't get too involved.' Liam was her guide and her counsellor. Such a laugh. And yet it all worked. Even as she saw every word that fell from his lips for what it was, she fell for it.

How was it possible? Halley asked herself now. How did I do this to myself? Amazed, afresh, by her story.

CHAPTER NINETEEN

Halley and Aidan were drinking coffee in her car at Brunswick Heads. They had sat first on the riverbank, but when the weather turned cold and rainy, they'd gone back to the car, parking it so they could enjoy the river view.

'Halley, I've been wanting to ask you this for a long time. Did you ever worry about the victims?' asked Aidan.

Halley wanted to jump out and run, screaming. She wanted to slap her hand against her forehead and bash her head against the dash.

'There weren't to be any victims.' Somehow she kept her voice calm. 'We didn't want civilian casualties, from a moral and pragmatic point of view. We were going to telephone through a warning. It was meant for an office building, to disrupt the banking and finance industries.' She forced herself to sit very still in her seat. 'It was meant to happen at ten on that Saturday night. It was dead at that time, Aidan. There weren't even cleaners there then.

Aidan looked at her steadily. 'Bombs are a weapon of war.'

'I know that,' said Halley. 'But our governments send people out to die and drop bombs on women and children and they give no warning at all.'

'Six people were killed in that pub. They weren't warned.'

'It was an accident, Aidan,' whispered Halley. 'I don't know why that bomb went off when it did.'

'And so you never imagined there would be a body count to your involvement in the IRA?'

She looked down, training her eyes on her hands gripping the front of her seat. 'I don't ...' Halley closed her eyes, seeing that dingy classroom where they met for the final time.

'Wait down here until I call you, all right?' Liam told her at the foot of the stairs.

It had been snowing that night, she remembered. She watched from the doorway as snowflakes floated down like feathers, covering everything, grime and dirt, leaves and grass, in a white blanket. After twenty minutes she could have been standing in an alpine meadow, not a grimy North London street, and she marvelled at the power of nature to make everything clean again.

'We're ready for you,' said Liam, appearing at her side. She followed him up the stairs and entered the room, shedding her scarf and coat. There were only four of them there tonight, including Liam. Where was Karen? she wondered. It was just her and the men, including the businessy one, remembered Halley, although this time he wasn't wearing a suit.

'I'll drive the van,' agreed Megan when they asked her. 'You can count on me.' They looked at each other, eyes sliding to right and left, lips tightening, it seemed to Megan, in a collective withheld smile.

'Hang on.' That night when she was recounting the same story to Matt he stopped her. 'You said it was winter? Right? All that snow?'

'That's right.'

'But you said before that you were wearing thongs and a cotton dress.'

'I was, but ... ' It was as if a part of her brain caved in. 'I guess it must have been summer. June. Or July,' said Halley.

'You don't remember?'

At the beach, when you set up your towels against the slope of a dune and then something disturbs it, perhaps the sun dries it out a little, and the dune falls in on itself and over you, gently collapsing into a soft mound – that was her brain. That was her memory of that time.

'You must remember,' said Matt. He looked more shocked than he had when she first told him she had been a volunteer, thought Halley.

'There was an explosion, Matt. It all happened so suddenly. And then I was on the run. And then ...' She shook her head, frightened at herself.

'It was November,' said Aidan evenly when she asked him. 'November 12th, 1992. The height of the IRA's London bombing campaign.'

'You remember it so clearly,' said Halley. 'Is that because of Liam?' He had disappeared immediately afterwards, Aidan told her. He hadn't been in

132

touch with them for two days, and added to everything else she was dealing with, Nuala had been desperately worried about his safety.

'No,' said Aidan patiently. 'Because of Dom.'

A tide of something dark rose in her, a black panic, that Halley shied away from. Turning her head slightly. Shifting position.

'That was just a short while after the explosion. Black November, Mum called it.'

And Halley remembered exactly which day it was. The memories came at her like figures out of the mist. Nothing, nothing, as she edged her way forward, not knowing if she was still on solid ground, and then there he was. Dom, in technicolour red velvet and ermine. Shakespearean in his splendour. Majestic in his presence and reality. You would never think that up until a moment ago he had been lost to her, in the past. And the date, in stark black letters; there it sat in front of her.

'I remembered thongs and a blue summer dress,' said Halley faintly.

Was anything she remembered reliable? she wondered. Probably not. Not when you've worked this hard, all these years, to forget.

CHAPTER TWENTY

Megan talked to Dom just before she left to collect the van from the address Liam gave her on the morning of November 12th. She wasn't sure what she had rung him for. It was night-time in Australia and he was getting ready for bed. Whatever it was she was hoping for from him, he didn't give it.

'You sound so disappointed in me,' she said, interrupting his description of the work he'd been doing at the youth refuge.

'I'm just confused, I guess.'

At least admitting, thought Megan, that there was a subtext to what he'd just been saying.

'I don't understand why you're still over there. I thought by now you would be coming home.'

Megan swallowed.

'What's wrong?'

She couldn't speak.

'Are you laughing?'

She could only make a shuddering sound.

'Are you crying, Megan? What's going on?'

'I have to go,' she choked. The less he or anyone else knew about what they were planning, Liam had told her, the less danger there would be.

'Shall we speak later then? I can stay up late.'

'You need your rest. And I've got a busy day,' she said, cringing. She was a hopeless liar. 'I'll phone tomorrow.'

'All right.'

'All right,' she repeated, roughly wiping the tears from her cheeks with the back of her hand.

'I'm sorry.'

'For what? Shouldn't I be the one who's sorry?'

'For making you cry. What are you sorry for?'

'That I didn't come home when I said I would. That now I have to go.'

That was the last time she ever spoke with him. After the explosion she was too shocked and frightened to phone, and there were no messages from him, either. They had an arrangement that he would leave messages for her on his own answering machine, which she could access with a code if they couldn't get in touch any other way. But two days later, back in Sydney, the machine had no messages for her, and she took one of her greatest risks and phoned Nuala from a phone booth, breaking every rule she'd made for herself about running away.

'Who is this please?' asked a voice on the other end of the line.

'I'm a friend of Dom's,' said Megan, speaking low, trying to disguise her voice. 'Is he there?'

'A friend?'

It was Nuala, realised Megan: her voice sounded so different from usual she hadn't recognised her.

'You don't know?' Nuala said.

'Know what?'

That's when she realised something terrible must have happened, and, without meaning to, she hung up before Nuala finished speaking. A moment later she took hold of herself and forced herself to phone again, her fingers shaking as they dialed, and her voice trembling as she asked to speak to Nuala, but this time someone else answered the phone and told her Nuala was not available. Dom had died, a suicide – the voice explained – two days previously, and was she a close friend? Megan found herself unable to answer, to make her voice work even enough to say goodbye. 'I'm sorry,' she whispered soundlessly, her mouth moving but no sound coming out. 'Hello? Hello?' the voice repeated, until, after a few more seconds, they hung up.

'How did he do it?' she asked Aidan now.

'Hanging. He'd been dead in his room all night by the time they found him.'

'Ah, Dom.'

'Mum always thought it must have been because of Dad. A delayed reaction to the trauma. It's not that uncommon, actually. But I've always thought it must have been mostly to do with you.'

Halley remembered putting down the phone. Nuala must have known it was her, despite her disguised voice, she realised. But Nuala hadn't said anything, and that became the keystone of her grief. Nuala blamed her. They all did. On it she balanced whole towers and archways of stones, each with its own tonnage of guilt.

'Your mother knew what I'd done and she never wanted to speak to me again. I didn't have a name. I was nothing, I was dead to her,' said Halley.

'She didn't recognise your voice: she had no idea you'd phoned,' countered Aidan. 'She kept asking about you. She kept asking where you were.'

'No,' said Halley, unwilling to believe, thinking of that vast wall she had built around Dom's death, unwilling to even begin to dismantle it. 'She didn't ask who I was. That was the giveaway. She didn't because she knew. She knew it was me.'

'No,' insisted Aidan. 'Your parents came to the funeral, Megan, and everyone was wondering where you were. Mum would have said something if she'd spoken to you. Her heart went out to your mum and dad. They looked like they had been bereaved, as well.'

'My parents?'

'Are you surprised?'

Halley gave him a sharp glance.

'Oh come on,' said Aidan, almost laughing. 'What did you think? That we forgot about you? My mother never stopped asking about you – at Christmas, and Dom's birthday, every year.'

'What do you mean, asking? What would she ask?'

'Why? Why? Why?' Aidan moaned. 'They were so happy. So happy. A misunderstanding. Blah blah blah.'

'Aidan, stop!' said Halley, reprovingly. Just this short imitation brought Nuala back to life. Her river of words, like a weather pattern you entered, swirling around you with a logic and an energy of its own. You pulled on a raincoat if she was sad or got your sunnies out if she was feeling lively, but there was no point trying to stop or change the course of her emotions.

'Liam, Dom, Liam, Dom,' intoned Aidan. 'Dom, Liam, Dom, Liam, oh God, oh God, oh God.'

'Don't you think you're being a little mean?' said Halley.

Aidan yelped, a high, bitter laugh. 'You are unbelievable! You are just like Liam! Me? A little mean? You are the one who left, remember that. You are the one who never came back. You are the one, the last time you saw your parents was at the airport. Okay?'

Halley gasped, speechless at the shock of his attack.

'Your leaving broke them, you know. For a while I thought it might kill them, too.'

'I wrote them postcards every year at least,' said Halley. 'I told them I was okay.' Please stop talking about this, she silently begged.

Aidan shrugged, dismissing her. '"Do you understand what might have happened, Aidan?" your father kept asking me. "Can you think where she might have gone? Can we contact Liam, Aidan? Do you think *he* could tell us where she has gone?" They hired detectives! Who came and questioned me! That freaked Liam out. For years your mother kept calling me. Can you imagine what it was like for them to lose their only child?'

'All right,' said Halley, trying to placate him. These were the areas she must not go.

'I am the one, the only one in my family, who actually stood by my mum, okay?' said Aidan, pressing his point home. 'It's not my father's fault, I'll give him that, although you know they could have left Belfast ten years earlier like my mother wanted and none of this would ever have happened.'

Halley thought of Liam's uncles, of Liam's passion and commitment, and wondered. But she didn't say anything.

'I am the one who—' Aidan stopped talking abruptly, as if exhausted by his own rhetoric. 'It's all so old. It's over.' He slumped back into his seat.

Halley gripped the steering wheel, driving her hands down painfully into the thick leather stitching, remembering what it was like when she found out Dom had died.

CHAPTER TWENTY-ONE

She hung up the phone, realising what Dom had done, and turned away. Looking back on that moment, it still came to her as a stark choice. A choice she had made in an instant, just as when the bomb exploded she had chosen to run. Now she chose to turn away from her family, Dom's family, her friends from school and university, from the society of shared grief. She still could have shown up at that point. Her parents would have stood by her. They would have found her the best lawyer, provided her with the best protection money could buy. She could have, she should have – of course she should have! everyone says you should – expressed her grief. Felt it. Processed it. Like processed meat, thought Halley. De-boned and de-veined and compressed into something more manageable. Something that could be packaged and shipped and handled. Instead she turned away, choosing never to speak of it, or to any of them, again.

She was like a hitchhiker turfed out onto the side of the road. A track led away from the highway, a backwoods path through frozen trees and straggly branches. Making her way through this frozen, quiet place – that had been, she supposed, the work of her first few years in northern New South Wales – she found herself on a large open road where she was surprised to see others walking, their faces turned resolutely inward, just like herself. There were so many people she came across who didn't want to talk about what had brought them here. They didn't look at one another or talk. That was the point of this place. You came here to be alone. There were others before her, intimately related to her in their burdens of grief and guilt. And others coming behind. Out of every tragedy and failure, war or natural disaster, divorce or bereavement, there were the ones who just needed to keep moving, who didn't want to or who couldn't describe what they were leaving behind.

What would express her feelings now? she wondered. A scream? A howl? The impossibility of it intimidated her. One of the good things about coming here had been that it didn't have to be spoken of. The burden others imposed, of talking about what had hurt them – it was unbearable. And they had no idea they were doing it, Halley had come to realise. In their automatic assumption that anything felt strongly must be shared they had no idea of the damage they were doing by forcing someone to speak of their pain. By running away from her family and Dom's she hadn't had to. Until now.

Words came haltingly. Aidan was a slow man, though. He didn't seem to mind. Words for those first few days after she found out what Dom had done. Stringing them together to form whole sentences, to her grateful surprise, just as she had found weeks had passed at the time. The shock, she remembered, of waking up one morning to find that it was January, and that Dom's death had happened two months before.

That was like the relief of talking to Aidan, Halley was finding, amazed and grateful at the way an honest word could lead to a truthful sentence. And that a whole conversation might be managed in which she conveyed at least a part of what she had been.

'It was like two different existences,' she said to Aidan. 'Life with Dom, and then life with Dom gone.'

Aidan nodded, and Halley remembered afresh that he had lost Dom too. That was the trouble with the choice she had made to go it alone: she had forgotten, somehow, that there were others who were feeling a version of her grief.

'It was all my fault.'

Aidan nodded again. This was the strange thing, the weird thing, the most touching and surprising thing about talking with Aidan, thought Halley. Even when he was saying something terrible, or confirming her worst fears, she felt comforted. They'd just agreed on the worst thing of her life, and she felt better than she had a moment ago.

'I betrayed him.'

Aidan nodded again. And that was a relief, that they weren't going to argue about it.

Aidan focused on breathing deeply, looking out at the fast-flowing river. The sandy shoreline was empty of people as evening approached, the mountains behind Mullumbimby fading away into a wash of deep purple. A mist rose from the water, blending blue into green into the gold of the river merging into the horizon.

'His suicide shocked us all,' said Aidan finally, long after Halley had fallen silent. 'I don't think I'll ever get over it.'

Eleven-thirty in the morning it had been. The two of them, Aidan and his mother, were at home. He was doing homework, or pretending to, sitting in the den overlooking the backyard, and his mother was doing something in the kitchen. Working out her points for the week probably: she was devoted to Weight Watchers by then. She was singing along to something on the radio, something loud. Aidan never liked pop music, maybe because his mother did. Or maybe because of that morning. The phone rang, she answered it, not turning the music down, and then after she hung up she turned the radio off and he heard her footsteps coming down the tiled stairs. Somehow he knew before she appeared in the doorway that it was bad news, and his mind gave him the option – Liam or Dom. He looked at her face, and he knew. He didn't know how he knew, but he did. Something bad had happened to Dom. What he couldn't believe, what none of them could believe, was that Dom had killed himself. 'It's a mortal sin,' his mother said. They were her first words after the phone call. Her eyes were wide, her face open and young like a child's. Aidan could never do his homework in the back room after that, and when he finished high school a year later the two of them, without even talking about it really, left Australia.

'A mortal sin,' Halley sighed. It was the last thing she would ever have expected Dom to do. But not because it was a mortal sin. No, she was shocked at him for leaving her. Until then she'd still had some kind of a tortured future mapped out for them, which she'd devised on the plane home. The two of them getting in touch as soon as she was sufficiently off the grid. Him convincing her finally to turn herself in, or her convincing him to go into hiding with her. She was counting on him to steer them onto the right path. The whole time in London she'd had the comforting feeling that she would pay. That she would tell Dom everything when she got back to Australia, and that he would help her work out how to pay. After all, that's what Catholics specialised in, didn't they? Repentance and forgiveness and all that stuff.

'Do you remember the dress you wore to your formal?' said Aidan, breaking into her thoughts.

'My Year 12 formal?'

She hadn't thought of that dress for years. Decades, even. Tight in the bodice with a billowing skirt, it was made of red satin taffeta shot through with threads of green and blue silk that changed colour in the light.

'You looked so beautiful in that dress. So did Dom in that suit Mum made him hire. The two of you.'

His voice broke, and Halley didn't want to think about it anymore. Leaning awkwardly across the gear stick she pulled him into her arms.

'Oh Dom,' Aidan cried.

It was as if the car had filled up with the red satin taffeta of her gown, thought Halley, glowing and warm, changing colour around them like shot silk. Threads of greens and blues; emotions she hadn't felt for so long.

She kissed him, salt from her tears in her mouth, making her lips wet, pressing against his cheek. He hugged her tightly. After a long time his arms loosened finally, and she sat back in her seat. The warmth from the sun still concealed behind the clouds was strong, and the car felt to Halley like the inside of an egg, the two of them like twins, travelling in the past's fragile yet unbreakable shell.

On the night of the school formal Megan decided it was time for her and Dom to make love. She felt strong and powerful and imperious. Maybe it was the dress. Low cut and billowing to the floor, it swished regally. Diamonds sparkled in her ears and on her wrists, borrowed from her mother. Her parents had been full of admiration that evening when Dom and Megan posed for photographs in front of the view of the harbour that took up the living room wall.

'Beautiful girl,' said her father, as she walked past him to the front door.

'Beautiful young lady,' her mother corrected him, her lips full and her eyes gleaming, as if she was sucking on a smile.

'I want to have sex,' Megan said to Dom, six hours later. Her words sounded bald but she was all seduction.

They were sitting on the jetty in front of her house. At her insistence they had skipped the party afterwards and Dom had driven her home. She had been stroking his hair. She lay back, the warmth of the summer night caressing her bare shoulders, the slapping of the waves and the lateness of the hour making her feel sensuous and dreamy.

She had felt so confident that evening. It was his love for her, holding and warming her in the spotlight of her school friends' gaze all night. He had held her hand and danced with her. Although always aware of what people might be thinking about her father, about her family, she'd felt like a princess all evening.

'I love you.' She meant it as the preface to the thing she was about to say, but he interrupted.

'I know. And I want to wait until we're married.'

'And what if I don't?'

He looked out at the water, bothered, she could tell, but not annoyed. He was always patient in these conversations.

'Will you let me tell you about game theory?' .

'Wait. What does this have to do with anything?' said Megan. This was an unexpected turn.

'You study it.'

'It? What's it?' she asked, bewildered.

'The game. Whatever game you're talking about. You learn it. You work out the angles. If it was poker you would learn to count every card. You would memorise every play. Do the stats on which to use when. Work out every probability.'

'But you're terrible at games,.'

'Because they're for-fun games. You don't need to study them. Winning and losing at them doesn't matter.'

Megan admired that. Dom knew when it was a game, and when it was not – something she could lose sight of sometimes.

'I'm talking about the game—'

'The game of life?' said Megan, beating him to the punch line.

'Yeah.'

He was embarrassed, she could tell.

'Explain it to me,' she said, taking his hand.

'In game theory you look for the optimal way to play the game. You find the strategy that has the best odds of winning every time. And that way it doesn't matter what your opponent or any of the other players do. You just keep playing your optimal game.

'So you're saying Christianity is like game theory?'

'You won't always win,' said Dom, looking at Megan intently, as if willing her to agree. 'Life is random. There's luck involved. But you will never be beaten. And if you study and work and always go for the highest possible play, you will, eventually, win.'

Megan sat up, her legs slipping over the smooth old wood of the jetty, her dress rustling luxuriously. The most annoying thing about this was that she had never felt so beautiful. This was her movie ending. This was the time, the place, the moment to give him her virginity.

'Rats.' She tried to sound good humoured, to be gracious in the face of Dom's demanding, difficult-to-please God.

If only he had given himself to her, thought Halley, now. If only he had let her play her own optimal game.

'You know, I think I would have left him,' she said to Aidan.

'Who?'

'Who? Dom!' My love. My one and only, she thought. 'I think I was trying to leave him when I went to London. He was too good.'

'Too good for what?'

'Too good for who,' she corrected him. 'He was too good for me.'

The steady shining light of his love, never marred by bad temper or withdrawal. His generous, open-handed giving – to everyone, which should have made Megan jealous, except how could she be jealous when he already gave everything he had to her? Maybe that's why he was so determined, so extraordinary in his promise to remain a virgin until he married, thought Halley now. He was a passionate man, and Megan could never quite believe he was really going to place all of that importance on a single act, but maybe he wanted, needed, to retain something – something of his own, for himself.

'Maybe he didn't want to have sex for the same reason I decided to go to London,' said Halley. 'Maybe he didn't want to be possessed, either. Maybe he was afraid of all-consuming love, too, like me.'

'I think he'd already seen what jealousy and hatred and all that crap could do and he wanted no part of it,' said Aidan, gently refuting her. 'He just thought following the Bible was the best way. He always used to say to me—'

'Life's too short to work out the rules on your own,' said Halley, finishing his sentence for him.

CHAPTER TWENTY-TWO

As soon as Halley woke in the dark she sensed that something was different. She sniffed, and listened. The house was quiet. Benny must have gone out early, or maybe he just hadn't come home. Halley felt her familiar anxieties slithering into the room. Car crash, bashing, flash flood, snake bite ran through her brain, like the text they scroll underneath TV shows, advertising the coming attractions. She rolled over and felt with her hand for Matt's body. The same flannel leg, but ...

'Are you awake?' she whispered.

'Yes.'

Matt slept like a log, always, and she resented him for it regularly. Unable to sleep, she would listen to his gentle snores and his contented breathing, despising him, in a small part of herself, for his lack of complication.

'What are you thinking about?' she prompted him, when she realised he wasn't going to say anything more.

'Those people.'

'Which people?'

It was peaceful here. The white sheets glowed in the moonlight shining through the windows. Crickets chirruped, inconsistent at this time of year. A car drove by. Then silence.

'The dead people.'

His voice was soft, and so hesitant she thought she must have misheard.

'Pardon?'

'The people you helped to kill.' This time he spoke loudly, as if to a deaf person.

'I heard you,' she snapped.

'Do you?'

'Think about them? No.' Halley spread the fingers of her right hand over the centre of her chest, just above her ribcage. 'I've been too scared.'

'Let's find out.'

'What? Matt! No.'

But he was padding out of the room already, and came back holding Benny's laptop computer. She sat up, pulling the sheets around her as Matt sat down next to her on the bed.

'November 4th, 1992, Kilburn High Road victims. Here.'

Halley fell back against the pillows, staring at the ceiling.

'Maxine Carstairs. Twenty-seven years old,' read Matt out loud. 'Mourned by her parents, Julia and Ian Carstairs, and her brother, Alastair.'

'Oh God,' said Halley.

'David Ryan. Twenty-one. Bricklayer. Left one son, Simon, two years old. Mourned by his wife, Bernadette Ryan, and parents Molly and Geoff Ryan.

Lucy Ryan, three months old, mourned by her brother, Simon, mother Bernadette and grandparents Molly and Geoff Ryan.'

He paused for a moment.

'Sean McDonald, thirty-two years old. Mourned by his parents, Agnes and Cecil McDonald.'

'Shelley Mould, fifty-four years old. Mourned by her fiancé, Philip Sherbourne, and her parents, Solomon and Hilary Mould. Doesn't sound Irish, even. Oh, this is more like it.

'Michael O'Brady, forty-six years old. Mourned by his wife, Therese, and his brothers.

'Simon Dengate, thirty-nine years old. Mourned by his daughter, Megan, and siblings, Sarah Clarke and Victoria Hood.'

Matt fell silent, his voice fading on the last few words.

Seven people. Seven of them, Halley told herself. She leaned over Matt's lap to look into the screen. Maxine Carstairs stared back at her. It was like looking at herself from that time. Maxine's too thickly mascara-ed eyes opened wide, staring confidently into the camera, her glossy mouth smiling.

'You know, in a funny way it feels like there could be a photo of me up there,' said Halley. She was surprised, in a way, that there wasn't. She so easily could have been a victim. She came so close to bringing the body count to eight that day. That in itself had always made her role in it all seem different, more tenuous and less responsible somehow. Although now she wondered why.

'I can't believe you never did this before,' said Matt.

'I didn't realise that I could,' said Halley, staring at the faces. In all these years it truly hadn't occurred to her.

'What does that mean?' asked Matt, pointing to the word that had been stamped over the faces of Sean McDonald and Michael O'Brady at the bottom of the page.

'Collusion,' said Halley, trying the word out on her tongue. 'That means they were suspected of being IRA. So if it was true, they would have died at the hands of one of their own.'

'They don't sound like IRA. This one was a schoolteacher. And this one had two children.'

'No,' said Halley. 'But I'm sure I wouldn't have sounded like it, either.'

'Let's google you.'

'Matt, no!'

'What's your surname, again? Can you believe that I don't know it?'

'O'Dea,' said Megan dully. 'O. Apostrophe. D. ...'

He had already typed Megan O'Dea into the space bar and clicked on it before she'd finished spelling it out.

The first few entries were for lawyers and accountants in Canada and the States, but halfway down the page it was obviously her name that was coming up, in word groupings with her parents' names, and a Sydney law firm was seeking resolution of a will.

'Don't, Matt,' said Halley quietly, as his cursor circled over the details. She knew her parents had been looking for her. And she knew there must be legal documents and wills to settle sometime. But not now. Sliding her hand over Matt's on the mouse she clicked back to the page with the victims' faces on it. Had they been here all this time? she wondered. Their faces and details available to her in a moment, if only she'd thought to look? It was as though she had been unconsciously avoiding it for all these years, thought Halley, and now she thought she understood why.

As she moved the cursor over the victims' faces she learned that 'One Art' by Elizabeth Bishop had been Maxine Carstairs' favourite poem, and there it was written out in its entirety; Shelley Mould's mother had written a grief diary; grandchildren had been born whom Shelley had never met. She paused over a photo of Lucy Ryan's gravestone, with balloons and a colourful spinning-wheel planted among the flowers surrounding it.

'It was an accident, right?' said Matt, when they were lying down again, the laptop on the floor next to the bed. Halley wanted to touch him, to press herself all along him, but she was afraid. It felt as though she was more afraid than she had ever been. It made no sense. She was trembling, shivering with fear.

'You know it was. I told you it was. I've told you everything, Matt. Don't you believe me?'

'I want to believe you,' he said slowly.

'You have to.' Halley turned over and blindly sought his body with her own. 'You have to believe me.' Her eyes were screwed shut even though the room was dark. She forced herself against him, his body surprised but not unaccepting. 'You have to.'

He held her gently, not rejecting her, thought Halley, but not entirely willing, either.

Once Matt had left for work in the morning, taking Benny's bag and uniform to drop off at school, Halley opened up the computer again and found the photos of Michael O'Brady and Sean McDonald, the ones with 'Collusion' stamped over their faces. The photos were unremarkable – clean-shaven Sean smiling shyly; Michael obviously snapped on a fishing holiday. But they reminded her of something she couldn't quite place. Like faint pictures, underdeveloped and out of focus, and nothing like her memories of the day of the bombing – so vivid, yet so unreliable in its sparkling intensity.

'Who were these men, Aidan?' asked Halley, once she had pulled the car up to their spot in front of the river. She handed him a print-out of their photos.

Aidan scarcely glanced at the page before answering. 'They were the ones inside the Royal Arms at the time of the blast. It was closed that day because of a gas leak, and there was no one else there.'

'What were they doing there, then?'

'I don't know.'

He wouldn't meet her eye. He was looking at his hands placed flat on his knees.

'I think I knew them,' she said. 'Their names weren't the ones given on the website, though. When I met them they were called ...' and just as her mind reached for it there was the answer '... Lachlan. And Joe.'

An image appeared before her. Distanced and grainy. More like a scene from a film than a lived experience. Collecting them from the airport and driving them in a blue Ford Escort Liam had rented, to a storage area in Clapham. It was run by a sleepy-looking couple who took a fifty-pound note from Megan and handed her a set of keys and a wheelie trolley. She walked with Lachlan and Joe to a wire enclosure and watched as they wheeled away a large metal box, like the kind a carpenter uses to store his tools, and put it in the boot of the car. That was the box, Halley remembered, that Liam brought back to their flat.

'That box contained five pounds of Semtex, from Libya,' said Aidan, when Halley described it.

'I was the only one they would trust.' The words as she uttered them were bringing memories up behind them, rather than the other way around. 'They refused to meet anyone else from the group. They wouldn't even meet with Liam.'

'That's right.'

'How do you know?' Something about the way he was looking at her made her itch all over.

'Liam told me. He particularly wanted me to find out what you remember.' He was looking at her with stony eyes, his mouth set in a grim line. 'Liam offered you to them to be their driver. He sent some newspaper stories about your dad over to them in Armagh. He says it gave you a believable reason for being involved. They wouldn't have come over to London otherwise.'

Halley struggled with the images pressing upon her. No technicolour. No red velvet and ermine. No dates burned in black against the sky. Just a series of disconnected petty events. Drab and grey. There was none of the glamour of fiction, the mystery of half-remembered truths. These images had the same flat, factual lack of texture in her memory as brushing her teeth that morning.

'Lachlan and Joe weren't killed in the bomb blast,' said Halley. Something about this, the memories of these two men, had excavated another chamber in her stomach and her heart. Another place she was afraid to go.

'They died, Halley. That's a fact,' said Aidan.

'But they weren't killed in the explosion.' And here it was, thought Halley. Who would have thought revelation could feel so flat?

'How could you possibly know that?' he said.

'Because they were already dead.'

CHAPTER TWENTY-THREE

After going to the storage facility, Megan drove the men from Armagh to a house in Willesden Green, with the older one, Joe, sitting next to her, directing her from the *London A to Z*. In his mid-forties, his face already bore the red bumps and broken capillaries of a lifetime's drinking. He wore an immaculate cream parka the whole time – Megan suspected he spot cleaned it every morning – and blue jeans and trainers. Lachlan, in the back, was altogether a different fish. Ten years younger than Joe, he was fit and slim and sported a carefully maintained five-day beard. He didn't say much, but watched everything, including Megan, carefully. She would often glance up into the rear-vision mirror and meet his eyes staring back at her.

That day he and Joe were jumpy, getting out of the car and walking away quickly as soon as she pulled up to the white-brick terrace. It was a one-way street, with the cars parked tightly against one another on both sides of the road. The crowdedness of London was a surprise to Megan after Sydney. Cars, houses, people – they all had to make do with so much less space. Megan waited, engine idling, double-parked in the middle of the road.

'We won't be long,' Joe had told her, but it was a matter of seconds, it seemed, before they were sprinting back down the front path, jumping into the car and slamming the doors. At that moment a white Mercedes Benz appeared around the corner, slowly coming towards them the wrong way down the one-way street.

'Drive,' said Lachlan.

'Go. Go,' said Joe, his voice breaking into a cough.

'But ...'

Megan checked the rear-vision mirror and started to reverse. The Mercedes was approaching. It was occupied, Megan could see, by four large black men.

'Go!' Joe was shouting, Megan's ears ringing in the close confines of the car. 'Jesus Christ Holy Mary Mother of God, go!'

The Mercedes made gentle contact with their front bumper bar. Megan stared into the faces of the men in the other car, just a few metres away, yet unreadable behind their black reflector sunglasses.

Lachlan's appeared next to her, leaning forward from the backseat. 'Go, Megan,' he said, his voice low.

She pressed her foot down on the accelerator and rocketed back down the road, a part of her brain flinching at the contact she was making with the cars parked along both sides. A scraping feeling, a groaning sound, the crunching and grinding of side mirrors being knocked off and denting thick metal.

'You're doing well,' said Lachlan, his head still next to hers.

The Mercedes wasn't pushing them anymore, Megan registered, and a glance through the front windscreen told her a metre had opened up between their cars. They were just trying to scare them, then.

'Keep going,' said Lachlan. He obviously didn't trust that they would remain satisfied with that. She pressed her foot down on the accelerator.

Liam would be liable for any damage to the car, Megan's brain reminded her. She thought about accident insurance and no-claim penalties while she steered with one hand, the other hand pressed to the ceiling, bracing her against the shocks as she ground her way back up the lane.

The road at last opened up behind her. She swung the car around, hand over hand on the steering wheel, not looking to see if anything was approaching from behind. They were facing the right way on the high street and they were flying out of there. Through an amber light, through a red one, and onto a freeway that seemed headed straight for heaven the way it curved away from those narrow streets in a wide stretch of concrete, empty and high.

'Jesus Christ,' said Joe, extracting a hip flask from his pocket and taking a long gulp. He wiped his mouth with the back of his hand, and passed it over to the back, his eyes trained on the road.

'Do not fuck with the Jamaican man,' said Lachlan, in a lilting voice.

'Do not ... Oh God,' said Joe, smacking his lips and shaking his head.

Although Megan's heart was racing, her mind was calm. Her hands and feet working the car automatically, she felt disembodied.

'What just happened?' Her voice shook.

'A fuck-up,' said Joe, drawing the silver hip flask back from behind the seat where Lachlan had been drinking from it.

'A major fuck-up,' said Lachlan.

'We could have been killed back there in that house,' said Joe.

Megan tightened her grip on the wheel.

'You did well, girlie.'

'That was some good driving,' said Lachlan.

Something was digging into her shoulder. Megan took her eyes off the freeway for a second: she had no idea what she was about to see. It was the hip flask. Joe was nodding at her. 'Won't you have some?'

She chauffeured them around for another two days after that. To different houses in Kilburn and Willesden Green. The two of them bringing something out to the car sometimes, a bag or a box or a bulging manila folder. They'd hold it with them in the back seat of the car, drive a little way and drop it off somewhere. They also stopped at betting shops and McDonalds outlets, Megan sharing in the pleasure of a Big Mac and fries eaten together in the car, parked on the side of the road. Some barrier had been broken through, a test had been undergone and passed, and they didn't hold back.

'There's a darkie,' Joe might say, gesturing with his hip flask, in use increasingly, noticed Megan, as the days went on.

'Don't mess with the ...' Lachlan would start, and not have to finish, because Joe would be laughing, holding his face in his hands, getting his handkerchief out to wipe his eyes once the fit had passed.

They were warm to Megan, reminding her to let them know if she needed anything or wanted to stop for any reason. The toilet, she supposed, was what they meant. She couldn't think of any other 'reason'. She drove them around for about five hours each day. The rest of the time she spent in Liam's flat, waiting for them to phone.

'You're doing a good job,' said Joe, when she dropped them off at their hotel on the third day, a modest-looking place on West End Lane.

Liam was pleased when she proudly reported that, and he echoed what they'd said.

'You're a good girl.'

CHAPTER TWENTY-FOUR

Liam instructed Megan to ask Lachlan and Joe to meet him in the upper room of the Royal Arms on their last afternoon in London. She was booked to drive them out to Heathrow and return the rental car the following day. Megan thought nothing of it, but the two of them looked at her strangely when she passed on Liam's request. They'd been about to get into the car, and were going over the day's itinerary. There was an easy familiarity to the way the woman rang straight through to their room for Megan when she showed up at the reception desk of their hotel in the morning. She would retreat to the street to wait, enjoying the crisp weather and the school children and older people with dogs walking by. A few minutes later Lachlan and Joe would emerge. Intimidated by them at the start of the week, she was almost fond of them now. Joe was wearing a black windbreaker that day: she noticed because she'd seen him in nothing but his cream parka before. Lachlan was in his usual uniform of white shirt and trainers, a bomber-type leather jacket and blue jeans.

'He wants to meet us?'

Megan glanced up at them as she unlocked the car door. 'After lunch. I thought we could have it at the pub.'

'What's he want to meet us for?'

'I don't know.'

She slid into the driver's seat and the two of them took up their usual positions. In the rearview mirror she saw them exchange glances, but neither of them said anything, or if they did she didn't hear it as she started the car.

That morning she took them to electrical shops in Charing Cross, double parking or slowly circling around the block while they went in and out of various stores. They ate lunch as she'd suggested in the bar of the Royal Arms. Meat pies with side orders of hot chips and lashings of vinegar all round. They didn't talk much, and then they filed upstairs, into a red velvet sitting room, where Liam was waiting.

'This is not usual,' said Lachlan as soon as they came in. 'We don't need to meet anyone.'

'What's it all about?' asked Joe.

'Ssshhhh,' said Liam. He winked at Megan and shut the door.

They all turned to watch him, something in the room changing, rising, and then falling, like a breath expelled, or a wave being sucked back towards the ocean, as he locked it. He left the key in the lock, and Lachlan moved a little closer to the door.

'Liam, isn't it? What are you locking us in for?'

Liam gave a wry laugh.

'This is not funny,' said Joe.

'It's not meant to be,' said Liam.

So tightly wound these last few days, he was relaxed and expansive, thought Megan, as if they were dinner guests and he their genial host.

'Liam Rafferty. That name doesn't ring a bell?'

Joe squinted at him. Megan was standing against the far wall, next to the red velvet lounge, feeling like a useless lump, not understanding anything of what was going on.

'No.' Joe was defensive. Wary. 'Should it?'

Liam was looking from one to the other of them, his eyes bright. 'I'd say so.'

'No,' said Lachlan.

Joe shook his head, certain.

'Well it should,' said Liam, and that was when he shot them.

Megan had never seen or heard a gun before, and everything about it terrified her. Its sleek, heavy, black charisma. Its understated 'whomp' when Liam fired it into the side of Lachlan's head.

It took her a moment to understand the cause and effect of Liam drawing a gun out of his pocket and Lachlan doubling over, a red stain ruining the crisp whiteness of his shirt. Liam turned and fired at Joe, who had dived to the floor, so that when Liam moved two steps closer and fired into his body again he didn't move much – just his legs kept cycling in the air for five more seconds before they stilled.

Megan's chest felt as if it might explode, blasting her apart.

'Shut up, Megan,' said Liam, his gaze intent as he examined Joe.

She stuffed her terror back down, her hands against her mouth to make sure no sound forced its way out. Her legs were wet. She looked down and saw a puddle spreading against her shoe.

'Liam,' she whispered. Her voice was hoarse and her throat hiccuped, as if she had been crying for a very long time. 'What have you done?'

There were people in the pub downstairs, she remembered. Someone must have heard. Any minute the police would arrive.

Liam looked at her, his gaze level, his voice calm. 'I've just rid the world of some very bad men.'

In the last few seconds the light seemed to have faded, and the carpet and the armchairs were the sticky dark red of blood.

'Got everything?' said Liam. He was standing in the doorway, his hand on the key.

'We're ... I mean you're ...' She was shivering. Her arms crept around her chest to hold her elbows. 'I mean, are we just going to leave them here?'

'Megan, it's okay. I promise you.' He let go of the door handle and crossed the room, stepping carefully over the two bodies on the floor, and took her in his arms. She was rigid with the cold, a growing ice sheet expanding its tentacles and shards into every part of her. He held her tight, the complicated zippers on his leather jacket digging into her breasts and her arms. His sudden tenderness shocked her, too.

'We've done well, Megan. This is a great day.' He held her away from him and grinned at her. She had never seen him like this before. Unguarded for a moment, and triumphant. 'This is a great, great day.'

She followed Liam down the stairs, past a man standing with his arm on the railing at the bottom. Oddly, he didn't acknowledge them as they walked past. The jukebox and poker machines competed with the chatter of patrons to make a general din and Megan realised no one would have heard the gunshots fired two metres above their heads a few minutes before. No one noticed them, it seemed, and Megan felt like a ghost as they walked through the crowded room. And then they were back outside on Kilburn High Road, climbing into the Ford Escort and driving it back to their flat, parking it in the street behind theirs next to a line of garbage bins. From that day to this she had never thought to wonder who eventually had returned it.

'I don't understand,' Megan kept saying, as Liam bustled around the small kitchen, making tea and burning the toast. He was shaken too, she could tell. His hands fumbling as they spooned sugar into the cups, his body standing so close to hers, as if together they could summon up some heat.

'I thought they were on our side.'

'They were not.'

'The others should be told about this, shouldn't they?' They should have gone over all this in the meeting. And they hadn't. She was sure of that. No one had ever spoken of shooting anyone, let alone Lachlan and Joe.

'You're not to say a word about this to anyone.' Liam turned to her, the steadiness in his gaze frightening her.

'Before you go to bed, I need the car keys,' said Liam, when he chastely kissed her in the hall, his lips brushing against her forehead. The antithesis of sexual, they were waifs. De-sexed and comrades in arms. Two souls lost in a whirling, amoral void.

'Car keys?'

'I need the boxes from the shops today.' Liam was looking at her, willing her to understand, as if he didn't want to have to say.

'Boxes?' It took seconds for her to understand what he was talking about. To remember that once, a long time ago, she had chauffeured Lachlan and Joe, those sprawling deadweights on the red carpeted floor, around to electrical shops. Could it really have been only that morning?

'In the boot. They're in the boot.'

'I'll go and have a look at them.'

'In your pyjamas?'

He looked down at himself. 'Wouldn't be the first time I got out and about in my trakky dacks.'

She remembered that she'd smiled weakly at that familiar Australian expression. They were caught here together. Locked in a strange, eternal intimacy. The intimacy of having harmed someone. The intimacy of having killed. She gave him the keys and he waited in the doorway while she climbed into her bed.

'Go to sleep, Megan. Tomorrow's going to be another long day.'

'Tomorrow?'

'We're going out in the van.'

How could she have forgotten?

'You can talk to the others all you like, after that.'

That night Liam was gone for a long time, and Megan couldn't sleep. Instead, the day kept reappearing before her as a scene of Gothic horror, projected like a movie reel onto her room's dark ceiling. The red velvet upholstery of the chairs in the meeting room drenched in blood. The curtains at the window flapping in an evil wind. Herself, terrified then paralysed. Growing colder and colder, frozen in time. Liam's gun going off with a thick, deep thud into the stomach and the skulls of those two men.

At 2am she got up to go to the bathroom and ran into Liam, who had evidently just got in. His cheeks and his nose were red with cold, his eyes bright and sparkling.

'Where have you been?' asked Megan.

'Out,' said Liam, peeling off his coat and kicking off his shoes. 'You should get some sleep,' he said. 'Lots to do in the morning.'

On her way back to the bedroom she decided to ring Dom, and picked up the phone in the living room. She needed to tell him she was coming home. It took her a few seconds to understand that Dom was already on the line. That he and Liam were speaking.

'You promised me you wouldn't hurt her,' Dom was saying.

Megan pressed the phone to her ear.

'She isn't hurt,' said Liam.

Megan hung up quickly, not caring if either of them heard the telltale click as she put down the receiver.

'Why did Liam kill those men?' Halley said, turning to Aidan abruptly. 'You know, don't you?'

'Why do you think?'

'I don't know,' she whispered hopelessly, staring at him.

'My father.'

'Your father ....' Halley gazed into Aidan's eyes, wondering if he expected her to guess the answer to this.

'When my father was murdered ...' Aidan swallowed. He looked up. Sunlight was glinting on the water, the sound of the surf strong over the clanking of the sails against the mast of a boat moored nearby. Someone was gutting fish, he guessed, from the swirl of pelicans rising and falling over the trees twenty metres away. This was the best place to talk about these things, he decided. So safe. So beautiful. So far away from it all.

'You know, no one has ever told me what actually happened with your father,' said Halley.

'I wasn't there.' So much guilt. He should have been. Aidan always thought he should have been at Dom's side, sharing in whatever there was to be endured. Instead he'd been in the kitchen out the back with Dearie, who didn't hear the knock at the front door. In his memory it resounded. Liam was out with his mother, shopping, but he'd told Aidan what happened so many times, like a bed-time story, that it was almost as if the two of them had been there.

'Your father home?' the men at the front door had asked Dom.

'Upstairs,' Dom had told them, and opened the door wide.

Two men wearing jeans and green jumpers with patches on the shoulders ran past him. One of them turned back to where Dom was standing, watching them at the foot of the stairs.

'Sshhh.' He put a finger to his lips.

Dom heard a shout, and bangs and thuds, and then the men came loping back down the stairs. They were carrying guns with muzzles on the end of them, their hands held low to their sides. Out the front door, the gate clanging shut behind them, arms flung wide and legs pumping down the road.

The ambulance came – as if they were able to do anything for their father who'd been shot point-blank in the head. The detectives came and brushed everywhere for fingerprints – as if they were going to find any. They cordoned off the area and asked around for witnesses. As if anyone was going to say that they'd seen anything, even if they had.

Dom was twelve at the time. Old enough to recognise faces, people said. But he shook his head mutely at all the photographs. He refused to speak of it. They must have threatened him, they said to Nuala.

'He blames himself,' their mother replied.

Liam blamed everyone else, getting into fights constantly after that, and falling behind at school, even though until then he'd been a capable student.

There was a big funeral, and that made Aidan proud, and a grand reception after. 'Poor fatherless boys,' everyone kept saying, and Aidan hadn't known how to answer. Dom was silent. He had never been talkative, but after that he said even less. It wasn't until they came out to Australia and he got involved with the youth mission at Lavender Bay that he began talking again. 'As if the sunshine got into him and opened him up,' said Nuala. It was just what she'd been hoping for by emigrating.

'He used to say God's love could heal anything,' said Halley, once Aidan finished speaking.

'Over and over again,' said Aidan, shaking his head.

'Vengeance is mine, sayeth the Lord,' said Halley. 'That meant you could be sure justice would be done, but that it wasn't something to be worried over by you. All you had to do was love. Love took away all the wrongs done and hurts you'd suffered and made you whole again. Dom told me he knew that from personal experience.'

'Not for me,' said Aidan. 'I've always been with Liam on this one. What's love worth if you won't fight for it? Or die for it? If you just forgive the people who killed your father, then what's anything worth? They came into our house in the clear light of day and murdered him. To me, all that turn the other cheek and give peace a chance horse shite is just another of way of keeping you down. And all you want, in the whole wide world, is someone who'll stand up for you.'

'I'll stand up for you.'

Aidan eyes were half closed against the water's reflected glare. 'That's what I'm talking about, Halley. That's why I want you to know about this. You already have.'

He reached over the gear stick and grabbed her hand, threading his fingers through hers and enclosing their hands together in a fist. His palm was warm and dry. This was the story of their lives, thought Halley. They were entwined.

'Those men. Who you helped to kill,' said Aidan. 'Dom identified them for Liam on his last visit to Australia. 'They were the men who killed my father.'

She felt something settling in the region of her chest.

The sun came up in Halley's heart before she even had a chance to think it through. Her next breath, it seemed to her, was deeper.

'Lachlan and Joe were informers. By then the IRA was riddled with them. They were paid by the Brits to kill our father. All that time, Dom was the only one who knew who they were. And all that time he was trying to resist what Liam kept tempting him with.'

'You're saying Liam got Dom to identify the men who killed your dad ten years earlier? Is that possible?'

'It's not something you forget.'

'Yet I forgot. All of it, somehow.'

Aidan looked at her sympathetically. 'Anne says trauma affects people in different ways. She studied it as part of her degree.'

But Halley wasn't listening. Her mind had clouded over. It didn't compute. If Dom identified those men for Liam it would mean he was implicated in their murder. It would mean he had taken revenge.

Sex is the ultimate connecting, Megan used to think, back then. Maybe killing is, thought Halley now. The necessary energy transfer. The only way to change what otherwise never would. And if you didn't do that thing you most needed to, what happened to all that energy? Of love, or lust, or hatred? What if it backed up, or dissipated, or exploded? What then?

'It's not a mineral or a fossil fuel,' laughed Dom when she had tried to explain this to him on the night of the school formal.

To deny her love for him felt like hypocrisy, Halley remembered. Not moral hypocrisy, but physical. Her desire for him was a truth more real to her than any metaphysical one. To dam it up made no sense. To hold it back when it wanted to rush forward was wrong. They loved each other, and their bodies loved each other, too. To keep denying them felt hateful. They were controlling something that needed to be free, thought Megan, and something warped and terrible would be created from it. Was that how the desire for revenge had felt for Dom? At the time, it felt to Megan as though he was finding the upper hand in their relationship – even if unconsciously – and using his fealty to the Church's teaching about sex to control her. Now she thought maybe he had been trying, with every fibre of his being, to resist temptation in all its forms, so he could resist what Liam was offering.

'It's a desire and when we're married it will be a fulfilment,' Dom had answered her then.

'When we're married ...' Megan's hands clenched when he talked like this. 'Marriage is just a ceremony. A feast and a white dress. What difference does it make?'

'It wouldn't be there in the Bible if there was no reason,' said Dom.

Was he so stubborn about following the Bible because it promised to teach him forgiveness, too?

'So you're saying you'll just follow everything it says in the Bible without question?'

Dom conceded with a dip of his beautiful brown eyes.

'It's sacred, the human body, if you want it to be,' said Dom. 'If you treat it as such. And it can do sacred things.'

'Like make a baby?' she pre-empted him. She had a horror of hearing him say it.

He leaned over and lightly kissed her mouth. "With my body I thee worship."

Megan fell against him helplessly. My body worships you, she wanted to tell him. Already.

'If you respect its ways, your body can help you love someone,' said Dom. 'Really love them. Physically, spiritually, in every way, for richer, for poorer, your whole life long.'

It was hard to believe that Dom, who had withstood her all that time, who believed in the sanctity of all human acts, of all human bodies, had given in to that other temptation. He had participated in having two people killed. It would have been a betrayal of everything he believed in.

'Dom didn't kill himself because of me,' said Halley.

'I don't think so anymore, either.'

'Why didn't he tell me?' she burst out. 'Why didn't he explain?'

Aidan stared out the car window, his shoulders hunched.

'We were together four years, Aidan. That's a long time. He just told me your father was murdered, but he never told me that he knew by who. That your mother brought you out here just like they'd planned. All three boys, as far away as possible from all that, she used to say. And how can you get further away than Australia?'

'But Liam never settled here,' said Aidan, still staring out the window. 'Even then I think he knew he had no business here. Even then I think he always knew he would be going back.'

'What if he'd become an actor?' said Halley. 'What about that plan he had for getting on *Neighbours*?'

'They'll cast me as the ne'er do well Irish cousin,' Liam had told her. He always ended up talking to Megan when she visited, because Dom would fall silent and chain smoke, staring into his beer. 'Come to steal your women.' The fact that he was so obvious about it made it all a joke. Or Megan thought so, anyway. She didn't take his flirting seriously the whole time he was in Australia.

'"Neighbours, everybody needs good neighbours"', Liam had sung. His voice was powerful, but off key. 'Dum de dum de dum de duum. I could get together with your Kylie Minogue.'

'She's left the show,' Aidan piped up. Always there, remembered Halley. Hanging around and getting underfoot. Always trying to be helpful.

'"Neighbours,"' Liam wailed. '"Should be there for one ano-other …"' He got up and put his arm around Dom, drawing him in tightly so his face was squashed against the mother-of-pearl buttons of his shirt. He put his hand on Dom's face and squeezed his cheeks, looking him in the eyes for a moment before kissing him square on the mouth. Then, noticing that Megan was watching, Liam winked at her.

'Oh fuck off,' Dom spat, pushing Liam away.

Why hadn't she confronted Dom? Halley wondered. Why had she never simply asked him why they hated one another so?

'Because he didn't want you to,' answered Aidan. 'He was ashamed.'

'Of what?' said Halley.

'Of himself, I think,' said Aidan slowly. 'Liam was always getting to him. Tempting him. Provoking him. Reminding him. And he didn't want that to be our story.'

'He knew my story,' said Halley. 'All those terrible things about my father, and yet he never confided in me.'

'Dom was an honest person,' said Aidan doggedly. 'One day he would have told you everything, I know he would.'

'Oh Aidan.' He was still the same hopeful little boy, thought Halley. Still trying to find a way to make it all come out okay.

'You used her to get to Dom, didn't you?' said Aidan when Liam phoned the next morning. 'You used her as leverage to make him identify the men who killed our father.'

'No. They were two separate things. I promised to keep her safe, yes, and yes, he finally confirmed who killed our father.'

'You forced him.'

'I didn't.'

'Come on, of all people she was your brother's fiancée. Your brother who had the information you needed all these years. It was never a coincidence, was it?'

'There are no coincidences, Aidan.' Liam's sounded almost bored, thought Aidan. 'Don't you know that?'

'If it wasn't to force Dom's hand, then why, of all people, did you have to pick her?' Aidan felt itchy and restless all over. He wanted to tear his clothes off and jump into the fast-flowing river, the tide taking everything with it – twigs and sticks and dirty-looking foam – out to sea.

'I told you. She recruited herself. She landed in my lap. And they were putting pressure on me in London. Everyone at that time was untrustworthy and I needed someone I could trust. Someone the others would trust. Someone with no criminal record. With no previous involvement. A cleanskin. Someone to come over, do the job, and go home. Without her it wouldn't have mattered what Dom told us, we could never have got the job done.'

'And what was the job?'

'What do you mean what was the job? Have we not been over this a thousand times?'

And it never came out the same way twice, thought Aidan. 'None of it adds up,' he said.

'That's because she was an amateur,' said Liam. 'One minute she was enthusiastic and the next she was shocked by what she's even thinking she might do. You give someone like that one job and it lasts them a lifetime.'

'And you, Liam? What are you?'

'I'm a professional.'

His accent had become more Irish, noticed Aidan. He used to think Liam did this when he was expressing true emotion, speaking with the voice of his heart. Now Aidan thought he did it for theatrical impact.

'I don't make mistakes. I don't change my mind.'

CHAPTER TWENTY-FIVE

When she arrived home Halley collapsed onto the sofa, staring at the wallet-sized photo of Dom that Aidan had lent her. He looked so young, although he had seemed old to her then, his forehead prematurely wrinkled, his hair speckled with the first signs of grey. Her fingers traced his prominent ears. His gaze was focused and confident. His full mouth almost smiling.

'Halley? What is it?' Matt stood in the doorway.

'This is Dom.' She thrust the photo at him.

Matt was kind, thought Halley, as he looked at it. The respectful way he held the photograph. The time he gave her. Why was she noticing these things? He sat down next to her as though he had nowhere else to go, and nothing better to do. A fact which on so many other evenings would have annoyed her.

'He was only twenty-three.'

Matt looked at her, about to speak, but Halley shook her head, unwilling to accept any comfort. She shouldn't say this, but she had to. 'I miss him.'

Over the next few days, Dom's face appeared before her every time she paused for a moment, at the cafe, or at home. I don't think I've ever loved anyone but him, she wanted to say to Matt, but stopped herself. I don't think I've ever wanted anyone but him. I don't think I'll ever get over him.

'No,' said Aidan, when finally she cracked and said it to him instead. 'You won't.' It comforted something in Halley to hear it. 'You can't expect to.'

Halley thought of his fiancée – gone, he'd told her. He had no home to speak of, and no children.

She burst into tears when she was peeling carrots in the cafe kitchen.

'Are you all right?' asked Drummond, who was working next to her.

'No.'

He shrugged, and went right on working.

'I've had a loss,' she said after a while, curious to hear how that might sound.

'Haven't we all.'

Halley had to stop herself from snorting. He was only seventeen.

Seventeen, she told herself later. That was the age she had been when she had her first terrible loss, when her father's betrayal of her family had been broadcast to the world. And how old was she when she experienced the worst loss? The loss of Dom? The loss of her family? Of her innocence and identity and everyone and everything she'd ever known? Only twenty. Still, from this vantage point, just a child.

'So you came up here and ...'

'Started again.'

Matt came into the kitchen each morning with a new question. She could tell it was coming from the determination in his step. The unaccustomed weight he'd give to his every movement before asking her. Placing his coffee cup down on the edge of the table and smoothing the tablecloth. Arranging his fingers just so.

'Did you ever love me?'

'Of course I did.' She glanced at the clock. She should have been in the car two minutes ago.

'I mean, when did you decide you would lie to me?'

'I can't remember.'

'Thank you.' He nodded formally, put his cup in the sink and walked out.

And that was it. Question time was over for today. Halley felt strangely lighter as she walked out to the car.

'Did you love me when you married me?' Matt asked the next morning when he came out to breakfast. As usual, lately, Benny wasn't there.

'I think so.' Something strange had happened. Now that she had been shorn of her lies, now that Matt knew the truth, she found she had no story for him anymore. She had no more ready answers.

She remembered when she first learned of her father's infidelities, trying to catch glimpses of him unawares, trying to find evidence of that other person she had only just discovered also lived inside his skin. Like Matt, she thought. What was it he was looking for in those fleeting glances he kept giving her when he thought she wasn't looking? What was it he was afraid to see?

Late that afternoon in the cafe, Halley pushed up her hair behind her ears before letting it fall down her back again. 'Some days I think I'll cut it all off.'

Lisa, working at the espresso machine, shrugged.

Once upon a time a statement like that would have drawn forth a hail of protest. Not your beautiful hair! Now, no one cared. She looked around for Matt, so she could say it again in his hearing. He would care. And then she stopped herself. She could go whole weeks, sometimes, without liking herself.

Matt was on the phone, standing outside. Who was he talking to? She wondered, as she collected her things to take home. A box of cutlery that needed de-mangling–fifteen minutes at the kitchen table with a pair of pliers would do it. The lamp with the flickery switch – that was one for Matt to sort out. Some chipped soup bowls that were no use to the customers anymore but would work nicely as little pots in the garden. Was he talking to a surfing mate maybe? He was smiling, a warm smile that put his age back a decade. He was a handsome man when you looked at him through a stranger's eyes. She glanced at Lisa. She was looking at him, too. Matt was a handsome man, period. And you're a hateful, jealous, deceitful, looks-fading woman, Halley told herself. You really ought to be more grateful.

The day she came north she cut her hair short all round and dyed it blonde. She looked terrible, the awful yellow colour highlighting the circles around her eyes and the wanness of her skin. It was like that when she met Matt. Cut in a salon by then, but still doing nothing for her. It was a testament to his love for her that he took her on anyway. Or her amazingly hot body. She smiled at the memory. That had been a long-running joke between them. Gardening had given her muscles, but there was something immovable and unchanging about Halley's strong flesh. While wrinkles emerged around her mouth and the skin between her breasts sagged, her body was still strong and lean. Matt always said it was no joke, she had a beautiful body, but Halley could never see it.

Some time after Benny was born she grew her hair out. A combination of not having the time or the money to go the hairdressers, and a relief at seeing her own face – with her natural hair colour returning, her skin's olive hue was restored – staring back at her. She tied it up, mostly, with an elastic band. Like a horse's tail, said Matt, and later Benny, when he started to talk. She'd whinny and gallop around the house with him, shaking her hair, neighing and blowing, making him squeal with laughter.

It had been eleven years since she'd seen her parents when she chanced upon the 'Missing' poster with her name and photograph on it, pinned to a noticeboard in a corner of the verandah of the courthouse in Mullumbimby. 'Have you seen this person?' it demanded in black capital letters, almost concealed under the memos and newsletters pinned on top. And there she was. In a grid of eight passport-style photos of strangers, her own eyes smiled back at her. The woman in the photo was a vital, hopeful young person – no wonder no one had connected it with her. 'There are many reasons people go missing,' the poster said in smaller writing above the tapestry of faces, the names and age of each person listed underneath. 'Phone home, or send a letter. If you know someone you think is missing, encourage them to get in touch.'

During those years she hadn't been able to think much about the past, because her present was difficult enough. Benny learned to walk early, at eight months, and after that, for the next eight years, it was all on. Running, destroying, tearing, screaming ... he would be out of the house and in the river within seconds, or under the house playing with matches, or going through the cupboards smashing things and cutting himself on the shards. They were asked to leave restaurants and holiday campgrounds, fast-food chains and indoor playgrounds. Everywhere they went they were never welcome – and most certainly not at pre-school or kindergarten. 'Benny is so high spirited,' was the kind way people put it. 'Benny is a danger to himself, the staff and other children,' was the more truthful report. Every day was a struggle to get through, without Benny hurting himself and, sometimes, thought Halley, pushed to the edge, without her hurting Benny. The most she had ever done was smack him hard on the bottom, and for that, the relative mildness of it, she was eternally grateful.

Matt was better with him. 'I was just the same when I was young,' he told her, 'and look how I turned out.'

It was a comfort then. Halley thought of it constantly, to counter her sense of despair at what she thought of as her terrible mothering. And then, around eight, Benny developed impulse control, his behaviour calmed down, and the whole thing slowly faded, its nimbus of worry lasting longer though, like the emotions you grapple with all day after waking from a dream.

That day Halley was at the courthouse to argue over a speeding fine – she lost, of course. She always lost, probably because she was always speeding. That day she spoke faster than usual, and was more rattled. The judge had allowed her sixty seconds to make her explanation before pounding his gavel down and discharging her with a fine. Now that Halley thought about it she'd been mad to go anywhere near a courthouse, but after the first ten years up here she'd almost forgotten she wasn't legitimate. No one checked, anyway. Why would they? It would have to be something pretty bad to make anyone look beyond your driver's license, which she'd obtained by swearing she'd lost all her documents in a house fire. By that stage everyone in town knew her anyway, from the cafe.

'Just call. Leave a message telling them you're okay,' the poster begged. How long had it been up on the noticeboard? she wondered, surreptitiously removing it. She'd sent her parents a postcard every year under a different name – from the references in the cards they would have known they were from her – but obviously they needed more. Of course they did. She needed more from them, too – if it could be safe. If it wouldn't hurt any of the people she loved more than their separation did. For a few weeks afterwards, she grappled with the idea of somehow making contact.

And then, just a month after she first saw the poster, she happened upon the newspaper article. 'Prominent ex-lawyer dies in Spanish road accident,' ran the headline. 'Jimmy O'Dea, the former barrister, and his wife, Faye were killed in a head-on collision in the southern Spanish town of Alicante on the weekend,' began the article. 'O'Dea was known for his relationship with Justice Patrick Cooney of the Supreme Court, which was the subject of a year-long enquiry ...' And there it all was, laid out before her yet again. 'O'Dea, convicted of attempting to pervert the course of justice, was in the midst of an appeal when he dropped the case and gave up his practice as a lawyer. He became a well-known racing identity and his wife a valued contributor to the research and family support activities of the Mater Hospital in North Sydney. They are survived by their daughter, Megan O'Dea.'

Dead? thought Halley. But she'd never had the chance to explain. She'd never introduced them to Benny, or told them how much she had always loved them, and loved them still. Dead? How could it be? How could it be? she kept asking herself, for months afterward.

The most difficult days of her life had been warmed by the thought, at the back of her mind, that she could always go home. It made the physical and emotional exhaustion of her life easier to bear. It made the worst days with Benny and worrying conversations with Matt okay. Somewhere inside she knew that her parents would always embrace her. Once they were gone she looked at her life differently. All this time she had been surviving without them, but now she wondered how she could go on.

CHAPTER TWENTY-SIX

Sug had grey hair streaked with white, yet he was younger than Halley. His face was etched with the deep lines of a man who'd spent most of his life in the sun. He might have been handsome if his expression wasn't so intimidating. Cooking for people was one of the few things he'd been able to think of that didn't involve lying, he told Halley. He refused to sell anything to people that they didn't need. Like a modern day Puritan, he refused to advertise. And yet like some modern day parable of integrity, customers flocked to him. Workers stayed with him. Women flirted with him. Halley wondered if he had any other women on the go.

'No,' he said, when she asked him, sprawled languidly on his mattress on the floor.

'Really?' She felt tousled and luxurious. More at ease in this ramshackle studio than in her bedroom at home.

'I don't lie.'

'What are we doing here, then?'

'You're lying, maybe. But I'm not. I've made no vow of fidelity to anyone.'

'So what are we doing?' Halley felt lonely, suddenly.

'Having sex.'

She rolled away from him, across the strangely cold, slippery sheets as far across the side of the mattress as she could manage. She listened to him light a cigarette while she stared at the checked linoleum tiles and in a few minutes she felt better. That was the mysterious thing about the truth. It often sounded harsh. But actually it was somewhat comforting.

'What's your real name?' she asked, rolling back.

'We've been over this.' He shifted away from her to turn over his pillow, thumping it with his fist before lying his head back down on it again. 'I won't tell.'

'What is it?' she insisted, pulling the sheet up so that her breasts were covered.

'You don't think this is my real name?'

'No one's real name is Sug.'

He put his arms behind his head, drawing up thick ropey muscles and exposing the patches of orange-grey fuzz in his armpits.

'You're not getting mad at me are you?' He narrowed his eyes at her.

'I was just thinking that you have a Byron name,' said Halley, referring to all those Hindu gods and Buddhist goddesses whose names so many people took on when they moved here, shrugging off their own culture so lightly in favour of someone else's.

'You know I don't believe in them,' said Sug.

Standing before him as she pulled on her jeans, the thought came to Halley that she had a Byron name and Sug didn't even know it. He had never truly seen her. No one, for the last seventeen years, had really known her, or touched her, except Benny. And that was partly the trouble. From the moment he was born he had invaded her barricades and shattered her defences. And she, always lying – and perhaps somehow he could tell that – was somehow driving him away.

She thought of Benny as he'd looked to her that morning. The thick curls on his forehead separating with sweat and the humidity. His hair was just like Matt's and his mouth was Matt's mouth, his teeth even and separated slightly, giving his smile a roguish look. Otherwise he was the image of her. The greatest cause of vanity she'd ever had.

'It's me!' she'd gasped when he was born, a surprised happiness flooding her. 'He looks just like me!' His skin was her caramel-coloured skin that quickly went from olive to dark in summer. His face was a fresh new version of hers.

Sometimes she felt her work on earth was done, just looking at him. But in fact it had just started, the day she had him at Mullumbimby Hospital. That's when she and Matt had decided to get serious about one day taking out a mortgage and opening a cafe. That's when they'd had to organise their lives into shifts so that someone would always be with Benny. And that's why, when Benny finally went to school, blocks of time, private, uninterrupted time, had arrived in Halley's life, disturbing her equilibrium and somehow serving her up here eventually, in odd places like this studio, with the likes of Sug.

'No one knows me,' she'd told Aidan, just after he arrived, when he'd asked about her life here.

'Not even your husband?' he'd replied. 'Not even your son?'

She'd shaken her head in reply. There had been a proud determination in it, all these years. A way of being stronger, of holding herself apart. But really, thought Halley now, no one knows me. What a terrible thing to say.

This morning Benny had walked up to her in the living room where she was ironing his school shirts. He was dressed in the black tracksuit he wore after his morning surf, his big feet bare on the rug, his hair hanging curly and still wet on his shoulders, his big hands holding a thin sheaf of paper out to her.

'Will you sign off on this for me, Mum?'

'Of course.'

She took the sheets of paper from him and rested them on the ironing board. He shifted from foot to foot as she read.

She stared at the pages for ten seconds before understanding what was wrong. He knew too, suddenly anxious, staring at her, worried. That familiar look, thought Halley. The same look he'd given her when he was a toddler. Always well meaning. Always her darling Benny. Always sorry when he'd done something wrong, even if a minute before she had reminded him not to. Still, he was heartbroken whenever she was disappointed in him. Like now.

'Is this the finished assignment?' she said carefully. She had never learned how to deal with this successfully, what to say or do.

'Yes.'

He made to reach for it but she held it away.

'What's wrong with it?' He was defensive already, and hostile. 'It answers the question. Look. It's written there next to the teacher's note.'

'I haven't read it, darling. Darling,' she repeated, holding him there. Willing him not to take fright and run away from her out of the room. 'But it doesn't have any punctuation.'

She held it out to him and he stepped forward, staring as though someone else had written the pages and he was looking at the work for the very first time.

He shrugged, and Halley's sympathy melted into frustration and ... here it was again, her all too-frequent friend when it came to dealing with Benny these days, it seemed. A bewildered rage. Was he careless? Confused? Or simply couldn't be bothered?

'No commas. No full stops. No question marks. No capital letters, even.' She glanced over the first page again. 'What happened?'

'Didn't think of it.'

'Well ... why don't you go away and fix it up ... and I'll make us a cheese-cake for dessert this evening?' She despised herself when she did this. Bribing him, coaxing him with his favourite treats as if he was still a little boy.

'Nah. I'll eat when I'm out. Could you just sign it please?'

'You're going to hand it in like this?'

'Yeah.' He looked bored almost, his widened eyes and raised eyebrows giving him a cartoon face of mock despair.

She forced herself to remain silent as she handed him back the pages.

'This is nothing to do with his style of learning,' she'd railed to Matt as they started the lunchtime shift at the cafe. 'It's slackness, is what it is. Our son is incurably slack.'

Matt didn't say anything.

Of course he didn't, Halley told herself, furiously assembling salads – order number six on her list. Matt was no longer whisking eggs. It wasn't clear what he was doing. Just standing there, it seemed. In deep thought, you might assume, if you didn't know him. In a prolonged brain skid, you would assume, if you did. Matt was incurably slack too, she decided. The two of them, father and son, were as bad as each other.

'I offered to help him,' she continued. 'I offered to show him how to make it better. But he won't even punctuate! He won't even ... He couldn't even ... he couldn't even be bothered to put a full stop at the end of a sentence!'

'He thinks you hate him.'

She shook her head, not trusting herself to speak, and went back to her chopping. She could feel Matt looking at her for a long minute before he turned away. The tears that had been threatening her gradually subsided. They didn't say a word to each other for the next few hours.

That night Halley waited until she'd finished cleaning up the kitchen after dinner. As soon as he'd finished eating, Matt had excused himself to go out to the shed. Halley could see, from the light escaping through its one small window, the shape of his hunched shoulders and his bent head, working on something intently. After taking out the compost and bringing in the eggs, Benny had retreated to his room. She wrapped the leftovers of the frittata she'd made for dinner in cling wrap and took the chocolate cake she'd brought home from the café out of the fridge, so it would be ready for eating by the time Matt came inside. She knocked on Benny's door, and after a few seconds of silence she pushed it open.

'Can we talk, just for a minute?'

Benny was lying on his bed, his hands folded together on his chest.

'Huh?' He took an earbud out of his ear.

Just the one, Halley noted. The other no doubt still blasting music into his other ear.

Cautiously, she advanced into the room, stepping over discarded clothes and piles of books that she knew from experience could any minute collapse, upsetting glasses of water over precious drawings or pieces of computer hardware.

'Is this about my assignment? Because I've talked to Mrs Moss and she said—'

'It's not about that.' She felt nervous, and she had to fight against the urge to make up some excuse for her interruption. She could pretend she was collecting his dirty washing, or that she needed to know his size for some new shoes. 'What are you listening to?'

'Just music.'

She nodded.

'You wouldn't have heard of it,' he added kindly.

He was a kind boy, Halley reminded herself, and that gave her courage.

'I want to tell you something, Benny, about me.'

He pushed himself into a sitting position, and Halley advanced a few more steps to stand on the sheepskin carpet next to his bed.

'I want to tell you about me, and ... and about a boy I was in love with, when I was your age.'

'So this is about Gretchen.' He turned his head away to look out the window. He hadn't pulled the curtains, so she could see the outline of his face reflected there, his set expression and jutting chin.

'No, it's about me. It's about what you said, remember? That I wouldn't really know what ... what being in love is really like.' Her voice broke.

'Oh Mum.' He turned back to her, his face screwed up in concern. 'I didn't mean ...'

'No. I know. But I want to tell you, I do know what it's like. I wanted to make love with him. So badly I ached. But we didn't.'

'Why?' he muttered, lowering his head so his face was hidden from her, his hands up under his chin like a marsupial's paws.

She stepped back, so he could see her clearly if he wanted to look up.

'It's important that you know me. I want us to talk.'

'But why?'

'Because I'm your mother, Benny! Because I love you. I love you.' He winced as she said that, his shoulders momentarily tightening, but it needed to be said, thought Halley. This was the thing that most needed to be said. 'I know I get angry with you sometimes. But of all people, Benny, I want you to know who I am.'

'No,' he said patiently. 'I mean, why didn't you? You know.' His face flushed.

'Oh.' She felt embarrassed, wrong-footed by her misplaced intensity. 'Why didn't we make love, you mean? He didn't want to. But I did. I thought it would be terrible not to act on that desire, that longing to make love, if you felt it. That it might even do something bad to our relationship if we didn't.'

He was listening to her, thought Halley. His body unnaturally still, just his fingers absentmindedly brushing over the controls of his MP3 player.

'Is that maybe how it feels to you? Or Gretchen?' she added, when he didn't move.

'Maybe. And what about him?'

'Dom.'

'What did he say?'

'He said I was too young, and that we should wait. That for the sake of our relationship we should wait.'

Finally Benny looked up at her, and the shock of looking into his unguarded face took Halley's breath away. He was so young. Still so much her little boy, staring at her through the face of this bigger one.

'He thought it would be bad for your relationship?'

'He thought if we waited until we were older, and more committed to each other, that we could make something really beautiful together, that would last much longer.'

'I like that.'

It was so long since she had really been seen, thought Halley, since she had allowed anyone to really look at her. And looking into Benny's face, so open now, his feelings written there so clearly – interest, hope – she realised how long it had been since he had allowed her to see him.

He swung his legs over the side of the bed so he was sitting facing her. 'What did he say again? I want to write it down.' He reached down to his school bag and brought out a scrunched-up piece of paper. He smoothed it out on his knee and began writing intently with the stub of a pencil.

Halley closed her eyes as she repeated Dom's words, resisting the nausea she felt, combining Benny and Dom in the same room.

'Mum?'

Benny had finished scribbling on his scrap of paper and was looking up at her expectantly.

'Yes?'

'What happened? With that guy?'

'His name was Dom.'

'Yeah.'

She waited for a moment, gathering herself.

'He died.'

Benny's eyes widened and his head jerked back. 'Really? Wow.'

'I know. Sometimes I still feel really sad about it.'

'What a bummer.'

'It was a bummer,' she said, stepping forward to bury her face in his hair for a moment before leaving the room.

CHAPTER TWENTY-SEVEN

Aidan missed London. Even the greys here were not real grey. The sky, for example, before it rained, was lush and full. Lush grey! It was ridiculous. In London grey was rich but restful. Not pregnant with possibility. No portent of change, but rather a reassurance of more of the same. London, where nothing but Anne had ever happened to him. Where Anne still was. No matter what her status – he didn't want to know if she was with someone – no place could be bad that had Anne in it.

It had been years, and still he thought of her every day. As another man might think of sex, perhaps, he thought of Anne. Without her he was dry and withered. She was his secret spring, his hidden source of the living waters and he drank from her daily. He imagined her with him whatever he was doing, and wherever he went. He made love to her in his imagination. He talked to her. Out loud sometimes, when he was alone in the flat.

Maybe some people just have a very slow emotional metabolism, Aidan told himself hopefully, and at some point he'd finish digesting her. At some point he'd meet another woman who wouldn't be so upset by the idea of Liam. Why, some woman might even like it – although in that case he didn't think he'd like her. But he'd meet some woman and learn how to love someone new and move on. Surely. But even trying to imagine it felt impossible. His father had been a one-woman man. And Dom, it seemed, had been too. Was it genetic, then? That comforted him slightly. Making it not his fault. Not something Liam should laugh at as he did. Not another demonstration of Aidan's weakness. Something Anne miraculously had seen as a kind of strength. There was courage in vulnerability, Anne would say – and that in itself had made him feel brave. That's what Anne with her love could do. She could reinvent you.

When he met Anne, Nuala had been dead a year, and he'd taken a job as an administrative assistant in the Legal Aid service Anne managed while he tried to work out what to do with his life. They went out to dinner at the pub near work. He ordered a lager and she ordered wine. The big size, she said to the bartender, and he liked that. He couldn't understand why someone like her would be interested in someone like him, but she'd had enough of the competitive intellectual types she'd met at uni, she told him. You're restful, she said, and he'd wondered if this wasn't a backhander, but he quickly discovered Anne was nothing if not straightforward. 'I'm not the radio,' she said that first night, when he fell silent. 'When I say something you have to reply.' She made him tell her how he felt, and to have opinions. They ordered risotto, Aidan remembered, although in those days Anne hardly ate. She smoked when they first started going out together, but soon gave up the habit. 'It's easy to be good with you,' she said, and after a few months he moved into her flat, around the corner from her parents' house. He liked that she wanted to live close to her family. He liked the area of London she lived in, too, straddling the poor and the middle class. He liked their garden, reminding him of the leafy suburb they'd lived in in Belfast before his father died.

'My brother's in prison,' he told her that first night. Stressing that Liam wasn't a criminal, or a terrorist, but a political prisoner.

'To me they're all the same thing,' she replied.

'It's state-sponsored terrorism that killed my father.' His heart rose in his chest, bringing with it an ocean of grief that stopped any chance of further conversation.

This was when it mattered that she was English and he was from Northern Ireland, and they could only stare at each other in fear. They would be silent at those times, and after they'd moved on, one of them would find an excuse to catch the hand of the other, and draw them close, and pull their head into the crook of their neck, and the two of them would connect again, bridging the gap that had opened between them with skin and breath and warmth. They could never talk about it properly. The only time they'd even come close had been that night in India.

'That's what it was like for my family,' he told her, after they'd walked Mrs Sharma back to her hotel and said goodbye in the lobby. She had arrived in Kochi that morning, and they'd just taken her out to dinner. Aidan had expected Mrs Sharma would be reluctant to recount her story again in front of him, but not at all. The only thing she didn't mention to Anne was her husband, and Aidan had already told Anne about that. But the riots, the loss of their apartment, the reason Dev had emigrated to Australia – she told Anne all about them and Aidan listened, as if listening to someone describing his own life, rapt.

'That's what it was like for me.'

Anne stopped him. They were about to step out into the crowded street – at 10pm, it was as busy and bright as day – and in front of the curious, thrilled gazes of the young men at Reception, she threw her arms around him.

'You've never told me.'

Madly, he began to cry. 'It's the malaria pills.'

'You always say you can't remember.'

'Because I don't want to remember! I don't want to remember a country that tried to kill me. I don't want a religion that gets you killed.'

'Then why,' she whispered, hugging him tightly, 'is Liam in our life?'

'I need a family.' He felt as if each word of this sentence was scooping out another vital entrail from his body.

Anne was crying, too. 'So do I, Aidan. So do I.'

Yellow party lights flashed from the chat stall set up just outside the hotel's front door, the owner bleary-eyed with tiredness yet standing to attention. Smiling at them hopefully, as if, after this difficult lovers' conversation, they might feel like a snack to revive them. The poverty here, and the gallantry and courage with which people like this stall-keeper wrestled with it, broke his heart.

'I'm going away,' he told Halley, the next time he saw her.

'Really? But I feel as if we're only just getting to reconnect with each other. And I want you to meet my husband, properly this time. Don't go.'

'I'm just going to Sydney for a couple of days.'

She looked at him steadily for a moment, as if deciding whether to ask him why. If she did he wouldn't tell her, decided Aidan. He wouldn't tell anyone anything about it until it was done.

CHAPTER TWENTY-EIGHT

Halley finished adding up the till and picked up the mop to have a last go at the floor. A cleaner would be coming in half an hour, but she liked to give it a quick once-over, hoping to encourage a generally higher standard among the staff. When she got to the threshold of the cafe she rested on the mop for a moment. In a minute she would grab her keys, cross the road to her car, jump in and drive out to McAuleys Lane, pull in to Sug's driveway and park. Walk over the grass to Sug's studio, take off her clothes and make love with him on his messy mattress. She would then accept a glass of wine. Look at his latest paintings. Maybe share a cigarette. Look at the time. She would dress. Walk back over to the car. Back down his driveway, her neck uncomfortably craning. Drive down McAuleys Lane out to the highway and then twenty minutes later arrive home. Halley let the mop fall to the ground with a clatter. She pulled out a chair and sank into it. What she really felt like was a cup of tea and a lie-down.

'I'm sorry,' she said half an hour later, sitting in bed at home, the phone pressed against her ear.

'No, I'm sorry,' Sug replied.

Neither of them sounded it, thought Halley. So maybe this wasn't going to be difficult, she told herself. Because sitting here, the knowledge came to her that it was over. Maybe, for the first time, ending it was going to be easy.

Once she'd put down the phone it seemed that she hadn't been lying to Sug about feeling unwell. Her joints ached. Her head hurt. The cup of tea she'd made perched invitingly on her bedside table, but she had lost the urge to drink it. The sheets were cool as she relaxed into them, the pillow so soft and inviting.

At 2am she woke covered in a clammy sweat that stuck her nightie to her thighs and wet the pillowcase beneath her cheek. She threw the covers off, and a minute later was huddled under them again, shivering. The effort left her exhausted. Halley thought of her woolly socks with longing, but the effort involved in fetching them overwhelmed her. She went over her plans, again and again in the eternity that followed. She would turn over and reach out to switch on the bedside light. She would get to her feet and walk over to the chest of drawers. That would be eight or nine steps at most. Her socks would be waiting there, she hoped – her thick pink ones. She would return to sit on the bed, pull them on, and then at last she would find comfort. Even better would be a hot-water bottle, but the effort required for that was far too great to even think of achieving it. The socks were a realistic goal. Yet every few minutes, or seconds, or hours – she was losing track – she would pull herself together with a start, brought to by the aching in her feet, and realise that she still hadn't managed to get them warm.

'Why didn't you tell me?' said Matt as he dressed the next morning.

'You were asleep.' Halley felt sullen and angry, although she didn't know why.

'Well, why didn't you wake me?'

She heard him padding in and out. She heard whispers at the door. A little while later something warm and furry was pushed against her feet. Oh, the relief of a hot-water bottle. There had never been anything so wonderful, thought Halley, turning to the wall and pushing her face into the pillow, hiding her tears of relief.

'I'm going in to work,' Matt whispered. 'Are you going to be okay?'

With great effort she brought her arm outside the bedclothes and flapped her hand at him.

'Of course I'm okay. I'm just tired.'

'What's up?' She forced her eyes open. Time seemed to have passed because the room was dark. Something smelled good. Matt was sliding clothes off the dining room chair that had migrated into the bedroom years ago. He dragged it over to the bed and straddled it, next to her.

'I want to ask you something.'

'Ask away.' Halley struggled into a sitting position. The cup of tea she'd made yesterday had disappeared and a thermos and a fresh cup sat in its place, a packet of biscuits next to it.

'Who else has there been, Halley? Who else have you loved besides me?'

The colours in the room were vivid, the bedside light so bright it hurt her eyes. The sheets felt extra silky and the paisley pattern on the curtains had a texture so thick and imposing she could feel it. Even their colour – deep burgundy – seemed to have a taste.

'Just one other, Matt. One person.' Halley's eyes leaked tears. A face. Black hair. Brown eyes. 'Just one.'

He put his arms around her, pushing her head into his shoulder.

'So what was she like?' Matt had climbed into bed so that they were sitting side by side, their arms touching and their faces turned to one another.

'Who? What do you mean?'

'Megan. How was she different from you?'

Matt's face this close to hers was unfamiliar, thought Halley. It had been so long since they'd lain like this, looking at each other.

'For lunch on her own she liked to cook messes, like eggs and mushrooms and avocado, all scrambled around together in the pan. It looked horrible, but it tasted great.'

'What else did she make?'

'That was it. That's all I could cook. My mother did all the cooking.'

'You're a great cook,' said Matt loyally.

Halley was quiet, thinking of her mother's well thought out, nutritionally balanced meals, always comprising an entree, main and dessert. Prawns and avocado, lemon sole and chocolate mousse; pear and goats cheese salad, grilled lamb chops with rosemary, and then a fruit salad with fresh whipped cream. It was amazing, thought Halley, when she let herself think about her parents, how much she could remember.

'What else?' Matt prompted her.

'She loved reading, and singing.'

'Like you. What else?'

'Well one thing about her ...'

'Yes?'

'She invented kissing.'

'She invented it?'

'You know. Down there.' Halley felt shy suddenly. She was embarrassed to say it, but she wanted to give Matt something intimate, something private from her life as a girl that she had kept from him.

'I found out other people had discovered it too, later, you know. But she made it up for herself.'

'Really?' He laid his hand on top of hers, where it was resting on the bedclothes. It felt comforting, thought Halley. 'You were that innocent? It hardly seems possible.'

She grasped his hand and squeezed it. 'I know.'

On a sand hill at Suffolk Park, just south of Byron Bay, during a church youth camp that Dom was leading, she had invented it. That night on the sand – the dark sky behind him and the prickly sense of people around, and waves crashing and dogs barking in the distance – it had felt to her that Dom was as much conjured out of her imagination as the act itself. So different was he to his daytime self. Daytime Dom of endless patience, playing guitar and leading the cooking and washing-up activities at mealtimes. She had waited all day. Helping as much as she could stand to. Reading in their tent the rest of the time. Making polite conversation. Waiting, waiting for dark.

Finally, the last firelight song played and sung, the last goodnight called out, the last homesick ten-year-old comforted, Dom came to the flap of their tent and reached out his hand. Grabbing a towel and kicking her feet into thongs, Megan let him lead her, the two of them silent as they padded through the camp site and down the track to the beach.

They saw a huge white kangaroo, standing in their path. Megan's instinct was to turn back, but Dom grasped her hand more tightly, as if he knew what she was wanting – to return, to go back to the safety and the celibacy of their tent – and held it firmly as he led her on. The creature was magnificent, his white fur gleaming in the faint moonlight. Megan imagined him launching himself at them, kicking and clawing, as she knew kangaroos could do. Dom wasn't afraid. He kept walking. Megan stared at her feet as they approached, stepping over roots and stumbling on a vine growing across the pathway. She looked up and the kangaroo was gone.

'Where did he go?' There had been no sound. It was as if he had been beamed up by the white moonlight.

'Shhh,' said Dom.

Staggering over the dunes, the sand still warm from the heat of the day, they emerged on the beach. Around a corner, and there at the edge of the forest was the patch of straggly grass they had been aiming for. Dom let go of her hand to remove sticks and rocks and then took the towel from her to lay it near a low-hanging branch of a white gum tree. This wasn't her everyday Dom. She wasn't the everyday Megan. This was all from her dreams.

'Why did you stop loving me?' Halley whispered, cupping the side of Matt's face with her hand.

'I never stopped loving you. What do you mean?'

'Why did you stop wanting me, then?' Halley felt grim. She hated even saying these words, let alone thinking of all those times he'd turned away. The failing of his delight in her. The lessening of their attraction. Like a life raft deflating from under her, the dying away of his special affection. The loss of that halo of peace and harmony between two people that making love could bring. She was sure this was when Benny had started pulling away from them. A funny thing to say in the light of his problems in his childhood. But she was sure this was when the true pall of unhappiness and dissatisfaction had settled upon her home.

'Matt?' she pleaded.

'That's not how it happened. You just ... as time went by ... you just always seemed so unhappy, and nothing I could do would please you. When we met you were soft, as well as so strong. But then maybe it was Benny, or me, or life ... I don't know. You became so hard.'

Halley thought of her face in the bathroom mirror in the mornings. She had thought that was just how she looked to herself. She'd never thought it might be how she was facing the world. 'It wasn't you or Benny.'

'Well, I know that, now,' he said, emphasising the now, and Halley felt a flash of her old irritation.

'Everything became so hard. I want things to be soft. I want things to be ...' His mouth widened in a smile. 'Like Greece. Like I imagine us in Greece.'

'And how's that?' Halley felt filled with nostalgia for the way she knew things would never be.

'Sunny. Easy. Beautiful.' Matt smiled. 'Like how I imagined living here was going to be before I came.'

Like heaven, thought Halley, thinking of those conversations all those years ago with Dom's youth group in the basement at the Lavender Bay church. She was feeling sleepy again. Matt's smile had started a warmth in her stomach that was radiating into her aching back and up through her ribcage. Like a kindling fire, thought Halley, as she fell back into sleep, softening and melting the ice around her heart.

'What's wrong with me?' she moaned on the fifth morning, when Matt was getting ready to go to work. He was doing all her shifts as well as his own. The first few days her worry about the cafe had been another source of agony to her, but she had given up on that. All she cared about was the aching in her bones and the stinking phlegm she was coughing up. She had to ask Benny to clean out her wastepaper basket, banked high with tissues like a snowdrift, every evening.

'You're sick,' said Matt, sitting on the edge of the bed and leaning down to pull on his shoes.

'I'm never sick.'

'You are now,' he said cheerfully, smiling at her.

His good humour – it seemed to be improving by the day – made her resentful. Just as during the night she resented him for sleeping while she spent hours awake. The selfishness of the well, thought Halley: they had no idea of their good fortune. Halley knew that until a week ago she had been one of their number, but she now couldn't remember the feeling.

'We used to do things together on Saturday mornings,' said Halley on Friday night. It was a week since she had fallen ill. 'Remember?'

They used to go swimming at Brunswick Heads and for walks to the lighthouse at Byron Bay, dragging Benny up the hill between them and keeping an eye on the horizon for whales. They had been killing time, really, trying to keep Benny out of trouble and entertained, but when she looked back it appeared halcyon.

'That was years ago, Halley. You work now.'

She did. And after work she had been going to see Sug. She had organised it that way.

'I don't see why we can't again.'

'Don't you?'

Sometimes she wondered if Matt didn't already know. Everything. The way he looked at her. As if it was all laid out between them, without the need for any words.

'No. Why?' She was almost afraid to ask. Afraid and excited that he would break this unspoken rule between them.

He shrugged. That wordless gesture he had become so good at lately. 'Because that's all in the past.'

Next morning, Saturday morning, she woke out of a restless, dreamless sleep. Almost without missing a beat the thought formed, the conviction spread.

'You're seeing someone, aren't you?'

'You're crazy,' said Matt, pocket change jingling as he pulled on his jeans.

She felt crazy. Her hair was matted from lying in bed all week. Her T-shirt had ridden up while she slept and the wrinkles had left red imprints on her midriff. The legs of her tracksuit pants were twisted and bulky. She scraped a hand over her face, as if removing the mask of sleep.

'Every Saturday morning for years you've disappeared. And the calls you get on the mobile. Who are you talking to?'

He pulled his shirt out of the wardrobe. Look at that, thought Halley absentmindedly. For the first time ever it was ironed.

'When you started disappearing on Saturday mornings ... that was when you stopped wanting to make love with me ...' Her tone was one of wonder. Wonder that she hadn't thought of this, or noticed this, before.

Four years ago, or more? – when every day was the same it was hard to remember these things – they had pretty much given up the ghost. He stopped stroking her arms with his fingertips – putting the question. She stopped kissing him with her mouth slightly open – giving the answer. For years before that, with Benny so needy and work so hard their lovemaking had been patchy. But good. Back then the unspoken assumption had been that they would make love more when they had the opportunity. But, of course, thought Halley bitterly, things are never like that. The thing you left behind is never there waiting, unbroken and intact, for your return.

'I'm tired, Halley,' Matt had shouted at her the last time she had raised it. She'd picked the wrong moment, for sure. After work when she had just hauled his boots off – let me do it, she'd insisted – and peeled off his stinking socks. His toes in her hand, she was giving his foot a massage, and she'd asked when he thought things might go back to the way they used to be.

He could have comforted and reassured her, she'd thought resentfully. Instead he acted as if this were the final demand in a long line of them, and his response, so battering, so mean, thought Halley, forever quietened her. He didn't try to fix it, he didn't even raise the question again, and Halley, furious with the sting of his rejection had at that moment, it seemed in hindsight, although not exactly then probably, decided she wanted a lover. Needed a lover. Was entitled to a lover.

After that they still made love sometimes. If you could call something that momentary, without prelude or postmortem, making love. Like last Christmas. It felt more like an accident. Something that, if she so much as breathed about it afterwards, would draw in its wings and scoot away, so easily scared, so timorous was this thing that still occasionally stirred between them.

'Are you ever going to tell me where you go?'.

'Give it a rest, Halley.' Dressed and shaved, all forward motion, he disappeared out the door.

That night, crying, she let him help her to the toilet. 'I hate this,' she sobbed. He handed her toilet paper, and supported her arms as she stood up. Even her tears infuriated her.

'Ssshhhhh.' On the way back to the bedroom he took her in his arms.

'No, no,' she protested. She was too heavy. He would never be able to support her weight.

'Shhh.' He swung her up, she felt his body brace, and she readied herself for the fall. He placed her down gently: it was like floating into a cloud, and not the clumsy tumble she had been expecting.

'Halley, I want you to come to the doctor in the morning.'

'No. I'm getting better. I just have a temperature. And anyway, it's too dangerous.'

That's exactly why she was never sick. That's exactly how you could come undone. They would ask your name. They would put you into their database. Benny's birth had been scary enough and after that she had always given Matt's name when she took him to a doctor.

Matt shook his head at her. Why did he look so sad?

In the morning she let him choose her outfit. Picking the skirt she liked out of the cupboard and carefully matching her underwear. He took her for a drive into the hills near Federal, playing Bach's orchestral suites on a new CD that she had asked for. When they came home he laid a new set of pyjamas out for her. Flowers were in the room, noticed Halley for the first time, and next to her bed a pile of books on loan from customers who left them for her at the cafe. All of it made her feel desperate. No no no! she wanted to cry. Why were they even thinking about her? They were going to all this trouble for someone they didn't know.

CHAPTER TWENTY-NINE

Aidan met up with Dev on Cleveland Street, which was one of Sydney's more unattractive streets, as far as he could tell. Garbage overflowed on the narrow footpaths outside crowded restaurants. Walking up from the bus stop he counted Lebanese, Turkish, Vietnamese, Cambodian, Nepalese, Thai, Indonesian, French, Italian and Indian restaurants, and the crowds of people walking past seemed to be of the same mix as well.

'What kind of food do you like?' Dev had asked him on the phone.

'All kinds, as long as it's not English.'

Dev laughed.

'Indian would be good,' said Aidan. 'Maybe you could recommend one?'

'Sure.' Dev gave him the address.

When Aidan walked in he was instantly reminded of Southern India. The ceiling fan circled slowly, insufficient to raise a breeze, yet just strong enough to ruffle the corners of the paper tablecloths and dislodge the dust. The smeared mirrors and tabletops reminded him of VS Naipaul's claim in the book that Anne was reading as they travelled that cleanliness in India tended to be a spiritual thing, a question of caste-based concepts of pollution and purity rather than hygiene. The cutlery in this restaurant was clean, though – Anne's perennial test for any establishment, private or public, anywhere. He'd stuck to this in India and only been sick once – and that was at a five-star hotel.

'Your regular?' he asked Dev, after they shook hands.

Dev shrugged. 'More like the regular for taking visitors to. I'm pretty obsessed with Japanese.'

'Oh dear, I'm sorry. I'd be happy to go somewhere else.'

Dev watched Aidan in his English fussiness – or so Aidan felt – and smiled. 'It's fine. I like it here. It reminds me of home.'

Lean and fit and young, dressed in jeans, new-looking trainers and a red long-sleeved T-shirt, Dev looked cosmopolitan and confident, thought Aidan, and he, dressed in his usual faded jeans and dull blue button-up shirt, wished he had more of a clue about what to wear. Dev's gleaming black hair was cut short. Aidan had half expected him to have resumed wearing a turban, and, without meaning to, he imagined what Mrs Sharma would have to say about that.

The waiter came up to their table and he and Dev launched into a lengthy conversation, neither of them bothering with smiles or gestures, just a barrage of melodious words.

'You know him?' Aidan asked, when the waiter left.

'Who? Him? No, man.' Dev laughed. 'We don't all know each other.'

Aidan had seen the same thing in Italy. The ability of the locals to talk at length on any topic. Asking for a street direction, or going over the wine list in a restaurant. He would love to have known what they were saying, but knew it was useless to ask for a translation. If you did you got a short answer – 'Asking about the wine,' 'Asking the way.' Well then, how could it have taken a thousand words? he wanted to say. So different from English discourse with its polite coughs and irritated sighs, the tentative 'Excuse me's' and absurd effort put into the most trivial of social exchanges. Maybe if he spoke Gaelic it might be this way, he'd suggested to Anne once and she'd laughed at him. 'It's what you have to say that matters, not what language you speak.' But he wondered if maybe English didn't carry with it a kind of essential reserve. Well, he would never know. He carried in him some kind of essential reserve and the only person who'd ever freed him from it was Anne. He wished for her now. She would know how to talk to Dev. She would know how to break the ice.

Instead they examined their menus.

'The bread here is very good.'

'Oh? Really. That's great because I like …' Aidan trailed off, too bored by the sentence he'd been going to say to go on with it. 'Listen, why don't you order?' He shut the menu with a bang. Some days he just didn't feel like living.

'So, you squired my mother.'

'I … what?'

It was so stupid. Aidan kept forgetting that for millions upon millions of Indians English was one of their main languages, so that when they spoke it articulately and well, and often better than Aidan, he was surprised. Was this racist? Some people thought the same thing when he said something rational in an Irish accent, he was sure. Not that he had one, really, anymore. He had a hybrid accent, which Dev asked about, of course, in the first few minutes.

'Australian, English, Irish,' Aidan explained.

'The mongrel mix.' Dev smiled.

'That's right,' said Aidan. Pleasantly surprised. Dev said things. He had a point of view. Was it being an exile?

Aidan looked around at the discoloured cream walls. The few pathetic – or poignant, depending how you looked at them – attempts at decoration. A plastic palm. A couple of posters of Goa. The relaxed, friendly waiter. The stuffy atmosphere. He could imagine everyone pushing back their chairs and drowsing off to sleep. And yet this restaurant stayed open thirteen hours a day, seven days a week.

'Don't you miss home?'

'This is my home,' said Dev steadily.

'What about your mother?'

'She is always welcome to come and live with me in my home.'

'But aren't you lonely?' Aidan battled on.

'Lonely? Why would I be lonely? Lonely is living in a country that's tried to kill you. Lonely is living with people who still want to.'

Aidan thought of Ireland. This was never going to work, he realised. He was never going to be able to talk Dev into going back home to live with his mother.

'She told you the sad story of my family?'

'Maybe. I don't know,' said Aidan, unsure exactly of what he meant. 'She told me about the riots.'

'That was just the latest, in 1984. During Partition, in 1947, they stopped trains in the middle of nowhere and jumped on,' said Dev calmly, looking through the window at the traffic. 'Strung women and children up from the ceiling fans and left them there. They were found blue, with their tongues hanging out and flies swarming, slowly turning.'

'Which side?'

'Hindus and Muslims. Both. They were just the same. My father's baby brother starved to death: my grandmother didn't have enough milk. My father says he can never forget the sound of him crying. My mother says it almost drove him crazy when I was a baby and I cried.' Dev's mouth twisted, as if he were about to say something else, but he pressed his lips tightly together as if stopping himself. 'There are lots more things I could tell you.' He shrugged, as if to say, 'But I won't.'

'The British did this to you, to your family,' said Aidan, suddenly eager for a connection with this man. Initially dismissing him as ... what? Frivolous? Too trendily dressed? He realised that what he had first judged to be lightness was in fact poise. Poise in the face of what his life had been marked by.

Dev was looking at him with a half smile. 'England did this to us?' He seemed to be turning it over. He nodded. 'Yes.'

'Like Ireland,' said Aidan. For some reason this conversation, so normal in his family, so normal among his friends, felt almost tasteless here. As if he should be making a wittier point, perhaps. Something not so obvious. 'England divided us. Divided you. Ireland was England's first colony, you know. We were the first ones to be dispossessed.'

'Yes.' Dev seemed almost bored. 'But it was Hindus who set fire to my home in Delhi ten years ago. My own people. And it was Sikhs who murdered Indira Gandhi.' He shrugged. 'It doesn't matter, Aidan. We're in Australia. Let's order.'

He called the waiter over with an almost imperceptible wave and it took Aidan a moment to realise they were both speaking English this time, so flatly did the words slip off Dev's tongue.

'You've got an Australian accent,' said Aidan, once the waiter had gone 'You don't.'

'So ... your father,' said Aidan. He wanted Dev to volunteer information, but so far it wasn't working like that.

'My father is a judge. He beats my mother.' From the expression in his eyes Aidan could tell that Dev knew he knew this already. 'My mother told you. Of course she did. How else could she convince you to try to convince me to go home? He beat me until I grew big enough to stand up to him. But my mother won't leave him, and after the riots I knew I couldn't stay. Pappadum?'

Aidan swallowed. He needed to find an argument for why Dev should go back to Mrs Sharma. This, after all, is what he'd come to Sydney for.

Dev leaned back in his chair, his hands clasped on the table in front of him. 'I was eight years old when they came with burning torches. The police disappeared. Not one to be found, for the next two days. They called it a riot afterwards, but it was really a pogrom. They knew who the Sikhs were, where we lived. Sikhs were killed on the street, burned alive with tyres around their necks. No one did a thing about it. Not that you could expect them to – what if the thugs had turned on them? It was only because the compound we lived in belonged to so many people – not just Sikhs – that it didn't get burned down. My mother wouldn't let me wear a turban any more after that. She cut my hair, but I would have done it anyway if she hadn't.'

Aidan bit into the pappadum's brittle surface, breaking and cracking it open like blistering flesh.

'So no, I don't miss India. And no, I don't care about my religion. I don't care about any religion, it only ever divides people.'

In Belfast, in 1969, they'd come with heavy boots and bricks that they put through the windows. There were no burning torches. They came with dozens of thick-limbed youths, paid by the Brits to do their dirty work. They came with jeers and insults that they shouted through the keyhole, Aidan's whole family cowering behind the bars of wood his grandfather had nailed there, listening. Be out of here tomorrow or you'll be sorry. They said it again the next morning and that was when his grandfather said they were leaving. That they were going to abandon Our House. That's how his uncles spoke of it, to this day.

Aidan knew the story by heart. There was never anything so wonderful as Our House. Even after Aidan's father made his money and they moved into a lovely leafy house on Malone Avenue, near Queens University, there had never been anything like Our House. Before that they'd been living in a Housing Executive place, two to a room and eating in the tiny kitchen. The living room was so close to the street you could open the window, Nuala used to reminisce, and spit on a passing car. And then his father's rich uncle had died and left them Our House and some money that they spent on repairs. A washing machine. A television, their first ever. Our House had a room for everyone, Aidan's grandparents and uncles included, and a study for his father. It was Georgian, with pressed tin ceilings that Nuala spent the whole first day looking up at, grasping the hand of whoever was passing to squeeze it and say, 'It's so beautiful.'

They only lived there for two years. And then they were forced back across Catholic lines with just a car load of their things – no removal van would come near them and no one they knew had a truck. The car was stuffed with their bedding and papers and his mother's jewellery. Fifteen hundred other Catholic families had to do the same thing, and three hundred Protestant ones. And then for weeks after, the awful regret, and the awful discoveries of what they had left behind. His mother's garnet ring from her sister that she'd left on the edge of the sink. She cried for days over that. Their football still out in the back garden. Liam had talked about it constantly until their father brought home another one. Who was playing with their ball? Liam had asked. A Protestant little boy? Not to mention the pressed tin ceilings, the grand ten rooms. Five years later they moved into their beautiful house in Malone Avenue, and then after his father died they moved to Australia and the lovely terrace in Balmain. But nothing could ever compare; nothing could be as grand or beautiful; they would never live in another house like Our House again.

'Aidan?'

'Pardon?' The waiter had come and was carefully placing small steel bowls on the table in front of them, each a different rich colour. Green. Red. Yellow. The breads charred and golden.

'I said what about your mother?'

'What about her?'

'You sit here guilt tripping me about my mother and yours is nowhere to be seen,' said Dev mildly, dipping his naan bread into his curry.

'She's dead,' said Aidan, staring at the dishes on the table. After looking forward to them so much the idea of eating now seemed like work. 'She got breast cancer after we

moved to London. We thought she'd recovered but then three years after that it came back and she died.'

'It's also a tragedy.'

Aidan looked at him sharply, wondering if there was irony in his words, comparing what his family had been through to a standard, if fatal, medical situation.

'I'm really sorry.'

No, realised Aidan. It was just his lilting Indian way of talking, despite the flat Australian vowels. That poise in the face of anything.

'It was a tragedy,' agreed Aidan. But his father's assassination – what was that? he wondered. After their eviction from Our House his mother had begged him, all through Aidan's childhood, to emigrate. Liam's lifelong career of incarceration – what was that? And Dom's suicide? And breaking up with Anne? His isolation and loneliness? What were they? If not all inevitable consequences of the same, original mistake?

'I think it's great that you're here,' said Aidan, pushing away his plate. He never should have come.

CHAPTER THIRTY

Halley lay on the couch, getting started on the weekend paper. She'd never read the news much before. Until now she'd avoided it.

'The paper is dead,' Benny informed her when he came out to the living room and found her there. 'It's all digital.'

'It's funny how people keep saying that, about DVDs, and books and yet ...' Matt waved an arm over Halley's legs, covered by all the different sections.

'That's really just for old people,' explained Benny.

'That's us,' Matt winked at Halley, 'just in case you didn't realise.'

'Oh, I realise,' said Halley. She wasn't sick any longer, but she still felt weak. Her legs felt like cottonwool and her back ached if she bent down.

'I'm off.' Matt leaned over to plant a kiss on top of her head.

'Wait for me, I'm coming,' said Benny.

'Like that?' said Matt.

Benny was wearing underpants and a T-shirt. He looked hairy and stringy, thought Halley, awkward and beautiful. She wished she could bottle some of what she saw in him and keep it in a vial on a necklace, close to her heart forever. The essence of her teenage boy.

'You've got four minutes, Benny. Four!' Matt thundered, as Benny went flying into his room, slamming shut the door.

'You're leaving me,' said Halley.

'For the morning.' He stood in the middle of the living room, feet widely planted, too far away from her.

'Don't go.' She tossed her head at him, her gaze on him steady, inviting him over for a real kiss. Matt nodded at her, smiling, as if appreciating her invitation, but standing firm.

'Don't go.' She meant it now. She couldn't behave seductively any more; she felt too vulnerable.

'Halley, it's Saturday morning.' He didn't move a millimetre from his appointed place on the rug. 'I'm going.'

'Where?'

'Not saying.'

'Are you having an affair?' she said quietly, with a quick glance at Benny's door.

'Give it a rest.' He turned his back to her and walked into the kitchen.

'I'm just asking where you take Benny. Do you drop him off somewhere? Why does it have to be such a big secret?'

'It's not a big secret.' Matt appeared in the doorway, holding an apple and running a hand through his hair, which was stiff with salt. Lately he seemed to be taking more pleasure in things, creeping out of bed before the sun came up to go surfing, so that when she woke she'd see his side of the bed was empty, and miss him.

'Then why won't you tell me?'

There it was, the tone she hadn't heard for weeks. Singsong, patronising, mean. Halley bit her lip, ashamed.

'Come on Benny, let's go.' Matt disappeared through the front door without looking at her again.

'Bye Mum,' said Benny, swooping in to kiss her and swooping out again so quickly that she had no chance to touch him, either.

Halley knew it was bad. It was terrible! It was nothing she ever would have considered doing before. Although that was partly because she hadn't the time to be interested before, she reminded herself. Before, she would have been at work since six on a Saturday morning. And Matt and Benny's habitual vagueness made it easy to overlook their evasiveness, the few times she'd asked them where they'd been.

She hovered in the doorway, just out of sight of the driveway until she heard Matt's old Volvo roaring into life. She glanced down at herself. Her skirt was baggy and her legs felt spindly in their unaccustomed shoes. She had to hold onto the bannister as she walked down the stairs.

The steering wheel felt good and solid between her hands as she followed the Volvo, always just out of sight around the road's many curves. She felt nervous for a little while, when they crossed the last stream and came up onto the plain. But why would Matt wonder if that cloud of dust behind him was her? There were plenty of silver Subarus in the world, and she would need to be much closer for him to be able to confirm it was hers. And coming into town, she had to drive closer than she would have liked to keep him in view. They cruised past the farm co-op, the vets, and then the cafe. She barely glanced at it as she drove past, but a few seconds later, when they were queuing at the pedestrian crossing, she turned around in her seat to have a proper look. That was her cafe! she told herself, trying to jolt herself into some kind of feeling for it. It was strange to see it from the outside, to see it functioning – better than ever, it seemed, if that crowd was anything to go by – without her. It was like seeing your heart on a plate beating and pumping without you, thought Halley. She braked, idling just out of sight as Matt neared the corner, waiting to see which direction he was going to choose. He was turning left, onto the bridge spanning the Brunswick River. She waited until the car disappeared behind the bridge's old plaster pilings before burning up the road behind him, following him past the Catholic school and church and turning left onto Main Arm road. She paused when he turned into the showground, slowing down to bump across the cattle grid. She hesitated, blinker on, considering what to do next. She wasn't going to lose him – this was the only way in and out for cars. A driver tooted his horn behind her and she pulled over onto the grassy verge, to give Matt time to get himself into a suitably incriminating position, and to prepare herself for what she might find. She sat in the car under the shade of a fig tree for ten minutes before gathering her courage and following him in.

The showground was an old place, dumpy but well-tended, like a beloved farm. She drove slowly down the dirt access road, looking for Matt's car. There it was, parked in a row of them facing the arena, a grassy oval surrounded by a white picket fence. She parked and climbed out of the car. There weren't any people about, except inside the arena, where a group of men was playing cricket. She put on her sunglasses and slowly scanned the rather ramshackle buildings scattered around the perimeter. She hadn't realised there were so many. *Brunswick Valley Pony Club,* one sign said, in pink lettering on a paler pink background. There was a shed around the back of the building, set up for morning teas, and another devoted to tack. He could be in one of the stables, thought Halley. He could be anywhere. She started to walk along the road, feeling hopeless about finding him, when the thwack of a cricket ball against a bat roused her. She glanced over at the arena. 'It's a six,' someone shouted.

A smattering of applause, a laugh and a shout. Her eyes found the cricket ball, a speck against the sherbet blue sky, and then followed it down, losing it for a moment against the glare of the sun. And there was Matt, bending over to retrieve it. Straightening up, his arms pulling themselves apart like an archer preparing his bow, before sending the ball flying back into the centre of the ground.

She gasped. 'Matt?'

Hunched, she crept closer, hiding behind a plane tree and peering around it into the arena. Matt was laughing, pointing at something, and then wiping his hands against his jeans. And there was Benny: her eyes had found him before she'd thought to wonder where he was. Walking away from the pitch and turning around, long legs smoothly gliding into a run, his arm moving back gracefully, ready to bowl.

Halley turned away before the ball left his hand, moving herself fast back to the refuge of her car, stumbling over the uneven ground. She got in and slammed the door behind her, her forehead pressed against the steering wheel and her eyes squeezed shut, trying to drown out the pain.

'Halley?'

She wound the window down without looking up.

'What are you doing here?'

'What are *you* doing here?' She whirled around to him, her voice too loud.

Matt glanced towards the arena.

'Did you follow me? I can't believe you followed me.'

'I can't believe you ... you and Benny ... that this is what you've been keeping a secret from me.'

He moved away from the window. She stared at her hands in her lap. She heard the passenger door open and in a moment his blue denim thighs filled the edge of her view.

'Why would you keep this a secret?'.

'I have a right to my own life. I have a right to my own friends.'

'But with Benny?'

'He's only joined lately. It's been good for us. We've needed it, to have something of our own.'

'It's just so ...' She shook her head, searching for the meaning of this. Of what hurt her so. 'Who's that on the phone that you're always talking to?' she asked.

Matt said nothing. He didn't need to.

'That was Benny,' she confirmed for herself. Her instinct told her it was true. 'What do you talk about?'

'His day. My day. It can be hard sometimes. To get through the day, you know, alone.'

'Yeah, Matt, I do know.' Her tone was acid.

'You've kept yourself apart from us.'

'Because I didn't want to hurt you.'

'If you say so.' Matt shrugged. 'But I didn't want Benny to be hurt by that. And so I made it like a kind of ... a kind of a game between us.'

'You made a game of excluding me? That's mean.'

'Yeah. I suppose it is.' He shook his head, as if he were clearing his thoughts. 'You're too much, sometimes, Halley.'

He used to say that about her in admiration, thought Halley. He used to often say that when they first met.

'You're like those drivers who expect everyone else to just keep driving reliably and predictably so they can be as haphazard and dangerous as they want. And then suddenly when they grow up and want to be good drivers too, all those car crashes and accidents they caused don't matter anymore, and they should be given back their licences because that's all in the past.'

Halley stared at him. This was the most eloquent she had ever heard him.

'You think you're the only one entitled to be mean, or to make a mistake. But there are consequences to the way you've been.'

'And I'm sorry,' said Halley desperately. 'I haven't known what to do all these years, Matt. If I'd known how to do it differently I would have. God, I would have.'

'And stop saying sorry, okay? It doesn't change anything. It doesn't mean anything.'

Halley bit her lip, swallowing the apology she had been about to make.

'I want it to be okay, too, all right?' said Matt. 'Just like you. That's all I've ever wanted. But I don't know how that's done.'

'Can't we try?' Halley whispered.

'I don't know.'

'What do you mean you don't know?' she pressed.

'I just have to wait and see how I feel.'

'Well, how do you feel?' She couldn't stop herself.

'Like I don't know!'

She stared out through the windscreen at the group of figures moving about in the arena, hazy in the glare. The men's faces were turned towards their car. One of the men was holding up a bat.

'They're looking for you.'

Matt glanced up. 'They can wait.'

'No. Go.' She forced herself to smile at him, and as she did, she felt lighter, as if the act of smiling in itself was lifting her despair. After all her dark imaginings it was actually pretty wonderful that this was where Matt chose to come in his spare time, Halley told herself. That this was the secret he had been harbouring. 'Go on. I'll see you back at the house, later on.'

Matt broke into a jog as soon as he climbed out of the car, as if he couldn't wait to get back to his mates. Or get away from her, thought Halley, as she watched him climbing over the fence to join the others. She waited to see if he might farewell her with a glance or a wave, but he seemed instantly focused on the man about to bowl, staring straight ahead as if he had already forgotten about her. Something had been settled between them, thought Halley, but she wasn't sure what.

She sat in the car for a long time, watching the cricketers without really seeing them, cast adrift. Without the cafe to go to, or Sug, and with Matt and Benny occupied, what was she supposed to do today? Or any day, for that matter? For the last week she had been floating around the house like a ghost. There was a way forward that offered a statute of limitations on the past, remembered Halley, or at least, that's what Dom had said. That put a no-limits promise on the present. That allowed things to move forward when they had been stuck. That released you and impelled you, free and clear, somewhere new.

An image flashed before her mind's eye of the orange beanbags in the church basement at Lavender Bay, where Dom had hosted the youth group. What would heaven be like? Dom had asked them. 'Apart from unlimited ice-cream and never any homework?' She used to think of it as a place of innocence, she remembered. Where we would all be seen for who we want to be. Where we would treat others as we would like be treated ourselves. Or better, maybe.

But what would that place be like? she asked herself, pushing herself the way Dom used to push them. Halley pictured a country cricket ground, where fathers played with their sons and their friends every Saturday morning. She saw a cafe, where people came to eat and drink and be together, or sit peacefully alone. She saw her own house in the rainforest, with the creek running next to it and the chickens in the garden, but she couldn't see herself. 'To love others as you love yourself,' Dom used to say, urging them on. 'What would loving yourself mean?' It would be to include herself in that picture, thought Halley, as she put the car into gear and started the engine. For her inside to match her outside. For there to be nothing to hide.

CHAPTER THIRTY-ONE

When Halley told Matt what she had decided that evening, he gave a bark of bitter laughter.

'It's not a joke.' She stood in front of him, her jacket still on, keys and bag still in her hand. She had been walking around Brunswick Heads all afternoon, and sitting by the river.

'Oh come on. You've kept this a secret all your life. All your adult life, from me, from Benny, from everyone, and now you're saying you're going to turn yourself in. Can't you see the funny side?'

'Of what? That my whole life has been a joke?' Halley walked past him into the bedroom, noticing automatically that Benny's bedroom door was open, but that he wasn't inside. She dumped her bag on the chair, and her jacket. She kicked off her sneakers and took off her earrings. She was still exhausted and needed to get as quickly as possible into bed.

'Hey.' Matt stood in the doorway. 'Sorry.'

'Sorry for what?' She managed to sound unconcerned as she pulled off her T-shirt and stepped out of her skirt.

'This could be the biggest decision of our lives. It's certainly the biggest decision of Benny's life. We need to think about this.'

She could change her mind, Halley told herself. There was nothing saying she had to go through with this. Couldn't she bury this and, somehow, move on? It's what she had always done.

'Don't punish me,' said Matt softly. 'Is this about this morning? The cricket?'

'No.' Although it was partly, thought Halley. It was her realisation of everything she had been missing for all these years, and the proof that they could survive without her.

But what if she could turn a new page, somehow, and start her life over? After all, if she was offered anything, any life, any choice, she would choose to spend her life here, with Matt and Benny. That's what she'd finally realised. She might even choose to run her own cafe. What if she could wake up tomorrow and just decide to make a new beginning?

But she had been living her life here for the last seventeen years, thought Halley, and for all that time she had been frozen in place by her lies.

'It's not just me. It's the families of the people who were hurt. That I hurt.'

'But they had a trial about the bombing, you said. And Liam's in prison anyway, and it was him who was really responsible. And it was all an accident,' said Matt wildly.

'The murders the night before weren't an accident,' said Halley quietly.

'And you were just a bystander! A bit player!'

'But maybe I can offer them something, somehow, by telling the truth. It might change things for one of them, somehow. The way talking with Aidan and you about what really happened has changed everything for me.'

'I wish Aidan had never come here,' said Matt bitterly.

'Don't wish that,' said Halley softly. 'Before he came I didn't have a very good life, and in some ways I don't think you or Benny did, either.'

'But what about Benny?'

'That's what I'm talking about. I think I was about to lose Benny, the way my parents lost me.'

'No way,' said Matt, shocked.

'I could feel it,' insisted Halley.

'But this might mean that he'll lose you.'

She wanted to tell Matt about the way Benny had looked at her when she'd talked to him about Dom. But she couldn't speak anymore. Her face had become rigid with the effort of talking, and her mouth felt frozen shut.

'What if they take you away, Halley? What if they send you to prison?'

She glanced at him, and then turned to face the windows, shivering in the cold.

'I'm scared, Matt,' was all she could manage to say. She felt his hands on her hips. She leaned back against him. His body was warm. His arms snaked around her waist and squeezed her, the soft blue flannel of his sleeves comforting against her goose-pimpled skin. 'I'm so scared.'

Halley woke in the night to a strange sound.

'Matt?' She sat up, her heart thumping. 'What's happened?' Her fingers found the switch of her bedside light. 'What's wrong?'

Matt was lying on his side facing her, one hand clenching the sheet in a ball that partially hid his face.

'Is it Benny?' She hadn't heard the phone ring.

'I don't want you to do it.'

His words were muffled and she was still only half awake, but something about the way he was positioned, and the expression on his face made tears start in her eyes before she understood what he was trying to say.

'Please don't,' said Matt, at the same time as Halley said, 'Don't cry.'

'Don't do it, Halley. I couldn't bear it,' said Matt, as Halley said, 'Everything will be okay.'

Their words collided. Each of them speaking, then stopping simultaneously. Pausing and then speaking at the same time again, so it was more the sense of their conversation that Halley was understanding than the exact words. The way it had always been, between her and Matt.

She slid down so that she was facing him, then grasped his hand and pulled it away, so she could see his face. She kissed his lips that tasted of salt. She gently smoothed away his tears.

'Don't do this,' he pleaded. 'You were the one who said nothing needed to change, just because I knew. How is this going to change anything, except in a bad way?'

'I don't know.'

They lay for a long time facing one another, their hands clutched tightly between them, before they drifted back to sleep.

PART THREE

CHAPTER THIRTY-TWO

'You fucking idiot!'

Aidan scrambled to move the phone away from his ear. When he did that, though, he couldn't hear properly. 'Something something fuck something,' was all he could make out.

'Stop shouting, Liam,' said Aidan, gingerly bringing the phone closer.

'I'll stop shouting when ...' Something something fuck something, heard Aidan, moving the phone away again.

'What's got into your pants?' he asked after a second or two, once the shouting eased.

'It's not a joke, Aidan.'

'No joke, Liam. What's troubling you?'

'You mean to tell me ...' His voice sounded tinny.

'Where are you ringing from?'

'Where do you think?'

He sounded different, thought Aidan, and the caller number that came up on his phone hadn't been one he recognised. Still, prisons were large places. You couldn't expect someone to ring from the same payphone month in, month out forever. On the other hand, prisons were systematic places. In a way, you sort of could. Aidan was getting that feeling, that Liam feeling. That something-is-wrong-with-this-story feeling that he so often had with him.

'I'm starving. Can we talk after lunch?'

He'd just put on his jacket and found his keys, about to ride around to Byron Bay for a bite, when the phone rang.

'No. We can't. Your little friend has just royally fucked things up for us.'

'For us? What are you talking about? There's no us.' Aidan had always been very clear with Liam on that point.

'Fine then. For me. She's just royally fucked up everything for me. I'm never going to get out.'

'I don't follow.'

'She was my exit plan. My superannuation, so to speak. The only way I was ever going to get anything like what I deserved from the bastards was if I had something to offer to the newspapers and TV.'

'The newspapers? You would have sold your story to the paper? What are you talking about, Liam?'

'Nothing, anymore. Thanks to her there's no fucking point.'

'Halley, you mean?' Aidan had been planning to see her after lunch. They hadn't spoken for a week, since he left for Sydney. 'What's she done?'

'You mean you don't know? She's just gone and ...' Liam's voice faded away.

He couldn't believe the way Liam had it in for her, thought Aidan, as he walked out onto the balcony, looking for better reception. It was incredible how long Liam could hang on to a grudge.

'She's just gone and turned herself in.'

Aidan had to sit down. He put his fingers up to his eye sockets and pressed hard. This is all your fault, a familiar little voice inside his brain was telling him. If you hadn't come and found her she wouldn't have done this. She has a family. A life. And you've wrecked it.

'This is all your fault,' said Liam.

It was like a snap, kismet, the perfect chimes of destiny, thought Aidan. How lucky he was, how fortunate, that that little voice inside his head should be the voice of his own brother.

'You have to turn this around,' Liam was saying. 'You can still stop it. She can still stop it. You have to convince her to say she was lying. You have to make her withdraw.'

Finding the arguments for that wouldn't be hard, thought Aidan. All those visits to Liam in prison would convince anyone, if he could describe it accurately enough. The ugliness, the dreariness of it all. The gain in weight. The loss of hope.

It was a few minutes after that, once Aidan had hung up the phone and was trying to work out what to do, that the question occurred to him: How did Liam know?

He sat down heavily on the couch. He took out his phone and dialed without thinking.

'You've contacted Anne Clemons. Please leave a message after the beep.'

'Anne?' he said uselessly. 'It's me, Aidan. Call me, will you please?'

That's what he always used to say if she didn't answer. When he rang her from the supermarket to ask what she needed for dinner. Or the video shop to check what she had already seen. Or the bottle shop to discuss how much they should spend on their hosts this time.

And then when they had parted there were no more phone calls and he had made his selection at the supermarket, the video shop and the bottle shop alone. Choosing what I want, he'd remind himself, although they had never argued over anything like that, anyway. They only had one argument, and that went on and on.

Blank, scared to think ahead, scared to move, Aidan sat back on the couch, his arms folded across his chest, to wait for her call. If it came in a few minutes or a few hours, a few days even, he would just have to wait, he decided. He wouldn't think anything or believe anything, he wouldn't allow himself to conclude anything, until he heard from her. He closed his eyes, blocking out the sunshine and river sounds of the bright Australian day, transported back to his flat in London three years ago, the last time Liam had visited.

'Don't tell me,' Anne said, as she came through the front door.

They'd been back from India for six months and were getting on better than ever.

'Don't tell me!' Anne said again from the hallway.

Aidan was sitting on the couch in the living room, staring at his hands, joined together on his knees as if in prayer. He wondered how she knew already that Liam was there. Aidan himself hadn't known he was out of prison, and had been surprised that morning to get his call.

'Well?' She stood in front of him, still wearing her coat and woolly hat, clutching bags of bulging groceries in her mittened hands. 'How long is it for this time?'

'Ah, love.' He got up and took the bags out of her hands, putting them on the coffee table, helping her off with her coat and hat.

'Well?' she insisted, throwing her mittens onto the table.

He shrugged, and shook his head.

'Oh Lord,' she sighed, putting both hands to her forehead and dragging them back through her hair.

'Did you buy anything special?' he said, nodding at the shopping, trying to change the subject.

'I was going to make us dinner.'

'What was you going to make?' Liam appeared in the doorway, wearing only his obscenely low-cut jeans, revealing the full glory of his naked chest. His hair was shoulder length at that point, and since Aidan had last seen him he'd grown a mustache and a goatee. He looked like a camp pirate, thought Aidan, trying to catch Anne's eye for one of their secret 'he's an arsehole' signs – mouths tightly pursed into the smallest possible pucker.

But Anne had closed her eyes, standing frozen, with a 'God give me strength' expression on her face like a statue of a saint.

'Well? What have you got for dinner then?' prompted Liam.

'Lamb and bean casserole with basmati rice,' she said, reeling off the menu like a waiter. 'Lemon pudding with cream.'

'Ah,' said Liam. His eyes serious, satisfied. 'That sounds mighty.'

Anne nodded. She never could be rude right to his face, and in fact when she let her guard down Liam charmed her. 'Oh there's no question of that,' she'd said to Aidan the last time he'd visited. 'He won't rest until you're charmed. It's too much trouble to resist him. But he's not as charming as he thinks he is. No one could be.'

Anne picked up the bags, placing her hand on one hip in a gesture of tiredness and resignation that made Aidan's heart ache. She was thirty-two and still not pregnant. As of yesterday that had been confirmed.

'Ready for dinner at eight then,' she said to no one, disappearing into the kitchen.

'That would be grand,' said Liam.

'Would you like a hand?' called Aidan, but maybe she didn't hear.

'See?' Liam said as he performed a chin-up in the doorway. 'I told you she didn't mind.'

She couldn't stop crying when Liam left finally, three days later, with his hair cut and outfitted with new luggage and clothes. Well-fed and bathed, he had even booked a home-visit massage.

'I was afraid, the whole time he was here,' said Anne.

'He would never do anything to hurt us. You know that, don't you?' Aidan had been about to spread out on the couch with the Sunday paper. Maybe get fish and chips for dinner with a good bottle of white and see what was on the telly. He had that lovely feeling of repose after a challenge, the relief that the next time couldn't be further away than it was this minute, with Liam just out the door.

'I'm not afraid of him. I'm afraid of you. For you. Of how much you would disappoint me this time. Of how much you would compromise yourself.'

'What are you talking about?' said Aidan, but he knew before she answered, and he couldn't look at her.

'You let him bully you. And us. And everyone. By letting him into our flat. By giving him a place to stay.'

He was staring so hard at the TV program the colours watered.

'I can't do this anymore,' said Anne. 'I can't have him here. Look.' She held out her hands.

'What?' She had pretty hands, white and delicate, her nails painted a new shade of pearl to flatter the engagement ring he'd given her just a few weeks before.

'They're shaking!' she exclaimed.

'They're not.' Just in case, though, he grabbed them and brought them to his lips.

He felt as if he'd swallowed a rock and it was going down his gullet, a big lump of matter pushing down his throat and into his chest. 'You were happy while he was here,' he protested. 'You spent the whole time laughing.'

'Laughing? I felt sick the whole time he was here.'

'I can't ask him not to stay. We're his family. He ...' He what? Aidan never knew what to say about Liam, really. He didn't feel he knew him well. He had no idea what he was really like. He was his brother, the only surviving member of his family, that was all.

'He's everything to me. Almost everything,' he amended, catching Anne's eye. But nothing, he was nothing, really, Aidan realised then. From the moment he met Anne he had known that he would make it. She was his everything. But Liam, whom he hardly ever saw, whom he hardly even knew, he was something, too. And terrible as it was he couldn't turn his back on him and what he stood for. He couldn't break with his birthright, his own flesh and blood, his family.

'I can't.' She pulled off the engagement ring.

'Don't do that, Anne. Please.' He backed away from her. If he could avoid seeing her do this, if he could avoid taking it back because she was holding it out to him now; if he could insist that she go on wearing it, he would make all of this go away. 'Don't.' The stone had settled in his stomach and was sinking, disturbing a nest of what felt like moths that were fluttering up through his chest and his ribcage, swarming.

The ringing startled Aidan awake, his eyes stunned by the glare and the light. He fumbled for the phone, dropping it into the sofa cushions, his fingers slipping on the screen and answering just in time.

'Aidan?' Anne's voice was hesitant. 'Is it really you?'

She was surprised, of course, Aidan told himself. Amazed, probably, to suddenly be speaking with him like this with no warning, after all this time.

'Is this a good time to talk?' he asked her.

'Aidan?' She sounded disbelieving. 'Where are you?'

'I'm in Australia. Anne, I need you to do something for me.'

No reply.

'I'm begging you to do something for me.'

She knew what the subject of his favour was. Asking, begging – that had only ever belonged to one conversation.

'So, no how are you? No how have you been?' she said at last.

Aidan was standing on the balcony of the apartment block, overlooking the river. On so many occasions he had wanted to tell her about it. To describe the colours melting into one another, and the sound of the waves slapping against the bank.

'I'm begging you,' he repeated, whispering.

'Aidan, this is finished.'

'Not for me.' He clutched the phone.

'If it's so important why don't you do it?'

'I can't.' I can't live, he wanted to say to her. I can't breathe with this question inside me. 'Please.'

'Aidan, don't ask me this.' Her voice broke.

'He's in prison in London, now. They'll let you in if you say you're there for me. He'll make sure they let you see him.'

He forced himself to keep waiting without saying anything through the silence. His fingers finding the packet of cigarettes in his shirt pocket and fishing one out. Sticking it into his mouth and then finding the lighter in his jeans pocket. He held it there, poised, the heat from the flame burning the tip of his thumb, still waiting.

'I need you to ask him something,' he said finally, breaking the silence. 'I need you to look at his face and tell me if he's lying.'

He flicked the lighter again and a spurt of flame came so close to his face he could feel the heat on his cheek. He put it to the cigarette's end and sucked back. Even talking to Anne like this – driving her away – he felt more alive than at any other time in the last three years.

'Anne,' he said softly. He would tell her that he loved her. He would tell her that he thought of her every day, that she was his invisible companion, everywhere. He heard her throat clearing. Perhaps she could sense it, thought Aidan. The welling of his emotion.

'What's the question?' Her voice was flat.

'You're the only person I can ask to do this,' he said.

She didn't want to speak to him, thought Aidan, flinching at her renewed silence. She didn't want to be on the phone with him. They had stumbled too quickly into intimacy and now they were in their old position of stalemate and there was nothing new to say. He had fucked it up again. This used to be a joke between them, from a favourite movie of theirs, where the best buddy screams at his irrevocably hopeless sidekick, 'You fucked it up, Walter! You fucked it up!'

'I want you to say this to him.' Aidan forced himself to continue. 'Do you want to write it down?'

'I'm not saying I will. Hang on a minute.'

A clunk as the phone was put down.

'Tell me,' said Anne, back on the line again.

'I want you to say to him ...' Aidan swallowed. 'I want you to say to him, who are you working for?'

He heard her quick intake of breath.

'I want you to ask him that question and tell me what his face does.'

'Aidan, I don't think I can.'

They were all business.

'He can't hurt you.'

She snorted dismissively. 'I'm not worried about that.'

'Then I'm begging you.'

'I'll try.'

'That's everything.'

She cleared her throat. He knew from the rhythms of their conversations that she was ready for this conversation to be over.

'All right then,' said Aidan.

'All right,' said Anne. 'I'll go this weekend. On Saturday, I'll go.'

'Anne?'

'Yes?'

'I fucked it up, didn't I?'

She laughed. He'd surprised her. Aidan smiled to himself. That was good. That was a little bit. That was something.

'Yes, Aidan.' Her voice was warm. 'You did.'

211

CHAPTER THIRTY-THREE

The federal police representative was half an hour late – the flight from Canberra was delayed, he said, although he made no actual apology – and casually dressed in moleskin pants and chambray shirt. When Halley introduced herself and Matt to him in the public waiting area of the Brisbane office building, he reciprocated with his name, Mr Scaviando, but that was all – no details of his rank or area of expertise, and Halley didn't feel entitled to ask.

Mr Scaviando consulted with the receptionist in a whisper, then led them into a room with just a desk and two chairs set up in one corner. It looked makeshift, thought Halley, as he went searching for another chair, and she wondered if anything they said in here would count.

'I am here in an unofficial capacity,' he began, when they were all seated, shifting the papers he'd taken out of his briefcase on the desk. 'Nothing we say here today will be on the record or noted, but we'll have the opportunity—'

'Then why have you come?' asked Matt.

He was nervous, thought Halley, his foot bouncing and his fingers laced together tightly in his lap.

'As I was about to say. We'll have the opportunity to discuss some of the options and likelihoods arising.' He gave them a moment to digest that, then continued. 'What Mrs Sorenson has admitted to is a very serious ...'

'Yes, yes,' said Halley, hoping that would cover it.

'Crime,' he continued.

'Yes,' said Halley.

'And the first problem I've encountered, that I thought I might raise with you today is ...'

'Yes,' encouraged Halley. He spoke in a disconcerting rhythm of cascading words and unexpected pauses.

He coughed. 'Can you prove it?'

'Pardon me?'

He'd done his research, he repeated, and there were a number of problems with her case, the first one being that he doubted she could prove it.

'I should have a lawyer,' said Halley abruptly. She'd been a fool to let this meeting happen without one.

'That's not necessary,' said Mr Scaviando quickly.

That's exactly what they'd said when she'd confirmed the appointment, and Halley knew without a doubt that she should have trusted her instincts and found one.

'You want her to prove she did what she said she did?' Matt was saying. 'What is this? Who would turn themselves in for something they didn't do?'

He seemed rough and unkempt in here, thought Halley. His accent more strident, his clothes more shabby than they had seemed to her just an hour ago in the car. She wished he'd brushed his hair.

'You'd be surprised,' said Mr Scaviando.

Matt's face flushed red. 'The bombing. It's on the internet,' he said. 'You can google it.'

'Precisely,' said Scaviando. He turned to face Halley. 'Who's to say you were really there?'

Matt made a noise of derision and pushed back in his chair.

She shouldn't have let him come, Halley realised. She forged on. 'What other problems are there?'

'This is a sensitive area, naturally,' said Scaviando, 'and there's a specialist branch. In London. But I've contacted them about this and they've twice referred it back to me.'

'What does that *mean*?' said Matt.

'We don't have the resources to deal with it.' Scaviando was looking at them curiously, thought Halley, as if daring them to protest.

'So ...' said Matt.

'So we're waiting for information,' said Scaviando, 'but until then ...'

'Until then nothing's going to happen,' said Halley. 'You're saying I can go free.'

'Not free, exactly ...'

'This is ridiculous. Can I donate money to the victims?'

Matt stared at her.

'I think my parents …' She took a deep breath. It was a risk to even mention them. 'It's possible my parents may have left me substantial assets in their will. Can I donate their estate to the victims?'

'You think you'll find your absolution?'

Scaviando said it dryly, thought Halley, and she wondered what made him think he was entitled to be her confessor.

'In any case,' he went on quickly, as if sensing her attitude beginning to turn, 'they're suggesting low-key measures.'

So the specialist branch in London had decided on a strategy, thought Halley. And he knew she knew that and he didn't seem to mind. He seemed awfully smooth at this, and for a moment she wondered what lay in his past.

'Is that guaranteed?' said Matt.

'No. It depends on the public's reaction. It has to go on the public record, of course. If there's a fuss they'll be obliged to … but even then …' He shrugged, and started packing his papers away.

As if the meeting was over, thought Halley. As if this had been the reason he'd come.

'There's always more to these things than meets the eye.'

'Isn't there,' said Halley sourly. They were being shunted into no-man's-land, she could feel it. Unable to go forward, unable to go back.

'And you can't guarantee that she won't go to jail?' said Matt.

Halley squeezed his hand under the table. Poor Matt. How terrifying this must be.

'I'm in no position to guarantee anything,' said Scaviando. He opened his hands and showed them his empty palms, as if to prove he had nothing for them.

'Why would he fly up to Brisbane just to tell you that?' said Matt in the car on the way home. He hadn't stopped talking since they left the police headquarters. 'Why wouldn't they, I don't know, send you a letter? Or just throw you in jail?'

'I don't know,' said Halley. There was still so much she didn't understand.

CHAPTER THIRTY-FOUR

'He's lying.'

It was just twenty-eight hours since Aidan had phoned Anne. He was out on his afternoon constitutional when his phone rang, watching pelicans landing in the little bay next to where the fishermen gutted their catch.

'I said he's lying.' Her voice was flat, her English accent more pronounced than it used to be, he thought, although perhaps she just sounded that way to him in Australia.

'How do you mean?'

'You said I should ask him who he's working for.'

'Yes.'

'I told you he was a liar. I always said so.'

'Yes.'

'Do you understand what I'm telling you?'

Aidan's mind had closed down. He was in a tunnel, with only her voice to follow. Suddenly he couldn't interpret her words, or find her meaning. He couldn't add two and two, it seemed to him, so afraid was he that he would get anything other than four.

'So. Right.' He ran his hands over his face. 'You asked him.'

'What you wanted me to ask him,' said Anne. Her voice was gentle.

Patient, generous Anne, he thought, looking at the beauty of the scene before him. The river widened here, just before it poured into the sea. He was standing on an island, an outcrop really, connected by just a rickety wooden bridge to the mainland, providing a haven for echidnas and little native rodents and birds. He felt a wave of protective tenderness towards them all. The sky was turning pink, the distant roar of the motorway part of the orchestral accompaniment for this revelation.

'Aidan?'

He couldn't speak. She knew that. She knew him.

'I asked him, just like you said. Hasn't he changed? No more fancy hair. I said that to him. He said it didn't work so well in prison and I asked him when had it ever worked? And he said, well it worked down the pub. When he realised girls went for you if you looked like a girl yourself it was all plain sailing from there.'

Why was she telling him all this? He was desperate for a cigarette.

'It was quite nice really, talking to him in prison, where he belongs. For once I felt we were on equal ground.'

He remembered her crying fits every time Liam left their place. 'How can you let someone like that into our house? A murderer!' she'd say.

'You don't understand,' Aidan always told her.

'You don't understand,' she would reply. 'They are terrorising us.'

'Just the English,' Aidan would protest, hearing how horrible that sounded. A five-year-old child had had her arm torn apart by a bomb in a bin once when Liam visited, just the day before.

'What are you saying?' she'd gasp, and then stop. At some point in these arguments the memory of Aidan's father would occur to them both at the same time.

'Did he mention us?' Aidan asked her now.

'No. He doesn't seem to know we've split.'

'Did you ...'

'I didn't tell him. What business is it of his?'

That, at least, made Aidan happy.

'It's you I've been scared for all along. What he would involve you in. What he would make you do.'

'And so ...' Aidan prompted her, afraid she might be about to ask him what he was doing in Australia. Afraid of having to tell her he was once again living his life for Liam.

'And so I said I had a message from you and this is what it was and I asked him your question.'

He didn't want to hear this. If it hadn't been Anne on the other end of the line he would have hung up.

But Anne talked on. 'He said, who did I think I was? He stood up and walked out and then about ten seconds later he walked back in again, all outraged. But he was lying. The whole thing, like you said, it was all a fake. I should be happy, really.' She caught her breath, just as her voice rose into a laugh, cutting it off abruptly.

Aidan squatted, his feet making a v position in their white trainers on the grass. He'd never said to Anne that it was all a fake. He'd said he could never get it to add up. He'd said he didn't understand, but that he never knew much, anyway. He'd said everything but that, he realised. He'd admitted to himself everything but that.

They say when your lover's been cheating on you that you know – that on some level, you know. He'd heard a relationship guru once on TV, who claimed that on some level everyone knows everything. He'd scoffed. But now he wondered: could that be true? 'It's your Teflon man,' Anne used to say when Liam called, because nothing he said would ever stick.

'I know it's not the answer you were hoping for,' said Anne.

Had he known, deep down? Aidan tried the idea on himself. Things never quite made sense and for all Liam's tactical stratagems and evasions they should have, once or twice, at least. Instead, with Liam, it was all free cigarettes and free fuel and trips across the Channel, and now he was in prison and now he was out again and nudge nudge and wink and wink and Aidan should have realised before now that it just wasn't plausible.

'Dear?'

Dear? It means nothing, he told himself, his fingers white against the phone. She was feeling sorry for him, that was all.

Her voice dropped to a whispered plea. 'What does this mean?'

It had all been for nothing. All that he had stood up for and stood by Liam for and all that he had put himself and Anne through. For nothing. What a fool he was. He didn't deserve Anne. He didn't deserve her.

'Did you ever ... did you ever ...' He struggled to get the words out.

'Suspect? Me? No. Never. Only when you said to ask him that it suddenly occurred to me.'

Aidan's head was shaking from side to side. As if he could shake his brain into some configuration that would make sense of all this. A new structure, where the support beams would become ceiling beams and the floor the roof. He couldn't manage it, and the past was crumbling, the present falling in, like slow motion footage of a building detonating.

'Aidan?'

Anne's voice sounded small and distant. The cicadas were starting their afternoon chorus. Soon they would make a wall of sound.

'That's all he said?' said Aidan. 'He didn't ...' He couldn't finish the sentence. Again and again his brain came at it like a horse at a jump, and then at the last moment shied away. Cantering away to come back around, to try again, and once again shying at the obstacle.

'I don't want to think about this anymore,' said Anne.

'I ... I just can't ...' He held on to the edge of the picnic table he was squatting next to.

'I don't want to know.'

'No, no, of course.' Would this be dangerous for Anne? he wondered belatedly. Why hadn't he thought of this before? Because he thought he knew Liam before. Because he trusted Liam before. What was going to happen now?

'Anne. Anne?'

'I'm here.' She sounded calm.

'Where are you?'

'Where am I?'

'Yes.'

'Now you're asking?' She laughed, a sad, soft laugh.

'Yes.'

'Well ...'

He could hear her, considering. But she had always trusted him. He had always been trustworthy. Not one of those men who feed on drama. He was one of those men who feed on domesticity, on peace and happiness and all those things he never really had much of before they met. There was no reason for her not to trust him.

'I bought a flat, in Belsize Park. I've got a girl, a student, living in the other room, to help with the mortgage.'

He liked that. It sounded safe. It sounded single.

'How about you?' she asked. Her voice softened. 'Are you okay?'

He closed his eyes. 'I'm great.'

They hung up a few moments later. Aidan unable to ask her more about herself, although he'd been planning to. The two of them lamely telling each other they wanted to stay in touch. None of it the conversation he'd been hoping for.

He went back to the flat, locking the door behind him. He threw his jacket down on the little couch in the kitchenette and went into the bedroom and turned off his phone and lay face down on the mattress and slept.

CHAPTER THIRTY-FIVE

Aidan woke with a start, the way he used to as a child. Wide awake instantly, the bright Australian light almost dreamlike in its clarity. He looked at the room with its neutral furnishings. His backpack. His bike helmet. He looked at his life here. He'd been thinking of a lunch date with Halley, maybe. A date with himself down at the pub this afternoon. He thought of his life back in England. That empty flat. That long walk to the station every morning. The morning's outcalls and then the afternoon at his desk until it was time to walk to the station again.

'Liam,' he said out loud. 'What kind of a brother are you? You took Dom's life. You've taken my life. Why?'

'What happens to terrorists when they get old, have you wondered?' Dev asked him, in the restaurant on Cleveland Street. Their food had just been served. The dishes had been explained. Aidan had made his compliments, Dev allowing them, judiciously. A silence had fallen, and Aidan had wondered if this was to be the extent of it.

'What do they do? What's Osama bin Laden up to, do you think?' said Dev.

Aidan ripped apart a naan bread as he imagined a terrorist camp – an amalgam of all the movies he'd seen. Tents and high tech equipment next to a sand dune, maybe?

'You couldn't live in a place like that,' said Dev, when Aidan proffered this. 'No. He's doing what we're doing.' Dev nodded, surveying their table with satisfaction. 'Eating a little bit of palak paneer. Snaffling up the mango chutney. Sneering at the Indian waiter.'

'Really? Do you think?' said Aidan. He thought of Liam getting old in prison. He talked about money a lot these days, and the costs of ageing. He'd asked Aidan to think about investing in a flat with him.

'What do you reckon they do?' Dev was saying. 'Part-time job in a video shop, maybe? Not like they get pension plans, is it? Not like they pull off something like September 11 and get a superannuation package from then on. Unless they die, maybe,' Dev amended. 'Maybe their family gets something then.'

'Don't you think they might be a hero in their community?' Aidan said. He thought of the people in the pub in Kilburn. Of the relatives of all the people Liam must have targeted and killed. 'Unless they're hiding from their community.'

'More like,' agreed Dev. 'The ones who killed Indira Gandhi, who started all the trouble for the rest of us in 1984. If I could get my hands on them, there would be no mercy.'

Aidan packed his bags. He booked his plane ticket at the internet cafe opposite the caravan park. He wrote a letter to Halley and posted it. He packed up his flat, slipped the key through the slot in the real estate agent's door and got on his bike to head up to the airport on the Gold Coast.

On the plane Aidan tried watching movies but he couldn't stop old scenes from replaying.

'They never want you to do anything with your life,' Liam used to say. 'Try as you might they'll never let you climb up out of the gutter.'

Aidan had assumed, naturally, that he was talking about the English.

'I've enlisted,' he'd overheard Liam saying when Aidan was around thirteen. He was walking down the hallway past Dom's bedroom to the bathroom at the other end of the house.

'We won,' said Liam, it must have been around fifteen years later, just after one of the important ceasefire agreements between the British government and Sinn Fein, in 2001. 'The longest war in history and we won. How many can say that?' Aidan and Anne had been tired that night, and unwilling to talk about this with Liam, or to participate in any kind of celebration, the two of them looking elsewhere as Liam popped the cork on a bottle of champagne, which he polished off on his own. Liam had insisted on Aidan clinking glasses with him. 'England's is the best anti-terrorist force in the world, you know. It's something to make us very proud.'

Aidan thought Liam had never said the actual words – IRA – for discretionary reasons. But now he understood it was because when he said 'we,' he was talking about the British all along.

'You know, it makes no difference in the end what you're in here for,' said Liam, the last time Aidan had visited him, before he came out to Australia. 'They say that it does, but it doesn't. It's the same shit food. It's the same boredom. It's the same horrible uniform.' His Belfast accent had become stronger since he'd last seen him, thought Aidan. But Liam's accent was a perennial wonder. When they came out to Australia Liam had sounded Australian within hours. Whereas when Aidan had been living in Sydney for five years already people still asked him what time he'd gotten off the plane.

'Some are very proud to be in here for the Cause,' Aidan had protested. He wanted them all to remain strong, to keep believing, he supposed. If someone had to be in prison for all those years, you had to hope that the conviction that made them get involved with it all in the first place could keep them going behind bars.

'Well,' Liam shrugged, 'they're like your brother.'

'Dom, you mean? He was your brother, too.'

'They're religious about it.' He leaned forward, whispering. 'And generally not that bright.'

'Why are you talking like this, Liam?' Aidan sat back in his chair, putting as much distance between them as possible. He had met the other families at meetings, although he'd attended fewer of those in the last few years. He'd met the mothers. He'd travelled here to the prison with some of them on the bus. He wanted no part of talking about them in that way.

'I'm just saying.' Liam spoke patiently. 'No matter what your reasons or whose side you're on, when it comes right down to it, you – or I should say I – am still in prison. And I'm tired of it.'

'Well, and you'll be out soon. Didn't you say?'

'Yes. And then I'll be back, no doubt. According to Her Majesty's pleasure.'

Aidan, looking back, understood. Liam was saying that even though he was an operative, it was still prison. That even though he wasn't actually a prisoner he may as well have been.

This would keep happening, thought Aidan. Every conversation they ever had would reappear in his memory at some point, and offer a new angle for interpretation.

'I'm saving lives,' Liam told Aidan once, when Anne left the flat to go to her parents' place, crying, and Aidan had told Liam that he was the reason. 'You should tell her that. For real. I am saving lives.' And then Liam was crying, too. Aidan hadn't put much store by it. Liam was a good actor.

'It's Catholics killing Catholics I cannot stand,' he'd said during Aidan's last visit to him in prison. There had recently been death threats made against some of the prison wardens. The Real IRA was against the blending of Catholics into the police and prison services, even though nearly everybody else, including Aidan, thought this was exactly what was needed. 'They're going to get one of them eventually.'

Aidan had shivered. Liam was eyeing off a prison warden standing in the corner as he spoke, and Aidan wondered if Liam knew something about him. If Liam was telling him in code that this guy would be the first to go. That he would be set on fire, or stabbed, or his car blown up. Aidan usually tried not to think about these things too hard. He tried to endure the prison visits without listening to anything Liam said very carefully. He didn't want to hear. But a question, a favour, an unspoken plea would somehow worm its way into him on the way home and hound him when he got back to the office, so that soon he would be trying frantically to work out what it was Liam needed and would be sending parcels of deodorant and shaving cream to him, and getting ironic little notes back, saying 'You're too generous with me, little brother,' that made Aidan swear and vow never to do anything for Liam ever again.

Except give up his girlfriend. Except give up the best chance at happiness he'd ever had. What had Liam given up? he wondered, staring out the window of the plane. What about his chances of an acting career, or a family, or even just a steady girlfriend?

Aidan remembered the time when he was fundraising for Progress and visited them in Balmain. Aidan had walked into his mother's bedroom one day and found the two of them sitting side by side on the bed, holding a framed photo of his father, and crying. It had shocked him to see Liam like that, so messy and out of control, Nuala's arms wrapped tightly around his shoulders. Aidan had retreated into the hallway and softly closed the door. It never ended, he had accepted then. It would never be over, and Aidan would stand by Liam through anything, he had promised himself. Always.

In Singapore the plane stopped for refuelling and Aidan phoned Liam's prison from a booth in the airport's shopping area.

'Just to check in,' he said brightly, when the telephone operator at the prison asked him what was so urgent about his need to speak to Liam.

'You can't phone me unscheduled,' said Liam when he came on the line.

'What do you mean, I can't phone?' said Aidan. 'What's this, then?'

'Out of hours. It raises suspicion.'

'Yes, I thought it might. Nice how today they put me straight through.'

All those hours he'd spent on hold, waiting, thought Aidan. Back in London he used to phone Liam every Saturday. Anne waiting at the door with the recyclable shopping bags and the car keys. 'Just checking in,' Aidan used to say, when Liam eventually came to the phone. He fancied he could hear the gratitude in Liam's voice, to know that the only surviving member of his immediate family cared about and remembered him. He used to imagine it might be a relief for him.

There were their aunts and uncles, of course, and their cousins, and Aidan knew they visited Liam, too. Aidan sometimes used to stay with them on his trips to visit Liam, but more recently he had slunk into Belfast on a morning flight and returned home the same day. What would they say about Liam if they knew? wondered Aidan. What if he phoned them and told them?

'I like how they just put me straight through,' Aidan said again.

'Of course,' said Liam. He was speaking quietly.

'Where are you?' said Aidan. 'You're not in the corridor, are you? And you're not in the mess.' He'd be hearing reverb, or a crash or a clash in the background. At the very least he would have heard the long distance pips you get with a public phone. 'You're talking to me from an office, aren't you?' To have worked this out filled Aidan with a kind of delight.

'Aidan,' said Liam. 'My brother.'

Yes, an office, thought Aidan. He sounded as if he was standing on carpet.

'What would the uncles and the cousins say if I told them?' said Aidan. 'They'd kill you!' His voice was rising, but in this crowded place it didn't matter. 'They would fucking kill you.'

'Let me ask you this,' said Liam.

He didn't even sound stressed, realised Aidan. Maybe he'd come to the phone because he wanted to. Maybe there was nothing Aidan or any of his relatives could do to him.

'Who do you think killed our father?'

'What?' Aidan stared at the phone. A silly action, thought a part of him, like in a situation comedy. He put it back to his ear. 'Who ... what?'

'I'm not saying the murder was connected with anyone in our family,' said Liam. 'It wasn't.'

'Of course it wasn't,' said Aidan. 'It was the security forces. The Brits.' His father had been killed because he was always defending the toilers for the

Cause. But something in him had awoken and even before Liam told him Aidan already knew.

'What if I told you it was an inside job that killed our father?'

'I don't want to hear this,' said Aidan.

'What if I told you the assassins of our father were actually, for real, acting on the orders of the IRA?'

'I don't believe you,' said Aidan.

'They killed a Catholic judge, too, a week later. For giving legitimacy to the institutions of the British government. But I think really it was because he'd flown too high. Made too much of himself. Sparked some jealousy.'

Like Megan's father, thought Aidan fleetingly, except in his case he was brought down by the other side.

'Why did you never tell me?' he whined, the perennially left-out little brother, always in the dark. 'How could you and Dom keep something so important from me?'

'Do you really think you could have kept something that big a secret?'

'Our House, Liam,' said Aidan. He felt desperate, clutching the edge of the blue metal base that the phone was bolted to, his knuckles and all down the side of his hand white. That was the thing that bound them all together. The place where his father came from. The thing they had all been dispossessed of. The loss of which they could never get over. The thing that made them always and forever IRA. 'What about Our House?'

'Our House?'

All that they'd lost. Rings and tumble dryers and footballs and the friends they'd had in Percy Street and his chance of a happy family, thought Aidan. The first in a cascade of losses that even now would not stop unfolding. Their house in Malone Avenue that they'd lived in until his father died. Their house in Balmain that they'd lived in until Dom died.

He needed to get off the phone, thought Aidan, drunk with grief. He needed a shower, maybe, or something to eat. He had to hang up, to end this conversation.

'Our House, Aidan?' Liam was shouting down the line. 'What about our father?'

Aidan was staring at a photograph of a human-sized bottle of scotch, which was hanging on the wall outside a duty free shop. He felt as if he'd fallen into it. His head swam. Fire rose in his chest as if he had drunk it.

'Are you a tout?' he said, when he had regained control of his tongue. 'An informer?' He hardly even understood these words, except that that's what everyone was always so afraid of.

'No, I'm not a tout. I joined up,' said Liam. 'Right from the start I was in the British army. Pretty much from the day Dad was killed, when Dom told me they were IRA. Except they don't take fifteen-year-olds.'

'How did Dom know they were IRA?'

'He recognised them, from when they were represented in court by Dad. They came to see him a few times at home. He never would tell me who, though. For ten years he wouldn't budge, until Megan came to London.'

'You were lying, to me and Mum, and everyone, all along,' whispered Aidan.

'I had no choice.'

'You always have a choice.' That's what Anne was always telling him. 'Megan says you came on to her. She says she was a virgin, like Dom.'

'Oh Christ.' Aidan heard him swearing under his breath. 'I didn't think she'd blather about that.'

'Well she did. She was your brother's fiancée, you arsehole. How could you?'

'She was begging me, Aidan. I underestimated her.'

'The sex? You're saying she begged for that?'

'I don't remember,' he said vaguely, infuriating Aidan with his sudden withdrawal. 'It was all so long ago. You have to remember this isn't the only … thing I was ever involved in.'

'Thing?'

Aidan heard him sighing into the phone, bored, no doubt, by Aidan's finer feelings.

'It's been so many years and so many complications. I can't keep track.'

Yet he had the monologues from every Woody Allen movie off by heart, thought Aidan. What, exactly, was real to him?

'This is a war, Aidan,' said Liam. 'You never seem to get that.'

'A war.' Aidan's eyes filmed. He took in the white-tiled flooring and multi-coloured make-up stands, a faint smell of something frying and the hum of air conditioning. 'I'm not at war.'

He walked on shaky legs to his departure gate and sat for two hours in the lounge, his head bent, his fingers stroking the seam of his blue denim jeans. He tried not to think.

'I've saved lives, Aidan,' Liam had whispered down the phone as Aidan said goodbye.

Aidan couldn't stop himself. Stare as he might at the weave in his denim jeans, Liam's voice kept forcing its way through to him.

'What about the people you murdered, Liam?' said Aidan.

'More were saved,' said Liam instantly, with no need for thought or pause.

CHAPTER THIRTY-SIX

Aidan sat on the edge of his bed, clutching the phone. The flat smelled musty, more than he would have expected from an absence of five weeks. That picture on the wall – a photo of a brook in full flood rushing over tree roots, that he'd taken back in high school – how many years was it since he had looked at it? Since he had really seen it? And these couches of faded red corduroy, comfortably worn in patches, he used to think, he now saw as threadbare. The carpet was too, in every doorway and on every step. The only reason he never tripped was through steady practice, his feet adapting as the carpet wore away.

'Oliver Knowles,' said the voice on the phone. 'Who is this?'

'Liam Rafferty's brother,' sighed Aidan. That's all he was. All he had allowed himself to be. All he had left – his brotherhood with a man who no longer, so he was being told, chose to exist.

'Aidan. Hello. I'm afraid we have no details about Liam that we can share with you at this point,' said Knowles, repeating what the last person and the person before that had told him, before he finally got Knowles on the line.

'But I have to see him,' said Aidan, repeating the demand he had been making for the last half-hour.

'If he wants to he will contact you,' said Knowles.

'What if he doesn't?'

With every second of tactful silence that followed, Aidan felt himself disappearing. Liam's brother – Liam's brother whom Liam would not even see. Liam's brother who ... Before he could disappear completely he forced himself to speak.

'I have to see you.' His voice sounded reedy.

'You're in London, are you?' said Knowles. 'You can come today.'

Knowles' office could have been in any building, anywhere, rather than a prison. It was separated from the cubicle next to it by thin sheets of plyboard covered with a polyester grey felting. It felt oddly cosy, thought Aidan, as if they were insulated from the real nature of the topics they were talking about. Bank accounts – Aidan would no longer have access to Liam's, Knowles informed him. Belongings – just a small pile Aidan could lay claim to, if he so chose. Liam had left prison yesterday in a hurry, apparently.

'What about ...' Aidan paused. This room was so bureaucratic that he didn't mind so much, he discovered, about anything. The order expressed in the filing cabinets, the neat desk – neither grand nor too humble – and the solid dimensions of the phone. Things were disposed of in here. Memories, crimes, punishments. Decisions were made. 'What about the victims' families?'

Knowles shrugged, a sad little gesture of resignation. 'What about them?'

'They would be upset that the truth of what really happened has been hidden from them, for so long.'

'They don't really know. About anything,' Knowles continued quickly, in the face of Aidan's painfully obvious astonishment.

'Anything ...' Aidan grasped for a way of talking about such things in this grey, carpeted place. It felt tasteless, almost, to dip into such bloody territory. 'They should know that the bombing of the Royal Arms was never an accident. They should know it was never even the IRA!' His voice rising with the horror of it. 'They should know it was someone working for the Brits – it was you – who killed their families!'

Oliver Knowles seemed still to be listening after Aidan finished talking. The keen expression on his face didn't change. For a long time he remained frozen, leaning forward over his desk. Finally he spoke.

'We don't know that.'

'Yes. We do.'

'MI5 doesn't kill people. That's a fact, Aidan. That's the law.'

'Well. Whoever pays Liam's wages and instructs him, then. Whoever provided him with the technology and the opportunity to do it.'

'We don't know anything, really, that we can prove. Or not prove.'

Aidan had to look away from Knowles' sincere gaze.

'But we do,' said Aidan, lingering on the 'we'. 'We have a witness. A living witness. Megan O'Dea. She wants to testify. She's turned herself in.' His voice broke at the last word. He was so sorry she had done it.

Knowles still hadn't moved. He was treading carefully, Aidan could see.

'She'll remain where she is in Australia,' said Knowles.

'But everything she thinks she knows about what happened isn't true. It's the opposite.'

'She'll never know,' said Knowles. 'You know, Aidan, it is the nature of intelligence successes that they are rarely seen. This is going on, in various ways, around the world, wherever there is or has been, war. Secrets are unearthed, and then buried again.'

'You let Liam manipulate her, an innocent girl, into helping with a bombing. Into murder.'

Oliver Knowles' fingers came down and splayed out on the plywood in front of him. 'I must ask you to stop making accusations. I assure you ...' His voice faded away. His face crumpled in embarrassment.

Aidan remembered a day when Knowles had sat with him for an hour after Liam's unsuccessful parole hearing, fetching undrinkable coffee from the vending machine and quietly talking with him.

'You know I would tell you all that I can,' said Knowles quietly. His kind eyes made Aidan think he guessed something of what Aidan might be feeling. 'But nothing can be proven. Liam's case ...' His voice faded away again.

'Did he choose to go undercover?' asked Aidan, suddenly hopeful. 'Could he have been forced?' Because he knew the Brits did that, sometimes. They coerced volunteers into becoming informers. 'Was he ordered to recruit my brother's ... his brother's ...' Aidan corrected himself, '... fiancée?'

'I wouldn't know that,' said Knowles quietly. 'It's the not the kind of thing they would tell me.'

'Not tell you?'

'No. Because you see, as far as I'm concerned, it doesn't change anything.'

'Not change anything? To know that for your sake he betrayed his own brother? To know that pub was bombed deliberately and those people were murdered by your own side?'

'No. Because we don't know that. And if I am on any side, it's on the side of the victims. All of them. On both sides.'

'Spare me,' said Aidan. He could see where this was going. No one was responsible. They were all in the dark.

'But it's true,' said Knowles. 'We are just trying to end the bloodshed as quickly and peacefully as possible, Aidan. That's why I'm asking you to be quiet about this. That's why I know you will be.'

Knowles sat back in his chair and Aidan appreciated the way the clock on the wall played no part in this. In this grey felted place no phones rang, no one interrupted them.

'The only way we can go forward, Aidan, is to forget.'

'I can't forget. Megan can't.'

'I'm asking you to. For the sake of everyone. The families. Our countries. For yourselves.'

'And you.'

'And for me,' Knowles conceded. 'I'm doing my best here, in a very complex situation. This is how it has to be if we're ever going to be able to move on.'

'Has to be?'

'I'm afraid, yes.'

Aidan nodded. If he had learned anything, it was surely not to underestimate these people.

'But what about Megan? Halley, I mean? She's told the police in Australia. She's turned herself in.'

'We've asked that she be cleared on a technicality. We've made a request to the government that she not be charged and, on condition of her silence, that she remain free.'

Halley had been practically naked, Aidan remembered her telling him, soon after the bomb went off. Her clothes ripped and shredded, laden with dust and shrapnel. It was like being shorn, she said. As if she was being prepared for a whole new life. 'I wish that it had been a whole new life,' she said, the last time they'd talked. 'For a few years I thought it was. What do you think, Aidan?' She sat forward, staring at him, intent. 'Do you think you can be born again?' Aidan had laughed in disbelief. 'You're asking me a religious question?' 'I'm asking you a practical question,' she said shortly. 'I'm asking, can you start your life over?' Aidan shook his head, leaning away from her. Thinking of how he and his family had tried that, in Belfast, and then Sydney, and then in London. And how over and over again the past had dragged him back. 'No.'

'What's Liam going to do?' Aidan asked Knowles, as he was leaving.

'He's going to Iraq, I think. With his skills he'll be useful, wherever there's sectarian war.'

'I thought he'd had enough. I thought he wanted to get out.'

'He didn't give me that impression.'

Liam hated the heat, remembered Aidan. He couldn't cope with it in Australia as a teenager, and the thought of what he would go through in an even hotter country gave him pleasure.

'So what message shall I pass along from you?' said Knowles. 'Shall I tell him he can contact you on the same old number?'

Aidan looked through the windows, up and down the street. This was Dev's moment, he realised. This was his own opportunity, to break free.

'No.'

Knowles seemed confused. 'But what will I tell him when he asks for you? At some point he's sure to.'

'Just tell him I said no.'

Going home on the number twenty bus, Aidan looked out the window and thought how beautiful it was here, at 3pm on an autumn afternoon. All day in England was like the most beautiful time in Australia, at dusk. Australia, so light, so bright, so simple. So plain and unadorned. So forgiving and undemanding. He didn't want it, that easy life. Those easy answers, resolving into nothing. Even the ugliness here in London had depth. It had history, and meaning. So many hues and shades, in this light, and all of them in black and grey.

He'd phone Anne when he got home, he decided. He'd ask her out – there was no reason not to, anymore – and see if she was free.

CHAPTER THIRTY-SEVEN

Halley felt like a fraud. The two of them, she and Matt, standing here, dressed up in order to fit in with these other parents, who probably thought they had dressed casually. Her white shirt-dress and strappy sandals for Halley. Newish shorts and T-shirt, for Matt.

'Stop fidgeting,' muttered Matt, tickling her along her inner arm.

Halley bit her lip, bumping him with her hip and edging in front of him with her shoulder.

'Hey.'

They were stumbling, giggling and snorting like the teenagers surrounding them.

'Stop it,' said Halley, suddenly serious: they were here to represent Benny.

They were standing on the verandah of a Queenslander in the old part of town, next to the tennis courts and the river. One of Benny's classmates lived here, and his parents had invited them over to drink champagne, while they waited for their children to arrive, and enjoy the view. Which from this height, and at this time of day, was spectacular. Mount Chincogan looked close from here, and big. Birds called and the bats had begun their evening migration to the trees in the bush reserve opposite. Below them, the grassy verge looked as if it was swarming with butterflies. Young men dressed in ill-fitting suits and girls in stiff dresses stood in tightly packed clusters, preparing to celebrate what, for a lot of them, would be the end of school. Some of them would be finding jobs or joining the armed forces or taking apprenticeships, some of them would be going as soon as possible on the dole. Benny was staying on. Whether or not he'd make it to the Higher School Certificate Halley didn't dare to hope, but at least he was going to try. Vintage cars nosed through the crowd from time to time, horns blaring, stopping in front of the house to disgorge their charges, who generally were dressed to match the car, noticed Halley. Grey shot-silk fifties dresses this time, spilling out of a rusty grey Jaguar. The boys in matching grey cummerbunds.

'Oh they're gorgeous!' said Sandy, who was Tali's mum. It was her house.

Looking at the young people, the girls in home-made or second-hand dresses mainly, their hair and make-up artfully done by mums and friends, some of the boys as brightly and theatrically dressed as the girls, Halley was moved to tears. Grateful that they wanted to begin their rite of passage here, next to the bush and the river. Grateful that they weren't dressed by designers, as the girls at her high school formal had been, and weren't going to celebrate at a five-star hotel in town. All that wealth she had grown up in would soon be put to use. Her parents' affairs were being settled, finally, and their mansion on the water was being sold. Soon their fortune would be divided between a fund in the UK, to help families bereaved on all sides in the Troubles, and another one, in Dom's name, to aid his old youth refuge in Sydney. She thought her parents would be pleased. And here, in a few minutes, once all the young people had gathered, and class and individual photos had been taken, they would be walking to the RSL four blocks away, to dance next to the poker machines on the old parquet flooring, to eat from the plates they'd contributed to the buffet earlier in the day, and to all fall silent in front of the Anzac Memorial for a moment on the way home.

'You okay?' asked Matt.

'Fine,' Halley said, brushing away her tears.

'Hmm.' He was standing close to her, his arm around her waist, and he looked down into her face, smiling.

'What?'

'It's good to see you cry.'

'Why?' She bumped him softly, remonstrating.

'Not such a hardarse after all.'

'No.'

They had made love this morning, Matt standing behind her, her arms supporting her weight against the bed. She'd turned her head and he kissed her mouth and then buried his face in her neck. The truth is erotic, thought Halley. Now that he knew the truth about her, her love for him came bursting forth.

To distract herself from the memory she leaned over the verandah where a tree laden with spiky pink flowers grew against the wall. Brushing the petals with her hand, their scent clouded up into her mind, suffusing her body like a honey flood, seeping into and sealing every pore.

'Look!' Sandy was jumping up and down, her face alight, pointing in the direction of the corner. 'Here come our boys!'

Benny and Tali and a group of them had hired a car, although until this minute Halley hadn't known what kind.

'Oh my God,' gasped Halley, as she found it in the crowd. It was a covered truck, and the boys were springing down from the back over the fender, stark naked.

'Oh my God!' echoed Sandy, staring, frozen, as her son flung his arms above his head and began to run through the crowd.

'Yeah!' shouted Tali's father. He was grinning, but the women and men on either side of him seemed shocked. Halley looked down to where the crowds were parting like the Red Sea in front of Moses as the naked boys, six in all, ran among them. From up here she could see how strong and tall Benny had grown in the last six months. He and the other boys were chasing each other through the crowd, waving their arms above their heads and whooping, Benny's mop of hair covering his face, the matching fuzz between his legs a pale flash, sliced by his tanned thighs pumping as he ran.

Halley glanced up, shy for some reason, at Matt. He hadn't said a word. What was he thinking? He had turned away from her toward the wall, his shoulders, his back, his whole body trembling. 'Matt?'

He turned back to her, shaking his head. 'I can't.' He waved his hands. His eyes were closed, every feature drawn back and taut, tears running down his cheeks.

Halley giggled. It had been so long since she'd seen Matt like this, although it used to happen often, helpless with delighted laughter, his body out of his control. It was infectious, the way it overcame him, and a bubble of delight rose in Halley's chest.

'Woo hoo!' she screamed, waving her arms above her head in an echo of Benny's cheering below.

'Yee ha!' chimed in Sandy, and the other women and men on the verandah began hooting their encouragement too. They were like cheerleaders in the bleachers, the parents of these shameless, beautiful, liberated boys. Drunk on merriment and delight as the boys chased each other like overgrown puppies through the crowd.

The truck nosed its way behind them as they progressed, and as they reached the other side – it had only been a few minutes – it stopped and the boys piled back in, bouncing on the balls of their feet as they queued for their turn, vaulting sideways over the backboard, so as not to give everyone a parting view of their behinds. Once loaded, the truck roared off down the street and around the corner.

'Where are they off to?' asked Halley, breathless from laughing.

'Round the back,' said Tali's father. 'They're going to get dressed downstairs here, then they'll come out and mingle with the crowd.'

Halley was impressed by their forethought and intimidated, suddenly, by the realisation of Benny's strangeness. Not strange in any peculiar way, but simply unknown to her: making plans, dressing himself, conducting himself, outrageously or otherwise, without her. After all those years of watching over him, bossing him and worrying about him, he could do all these things for himself. He was no longer hers. Just as she had ceased to belong to her parents. She felt a start of terror. And quickly quelled it. She had been unusual, she reminded herself. Unusual for this place, and this time, anyway. In some parts of the world at this moment young people were setting out on missions even more dangerous than hers had been, facing betrayals and mistakes even more life altering. But not here. Not now.

Halley accepted another glass of champagne and chatted with the other parents, remarking from time to time upon a particularly gorgeous outfit.

'Where's Gretchen?' she asked Matt, when she saw that Benny had emerged. Dressed in a powder-blue tuxedo a size too small for him, he was standing awkwardly just outside a ring of chattering girls.

Matt shrugged, studiedly casual.

So they had broken up, realised Halley. After all her agonising, her foreboding of calamity and suffering, of a future stretching out in its awful passion, it had ended.

'He's taken it well, even though it was her decision,' said Matt. 'You did well, Halley.'

'What do you mean?'

'I think it was a relief for him.'

'What do you mean?' She was half ready to throw her glass at his head; he was so typically obscure. The hubbub of happy voices and revving engines resounded in her ears.

'That you backed off. That you just talked to him. He didn't need her as a shield anymore against you.'

Halley wasn't sure whether to be affronted or pleased.

'I was a bit worried he might get upset when she dropped him,' Matt was saying. 'That he might lose his balance somehow. But he's fine.'

He wouldn't have been fine before, thought Halley. Before Gretchen, the last time a girl had broken up with him he'd withdrawn. Staying alone in his room for weeks, not even surfing. Before Gretchen he would never have done something like this naked run, either. Somehow, in the last few months he'd matured, and grown stronger. It was maybe due to Gretchen, thought Halley, trying to be generous. Or maybe it was something to do with herself, as Matt was saying. Maybe it was Benny finally getting to know his mother. Maybe it was his mother getting closer to his father that had given Benny confidence. Maybe it was the truth, for the first time, living with them in their home.

It was dusk by the time the young people dispersed and the parents were ready to leave. The sky glowed with a lush pink that set every other colour shimmering. Foliage and grass and the nubbly carpet of trees on Mount Chincogan rose before them in myriad shades of green. All was gold to the west where the sun was setting. Birds called, fluting and random against the steady pulse of the cicadas' buzz. Swimming through colour and noise, Halley could forget herself almost entirely, and all that was left was a sense of gratitude for the glory of being included in this.

Matt took her hand as they left the party. The atmosphere here was prehistoric, thought Halley, as they walked along the riverbank to the car. As though human time was erased by the sheer weight of years, the memory of the millennia this country had seen. And still the river flowed, and the fertility of this place endured. You remembered how old the earth was here, and how you, despite the passing of the years, were young. You could imagine a new beginning here, no matter how old you were. It was no wonder so many people did. Here you could always imagine that it might be possible to start again.

ACKNOWLEDGEMENTS

Although there are similarities between some of the events in this novel and historic figures and incidents, this is a work of fiction.

This is particularly so in the case of Pat Finucane, the human rights lawyer killed by loyalist assassins in collusion with the British security services in Belfast in 1989, and also the Murphy Affair, involving the politically motivated smearing of a judge and prominent Sydney lawyer in 1984. From the proven facts of these events, I created the jumping-off points for my story, and the similarities end there.

The sources and books I drew on in the research and writing of this novel are too many to mention, but I would particularly like to acknowledge the influence of *'Rebel Hearts – Journeys Within The IRA's Soul'* by Kevin Toolis, (St. Martin's Press, New York, 1995) and *'Open Secret – The Autobiography of the Former Director-General of MI5'* by Stella Rimington, (Arrow Books, London, 2002) as well as the investigative reporting of the *Guardian* newspaper into the activities of the British security services in the 1990s, and the many articles published in the *London Review of Books* about the Northern Ireland peace process in the last twenty years.

I would like to thank Amanda O'Connell, Bernadette Foley and Lucie Stevens, as well as Melita Smilovic, Lisa Brockwell and Geoff Bloom for their careful reading, insights and suggestions; Linda Quinn-Jarvis and Lesley Branagan for their help with specific cultural questions to do with Northern Ireland and India; Stephen Powter, Kyla Slaven, Rebecca Grenfell and Kristin Dale for their friendship and practical support; Maurizio Viani and Douglas Frost, Caroline Wilkinson and Alissa Dinallo for their photography, web and cover designs respectively, and Margaret Connolly, Sophie Hamley, Jo Butler,

Alan Gold, Dana Slaven and Kim Kelly for their encouragement and advice at different stages in the writing of this novel.

I would especially like to thank Geoff Bloom, Lisa Brockwell and Melita Smilovic for making it possible for me to be a writer, and Lou Johnson and The Author People for blazing a trail that as a writer I want to walk on.

Laura Bloom

It's the people traditionally left out of the frame who interest Laura the most, as well as what happens *after* what would be the climax in many stories. A couple reuniting after the war, in IN THE MOOD; a woman who has changed her name and started a new life, only to find her old life catching up with her, in THE CLEANSKIN; what happens when you break up with the perfect person, in CHOOSING ZOE.

Laura's novels have been shortlisted for the NSW Literary Awards, the ABC Fiction Prize and the Young Australian Readers' Awards and published in France, the US and the UK.

Laura grew up in Sydney and graduated with a BA, Communications from the University of Technology, Sydney. She has worked in the areas of youth policy, social justice and health promotion, and has travelled widely, including living for spells in Germany, India, the UK, and New Guinea. She now lives in a small town near Byron Bay on the east coast of Australia with her family.

www.theauthorpeople.com/laura-bloom

ALSO BY LAURA BLOOM

In The Mood

Robert was surprised when he saw the atom blast on film, the mushroom cloud billowing up to the sky, so peaceful and final-looking. So natural-seeming that this was what would end it. ...

... Home was her, Catherine, in her blue cotton dress, dancing to the radio in the living room, the furniture pushed back against the walls to give her space. Him sitting on one of the chairs against the wall, entranced, not just by the glimpses of thigh and garter belt, her skirt in a perpetual flying ruffle, but her energy, her hips and hands and every part of her so alive.

It's February 1946, and Robert Booker is just home from the war. Home is a pretty weatherboard house in Sydney, where his wife, Catherine, is waiting. They haven't seen each for three years, yet they are separated by so much more than time.

Robert is haunted by the horrors of what he has seen and done, fighting in the humid jungles of New Guinea, and Catherine is carrying the guilt of her affair with a charismatic US Marine – and other secrets too painful to confront. With so much that's changed between them, can Catherine and Robert find their way back to each other again?

Through intimately exploring the experience of one couple, and one war, Laura Bloom powerfully humanises the damage wrought by all wars to people everywhere.

IN THE MOOD is a tour de force of understatement, of insightful and concentrated emotional writing.   -The Spectator

Crisply written and dramatic, IN THE MOOD is compelling fiction.
                                                                            -The Age

www.theauthorpeople.com/in-the-mood

FROM.
LINDA JULY 2018.

Printed in Australia
AUOC02n1646021116
280156AU00014B/132/P